Praise for the Allison Campbell Mystery Series

DYING BRAND (#3)

"Tyson paints image consultant Allison Campbell with an intricate brush, telling an emotional, riveting, and gripping story in *Dying Brand*. I loved it! A must read for mystery fans."

– Gretchen Archer,
USA Today Bestselling Author of the Davis Way Crime Caper Series

"Engaging, intelligent, and riveting, *Dying Brand* kept me on the edge of my seat—guessing until the end. Bravo!"

– Mollie Cox Bryan,
Author of the Agatha Nominated Cumberland Creek Series

"*Dying Brand* delivers a complex puzzle mystery with a colorful cast and plenty of twists. Image consultant Allison Campbell rushes back into action, and readers will find themselves racing with her to the surprising conclusion of this fast-paced whodunit."

– Carla Norton,
Bestselling Author of *The Edge of Normal*

"Narratives alternate in this continually shifting novel, as characters evaluate their relationships with old lovers and are surprised by new ones. The main plot holds all of the stories together though, and it is Allison who drives the mystery with her own compulsions and vulnerability...This is a truly unique and enjoyable series of reinvention and, oddly enough, acceptance."

D1566142

DEADLY ASSET

"The mystery is firm and well-explained, and great fun to follow, but it's the rich relationships Tyson has created that this reader will carry away from the book...I will be following Allison Campbell and her cohorts with a great deal of interest in all the books to come. There had better be a lot more."

– Stephanie Jaye Evans,
Author of the Sugar Land Mystery Series

"A mystery is only as good as its characters, and *Deadly Assets* is filled with vivid people who will keep readers turning the pages to find out what happens to them...Allison herself is savvy and likable, with an unusual job that promises many satisfying installments in this well-written series. Highly recommended!"

— Sandra Parshall,
Agatha Award-Winning Author of the Rachel Goddard Mysteries

"Tyson creates a tense, engrossing tale by weaving vivid descriptions with thrilling threads of family secrets, greed and the shadow of an unknown threat...not to be missed!"

— Laura Morrigan,
Author of the Call of the Wilde Mysteries

KILLER IMAGE (#1)

"An edgy page-turner that pulls the reader into a world where image is everything and murder is all about image. Great start to a new series!"

— Erika Chase,
Author of The Ashton Corners Book Club Mysteries

"Wit, charm, and deliciously clever plot twists abound...the author has a knack for creating characters with heart, while keeping us guessing as to their secrets until the end."

— Mary Hart Perry,
Author of *Seducing the Princess*

"This cleverly revealing psychological thriller will keep you guessing...as the smart and savvy Allison Campbell (love her!) delves into the deadly motives, twisted emotions and secret intrigues of Philadelphia's Main Line."

— Hank Phillippi Ryan,
Agatha and Macavity Award-Winning Author of *The Wrong Girl*

"Nancy Drew gets a fierce makeover in Wendy Tyson's daringly dark, yet ever fashion-conscious mystery series, beginning with *Killer Image*. Tyson imbues her characters with emotional depth amidst wit, ever maintaining the pulse rate."

— Deborah Cloyed,
Author of *What Tears Us Apart* and *The Summer We Came to Life*

DYING BRAND

**Books in the Allison Campbell Mystery Series
by Wendy Tyson**

KILLER IMAGE (#1)
DEADLY ASSETS (#2)
DYING BRAND (#3)

DYING BRAND

An Allison Campbell Mystery

WENDY TYSON

HENERY PRESS

To Barbara Young - Thank you so much for coming out. It's a treat! Lovely always to you!

Wendy

DYING BRAND
An Allison Campbell Mystery
Part of the Henery Press Mystery Collection

First Edition
Trade paperback edition | May 2015

Henery Press
www.henerypress.com

Copyright © 2015 by Wendy Tyson
Author photograph by Ian Pickarski

ISBN-13: 978-1-941962-59-6

Printed in the United States of America

For Marnie Mai, Stephanie Wollman and Amy Speiser.
Friends. Always.

ACKNOWLEDGMENTS

I owe deep gratitude to many people, including:

My agent, Fran Black of Literary Counsel. Your patience, support, sage advice and good humor are constants. Thank you.

Kendel Lynn, Art Molinares, Anna Davis, Rachel Jackson, Erin George and the rest of the Henery Press team. You've made this a better book.

Rowe Copeland at The Book Concierge. Thank you for your creativity and friendship.

All of my early readers and tireless supporters, with a special shout out to my mother, Angela Tyson, Sue Norbury, Marnie Mai, Mark Anderson, Adrienne Robertson, Laura Coffey, Edie and Sam Newman, Greg Marincola, Judy Kraft, Abbe Fox, Mandy Gohn, Stephanie Wollman, Kim Morris, Ann Marie Pickarski and Carol Lizell.

And, of course, my family—Ben, Ian, Jonathan and Matthew. Thanks for believing in me and helping me make the time to write.

ONE

Allison Campbell couldn't think of anywhere else she'd rather be. Sitting in the grand ballroom at the Four Seasons next to her boyfriend, Jason, and her business manager, Vaughn, both of them dressed in evening garb and looking quite dashing, was the last place the image consultant expected to find herself on this early November evening. She'd been scheduled to present at a university ahead of her next book release, but when the invitation to be a guest of honor at Delvar's award ceremony had arrived a month ago, she'd canceled her other plans and accepted without question.

Delvar's was a success story of the very best kind.

Allison watched her mentee with maternal pride and the tiniest bit of professional told-you-so from her perch at the stage-side table. Not only was Delvar a sought after designer, but a role model to others. And that second reason was why they'd all gathered on a Saturday night to celebrate.

The gentleman on Allison's left was engaged in a conversation with Delvar's mother, and on Allison's right, Jason was in the midst of a heated discussion with Vaughn. They were talking football, a topic Allison knew little about. Slightly giddy from Dom Perignon and a night away, Allison took advantage of her boyfriend's distraction to check her email messages. It was then, with her small clutch open and her hand on the mobile device, that her phone rang. Allison answered quickly, without thinking, a move she would later regret.

The woman's voice was one she recognized. The sound of it, rather like shattering glass or a fork scraped against a ceramic plate, made Allison shudder.

Her name was Leah Fairweather, and she was a phantom of Allison's past.

Allison rose from the table with her phone planted against her cheek and left the award ceremony without a word to her companions. The whimsical lights and excited voices of the grand ballroom receded to a dull blur of background noise.

"Are you listening?" Leah asked.

Allison swallowed. She was standing with her back up against the wall of the hotel lobby. She pictured Leah's white-blond hair as it had been not long ago: long, thick and curled on the ends. She saw Leah's hooded gray eyes, that twisted little smile, part vixen, part intellectual snob. Allison knew these memories were colored by feelings of shame and remorse. Her mind had turned Leah Fairweather into a symbol of past regrets, both bigger and uglier than reality. Allison's hand shook.

"I asked if you were listening."

"I'm listening," Allison said.

"Why? Of all the men, why him? You both *promised*. He said it was over, all of it. For God's sake, why? And now, this—"

And now *what*? Allison blinked, confusion overriding other emotions. "I don't know what you're talking about, Leah. Slow down."

"Bullshit."

A baby cried in Leah's background and the sound registered as another accusation. Allison watched as a man in a tuxedo left the ballroom with a fifty-something blond hanging on his arm. They headed toward the doors that led to 18th Street. Allison said, "I'm going to hang up now, Leah. You're upset. Confused. I haven't seen Scott in four years. Except for a brief encounter, but that was just happenstance—"

"I know you've been seeing him."

"That's not true."

"Liar."

Allison closed her eyes, then opened them, fighting for control. From the corner of her eye, she saw Jason push open the ballroom doors. He looked around, searching for her.

"Goodbye, Leah," Allison said.

"Wait!"

"I need to go."

"Scott's dead."

Allison grabbed the wall. Her vision constricted, the heady lights becoming starbursts of ivory dancing in front of her face. Scott Fairweather, dead? But she had seen him, what, three weeks ago? He'd seemed fine. Perfectly fine.

"He's dead, Allison."

"What happened?"

"I thought maybe you could tell me. What happened to my husband?"

Jason spotted her. He was walking toward her, looking concerned. Allison wanted to hang up. She also wanted to know—had a sudden, crushing need to know—what had happened to her former paramour.

"How would I know what happened to him?"

"You were supposed to have been together the day he died."

"Together?" The vise on Allison's skull tightened. She felt Jason's touch on her elbow, registered his eyes, full of questions. Allison turned toward the wall. She had to get off the phone. With a steadier voice, she said, "That's not true."

"You're in his appointment book."

"It's not true. I have to go now, but—"

"He was murdered, Allison. And I'm sure you know why."

"Hey, you're shaking." Jason took the phone from Allison and pulled her close. "What happened? One moment you were there and the next you were gone." He smoothed back her hair. "Are you okay?"

Allison clung to him. His strength was a comfort, but even more, she didn't want to meet his eyes. He knew her well. And despite the image consulting, the emphasis on poise and control, when it came to her own life she had no poker face. Jason's arms loosened. He reached for her chin, held her face up toward his.

"Your mom okay?"

Her mom would never be okay, but she didn't say that. Instead, Allison shrugged. "A former client was killed."

"Oh, I'm sorry. Anyone I know?"

Allison shook her head. "Someone from long ago."

"Pretty strong reaction for someone from long ago." His voice was soft, caring. Only that made it worse. "Were you close to this person?"

The sound of applause crashed through their cocoon and Allison took advantage of the break. She forced a smile. "I'm fine, Jason. We should get back in there."

But he held her stare a moment longer, looking unconvinced and so darn handsome in his tuxedo. "There's something you're not telling me."

Allison sighed. She owed him the truth. As much of the truth as she could muster. "An old client. He was murdered. With everything we've been through," she said, referring to two close calls in as many years, "it shook me up."

Jason looked relieved. Allison, still reeling from the call, glanced down at her Jimmy Choo-clad feet. "I love you," she whispered, not knowing what else to say. But she meant it. And a terrible misstep with a client four years ago didn't change everything that came afterwards, including the fact that Jason was with her now. "Delvar will miss us," she said. "I promised him I'd be there when he accepts the award."

Jason nodded. He kissed her gently on the lips and took her hand. She led the way back to the ballroom with Jason's body pressed against her own. They meandered through the standing crowd—two hundred guests straining to see the latest success story—hoping to get a glimpse of the fashions that would be trends soon enough. Allison, on tiptoe, could just see Delvar, with his spiky black hair and his snug leather pants. But the conversation with Leah had stolen the moment. Allison told herself it was all in the past. Scott's death was Leah's problem.

Then why, she wondered, despite the press of their bodies, could she feel the guilt wedging itself between her and Jason now?

Delvar Juan Hernandez accepted his award with characteristic grace. He had been a scrap of a twenty-three-year-old when Allison first met him a number of years ago at an art school charity function. When she'd had the chance to talk to the budding designer later, during cocktails, she'd been intrigued by his story.

Born to a single mom in Bethlehem, Pennsylvania, Delvar had known that he wanted to design clothes since he was four years old.

Family members thought he was odd. His mother saw genius. Delvar worked two jobs during high school to save enough money for art school. Even at that, he had to wait until he was twenty-one to start school, and his education stalled when he ran out of funds. Allison wasn't the only person who saw promise, but in a moment of tender weakness, she was the only person who offered the money needed so he could finish school.

Delvar had since repaid her twice, once with a check covering the entire tuition amount, and again with his friendship and gratitude. But even beyond that, he was determined to give back to the community. And so he had started Designs for the Future, a charity aimed at giving young designers who might not otherwise be able to afford it an education. It was for this new accomplishment that he was winning an award. He wanted Allison to sit beside his mother when he accepted the honor.

It was a tribute that touched her. And now she wished she could shake the icy fingers of dread that trailed down her spine. Leah's voice. Scott's name. Logic told her they had nothing to do with her anymore. She had no idea why her name had been in Scott's appointment book, but whatever the reason, she'd severed contact with Scott almost four years ago and hadn't spoken to him since. Well, almost. But the day three weeks ago didn't count. It had been a chance encounter.

Or had it?

Allison looked over at Vaughn, who was beaming like a proud father even though he barely knew Delvar, and Jason, who was still keeping a worried eye on her. When Delvar stepped off the stage, she cat-called her affection for a man who'd had a vision and pursued it, despite the odds.

Allison tossed her head back and glanced around the ballroom. The crowd loved Delvar. She took a sip of champagne, then another. Delvar was walking back to his table, trying hard to hide the grin blooming on his thin, angular face. Beside Allison, Delvar's mother was weeping. Allison swallowed her anxiety over the Fairweathers. This was Delvar's night. A mistake from the past wasn't going to ruin the celebration.

*   *   *

Only later that night, sleep eluded her. Allison crawled out of bed, grabbed a robe, and tiptoed out of her bedroom, trying hard not to wake up Jason or her dog, Brutus. Jason slept soundly, his sleep aided by late-night lovemaking and at least three vodka tonics, but Brutus stirred. He eyed her from his spot on the foot of the bed, eyes sleepy, jowly face heavy with slumber. When Allison slipped out the door, she heard him huff and jump off the mattress to follow her.

They padded along the carpeted hallway together and entered Allison's office. She closed the door before turning on the light. While her computer took its time booting up, she sat on her chair and stroked Brutus's head. He stared at her with adoring eyes that made her feel listless. Guilt, she knew, turned everything sour.

Scott Fairweather. Somehow, Scott's presence in her life had evoked many lies, more than she cared to contemplate. But now that he was dead...did she owe his wife the truth?

What was the truth?

Allison had an affair with Scott during that relationship limbo between her and Jason known as a trial separation. Or at least that's what Allison told herself. The truth was that she and Jason had just reached an impasse when the affair began. Jason had recently lost his sister. His parents were divorcing, and Allison and Jason's marriage had quickly and devastatingly unraveled. Allison hadn't known how to help her husband. He'd been so distant. Irritable. Unreachable.

Scott had been her client. He'd been easy enough to look at. Dark, wiry curls cropped close to a nicely shaped head. Small glasses that gave him an intellectual air. A warm smile. Long, lean body and broad shoulders that resonated strength. But more than that, he'd been a good listener. During that tumultuous time in their lives, Scott had been everything Jason had not: ambitious, attentive, and, most of all, present. He'd made her feel like the only person who mattered. He'd seemed like such a nice guy.

Silly girl, Allison thought now.

Once her computer was ready, Allison opened a search engine and plugged in Scott's name, not surprised to see that Leah had been telling the truth. She could find few details about Scott's death other than a date, a location, and the suggestion that his murder had been drug-related. He'd died the day before, in the early morning hours. It was still too soon for an obituary, but an article said he was survived by his wife and infant daughter. A brother lived in North Wales.

North Wales. Allison remembered the small Mexican restaurant off the main street where they'd first kissed. A late night of strategic planning for a sales pitch he had coming up, plus not enough food and too many margaritas, and Allison had leaned across the table and touched her lips to his. His eyes had shown surprise at first before becoming heavy with desire. It'd been a ten minute drive to his townhouse. Ten minutes of tortuous silence weighed down by the hand he kept on her thigh. As though he'd been afraid she would flee.

She hadn't. Instead, they'd had sex in his bedroom, his living room, the floor of his kitchen. They were all sweat-covered skin and pent-up aggression. It'd been the hottest sex of her life.

Passion mellowed to something tenderer in the weeks that followed. They'd met at his house, her house, hotel rooms in between. She'd thought she was in love. He'd said the same.

Tormented with guilt—after all, in her mind, she was sleeping with a client and cheating on Jason, even if she and her husband were separated—Allison had resigned as his consultant. Two days after the resignation, Leah showed up at Scott's house during a mid-day tryst. Allison and Scott had been in his dining room, braced against the wall. Leah had worn a gray cashmere sweater that matched the ethereal gray of her eyes. Her hands were clutching the sleeves of her sweater, digging holes the width of her nails. Allison had been too shocked to cover her own nakedness.

Leah had been Scott's fiancé. They were due to marry in three months. Facts Allison hadn't known at the time.

Scott apologized to Leah, not Allison. He promised Leah right then and there he would never see Allison again. He called Allison five days later, begging for a lunch meeting. He wanted to explain, he said. He still loved her, he said.

Allison had hung up on him.

To this day, Jason didn't know.

TWO

Vaughn was still tired. Normally an early-morning run and an hour or two at the boxing gym left him wide awake, ready for the day. But not today. This Monday, his lower back ached and a vague sense of anxiety plagued him, clouding his mind and causing him to drive right past the entrance to his apartment building. He made an illegal u-turn on Meadow and swung into the gated lot, cursing his lack of focus.

He parked, jammed the BMW's manual transmission into neutral, and sat back against the seat. Problem was, he couldn't say what, exactly, was bothering him. The last months had been good to him and Jamie. He and Mia were still together, if you could call what they had "together." His brother was gainfully employed by the police and he'd recently received his certification as an ethical hacker. Jamie even agreed to leave the apartment on occasion for purely social reasons, not seeming to mind as much the machines and contraptions that had to travel with him in the handicapped-equipped van. Actually, if Vaughn was honest with himself—and since the drug deal gone bad more than a decade ago that left his identical twin paralyzed and both of their lives shattered, Vaughn tried real hard to always be honest— Jamie seemed downright *happy*.

So then what the hell was eating at him?

Even things at First Impressions had calmed down since the Benini crisis. His boss seemed content for the first time since he'd met her. Although she and Jason weren't officially living together, Jason was there most days—and nights—and Allison was focused on work. Allison's second how-to book, *Underneath It All*, the sequel to her bestseller, *From the Outside In*, was due out in a few months. And they had more clients than they could handle at the moment.

All good stuff.

So why the anxiety? Vaughn shook his head, grabbed his gym bag, and pushed open the car door. He'd learned to trust this sense of restlessness, this heightened intuition, since he was a young kid in juvenile detention, but now maybe he'd crossed some line and was making shit up in his head. Hadn't the Vaughn men been known to do such things?

His father sure had.

Inside the apartment building, Vaughn jogged the three flights of stairs to his apartment, unlocked the door and headed down the hall to check on Jamie. It was only seven in the morning, and he didn't want to awaken his brother or Jamie's nurse, Angela. Jamie had two primary caretakers besides him: Mrs. T, a sweet older woman who cooked for them and shared Jamie's love of detective novels, and Angela, a younger nurse with a radiant smile and glossy black hair. They both took good care of Jamie. They both slept over whenever it was their shift.

Quietly, Vaughn dropped his duffle bag on his own bed. He passed the closed door to the guest room where Angela would be sleeping and gently pushed open the door to Jamie's room, expecting to see his brother dozing quietly, the respirator humming like unwanted white noise. Jamie *was* asleep. But he wasn't alone. Snuggled next to him, her head on his shoulder, her lithe body wrapped around his brother's skeletal contours, was Angela. Her eyes were closed, her hair fanned across Jamie's chest, and her right hand cupped his brother's shoulder in a gesture much more intimate than that of nurse and patient. They both looked serene.

Heart pounding, Vaughn shut the door. He still didn't know the root of his anxiety, but now he knew the reason for Jamie's happiness. His brother was in love.

The Fairweather house was a modern abstraction of the American farmhouse. It was situated on two acres of golf-course emerald lawn and surrounded by no-muss shrubs and strategically placed ornamental grasses. The home's beige exterior matched the beige exterior of every other house in the neighborhood. A former farm, the development, Lofty Acres, was situated on the highest spot for miles around. Allison had a clear view of a sprawling strip mall in one direction and the Pennsylvania Turnpike in another.

She turned her attention to the house in front of her. The two cars in the driveway, an Escalade and a BMW sedan, said someone was home. The car seat in the Escalade said Leah was likely one of them. Allison took a deep breath. She opened the door to her Volvo and stepped out into the frigid morning air. She'd fought with herself over making this trip, but a bitter mix of curiosity and guilt convinced her she needed some answers. Had she ever really had closure with Scott? She didn't think so. Certainly not three weeks ago when she'd seen him downtown. And now this.

Allison paused on the front porch, unable to knock. Maybe it was the wreath of pink and peach dried flowers on the front door. Maybe it was the baby swing tucked next to the white wicker chairs on the small front porch. When she'd known Scott, he'd lived in a townhouse. After that, she'd heard that he and Leah moved to the city, had purchased a half million dollar rehab in a trendy neighborhood. From hipster to suburbanite? The thought made her wonder about the years that had passed. Was she wrong to come here? She felt like she was breaking a unspoken truce. Only she didn't know whether the truce was with the Fairweathers...or herself.

She forced her arm up, her fist to clench. Before she could knock, the front door swung open and she came face-to-face with Leah Fairweather. Or at least a shell of the Leah Fairweather Allison remembered. This Leah had aged. The long white-blond hair was now a yellowed bob that lay in an unwashed circle around her head. Her face, once pretty in a plain, haughty way, was lined. Her features looked pinched and tired. A loose-fitting gray sweater hung limply down sloping, hunched shoulders. The eyes that met Allison's, once full of intellectual arrogance and unabashed hatred, flashed from surprise to anger to a sad resignation that told Allison coming here had been a mistake. But it was too late to turn away now.

Allison took a reflexive step back, pulling her coat tighter around her torso. She said, "We should talk."

"I don't think that's a good idea—"

"About your call the other night, Leah. I'm sorry. About what happened to Scott."

Leah glanced behind her. She frowned, but opened the door wider so Allison could come inside. "My sister is helping me. The police just left. This is the third time they've been here." She sighed. "Let's go in the study. We can be alone."

Leah turned and Allison followed. The house was gloomy, the lights off and window shades drawn. A house in mourning. Aside from the gloom, though, the house was the epitome of the American suburban dream house. New construction, vaulted entryway, hardwood floors, Persian area rugs. Someone—Leah? A decorator?—had once taken care to fill the home with high-end furniture and designer touches, but now the tired edges said no one had cared in quite some time.

A baby cried and Allison saw Leah's shoulders tense. She didn't stop, though, and instead opened a set of glass French doors, and then closed them furtively after Allison entered the room.

Unlike the rest of the house, the office was bright and orderly, despite what Allison assumed had been a sweep by the police. Vivaldi's "Four Seasons" played from speakers that sat on a mahogany bookshelf otherwise lined with business treatises. A massive mahogany desk sat against one wall, its top clear of clutter. A leather swivel chair had been tucked under the desk, and two armchairs, their cushions upholstered in navy blue and ecru stripes, a small mahogany coffee table between them, took up the empty wall of the office. It was an interior room with no windows. If there had been a computer on the desk, it was gone now, likely taken by the police. Papers and envelopes sat on a credenza, arranged in tidy piles.

Leah stood by the desk, looking unsure of herself. Finally, she sat in one of the armchairs and offered the other to Allison.

"I shouldn't have called you." Leah glanced down at hands clasped firmly together in her lap as though they belonged to someone else. In fact, her whole persona gave the air of someone in a trance-like state. Shock, Allison knew. After four years of graduate school in psychology, she was glad she remembered something. Leah said, "You shouldn't have come."

"You sounded so upset, Leah. I wanted to reassure you. And I want to understand what happened, why my name was in Scott's calendar."

"Don't be so naïve, Allison. Isn't that obvious? He still loved you." Allison heard the anger nipping at the heels of Leah's grief. To be deceived by a dead man, when there can no longer be answers? That seemed to Allison the ultimate betrayal. Even if it wasn't true, Leah believed it was. Sometimes fantasy was more damaging than the truth.

Allison said gently, "Leah, Scott was not in love with me. I have no idea why my name was in his calendar. Truly, I don't." When the other woman didn't respond, Allison asked, "What happened to Scott? The papers made it sound like he was involved in something...illegal."

Allison waited for a response. She felt uncomfortable in this room. The scent of Scott's aftershave lingered, the same one he'd worn so long ago. Or maybe she was imagining it. Allison tried to picture him here, working at the austere desk, sorting through these papers, but couldn't. The room seemed barren: no family photographs, no memorabilia. Another casualty of the police investigation, or did Scott prefer the antiseptic feel of the bare office, clear of sentiment? If so, what did that say about the man he'd become?

"I don't know. I don't know anything anymore," Leah said finally. "Scott was found on a street off Broad, in North Philly. Two gunshot wounds to the head. Money and wallet gone. It was early in the morning."

"Did anyone see it happen?"

"An older woman out walking her dog claimed she saw a group of kids running down the street sometime after Scott was killed."

"But she didn't witness anything more than that?"

Leah shook her head. "Not that I know of."

Allison wondered whether the older woman would talk, even if she had seen it happen. Witnesses to murder didn't always fare well, especially if it had been a drug-related murder. Or if a gang was involved. "Who found him, Leah?"

Leah twisted the sleeves of her sweater around her fingers. "Teenagers. A group of them."

"How old?"

Leah looked up. "The cops didn't say. Does it matter?"

"I don't know," Allison said. But she thought it did. Older teenagers made it seem more likely that they were the perpetrators rather than a random group of passersby.

Leah looked toward the desk. Her hands were now fully entwined in the gray wool of her sweater, and her fingertips kneaded the inside of the cloth. "Scott ran every day. Avoided red meat. Flossed." She shook her head, and a tear escaped. She untangled her hands long enough to wipe it away. "Why would he want drugs? Why?"

Allison didn't know why. The Scott she knew had been fit and athletic, a six-foot-four bastion of clean living. Could the stress of his job, or something in his personal life, have pushed him to recklessness? She reminded herself that he'd lied to her and cheated on his fiancé. Risk-taking behaviors. If his desire for risk had grown, she supposed anything was possible.

"Can I see the appointment book, Leah?"

"The police have it."

Allison thought. "Is it possible he had an appointment with another Allison?"

"Hardly." Abruptly, Leah stood and left the room. She came back a minute later with a sheaf of papers in her hand. She flipped through them, and then pulled one out and handed it to Allison.

It was a photocopy of Scott's daily calendar. Indeed, the words "Allison Campbell" had been scribbled in the margin in Scott's tight, slanted printing.

Allison shook her head. "I swear to you, Leah. We had nothing arranged for Saturday night. For *any* night."

But Leah refused to back down. "Then why are you in his appointment book?"

Allison didn't know why, and she said as much. She thought of her chance meeting with Scott a few weeks before. The way he looked at her. They'd both been at Thirtieth Street Station, downtown. She'd been in line to board an Amtrak train to New York City. He'd been rushing through the concourse, toward her. He'd mouthed something she didn't understand. Still hurt, still angry, and wondering what those feelings meant all these years later, Allison had descended the steps to the waiting Acela. Security had blocked Scott's path. At the time, Allison assumed it was a chance encounter, that he'd seen her across the great hall. Had it been more than that? Had Scott Fairweather been trying to tell her something?

Suddenly the Vivaldi was too much.

Allison was rising to leave when the French doors opened and another woman walked in. She was the spitting image of Leah that day Leah had stormed into Scott's townhouse and found Allison and Scott in the dining room. A younger, prettier, fresher version of the widow standing before her now. It was déjà vu. Allison's stomach tightened.

"Someone wants Mommy."

Someone was the infant in this other woman's arms. Chubby. Tow-headed. Adorable. The little girl stared wide-eyed at Allison.

The woman said, "I'm Leah's sister, Heather. And you are?"

But Allison was no longer listening. Vivaldi's violins rang out, a melody echoed by the deeper tones of cellos. Allison's chest felt heavy. To Leah, she muttered, "I'm sorry to have bothered you."

Leah opened her mouth to speak, but Allison didn't wait to hear what she had to say. She left that house quickly, more confused now than she'd been when she arrived.

Vaughn showered quickly, changed and drove to First Impressions. By the time he arrived at the office, he saw Allison's Volvo in the parking lot, next to a pearl white Cadillac Seville. He recognized that car. Midge Majors.

Inside, he walked past the client room, trying hard not to listen to Midge's high-pitched voice going on about something and pulled on the door to his office, leaving it open just a crack. There was a stack of mail on his desk and he began sorting through it, filing away bills, fan letters and the occasional circular. He came to a 6" x 9" brown envelope clasped shut and then taped. Someone had typed "Allison Campbell" in black blocky letters across the front. The envelope was smudged and dirty, with two square indentations, as though it had been rescued from beneath a heavy chair or caught in a door. Probably some hand-delivered fan mail. Vaughn figured the cleaning crew had left it on his desk. But where had they found it?

Before he could give it another thought, he heard Allison calling for him. She opened the door to his office, gave him a quick, quizzical look—it was unusual for his door to be closed—and then pointed to the woman standing behind her. Midge Majors was dressed in a powder blue button down dress and matching heels. A small black hat perched on her ebony-dyed hair, and circles of red rouge graced the sagging skin of her cheeks. There was a twinkle in Midge's eyes, though, a mischievousness that had to be the cause of the amusement on Allison's face.

"Tell him, Midge," Allison said. "He'll give you an honest opinion."

"Tell me what?"

Midge cleared her throat. "Sexy seniors."

"Sexy what?" Vaughn looked from Allison to Midge and back again. What were they up to now?

"Sexy seniors," Midge repeated.

"It's Midge's new group idea. The next phase for some participants in the recently divorced group."

Midge nodded with such vigor that her cap nearly flew off her head. "You know, for those of us over sixty who are ready to get back in the dating pool. We can help each other. Seniors have some special issues in this area, and it would be good to talk about them. Learn, you know...techniques."

Her face flushed beneath the garish rouge. Vaughn swallowed. It was nowhere near Valentine's Day, but already everyone was thinking about love, love, love. He smiled and nodded, because that was what Midge wanted. These groups of Allison's were always a hit, but he didn't know how she'd find time to squeeze in another.

"Sexy seniors." He made a note on the pad on his desk. "I'll set it up and include an invitation in the next client newsletter."

Midge clapped. "So you like the idea?"

Vaughn smiled again. He saw Allison staring at him and shifted his eyes toward the window. "Midge, what's not to like?" he said a little too heartily. "Sexy seniors. You may have given Allison a new book idea."

Thirty minutes later, Midge was gone and Allison was standing before Vaughn while he signed checks at his desk.

"You okay?" she asked.

She was letting her blonde hair grow, and it fell in soft waves around her face. He noticed a few crow's feet around her eyes, a crack in her armor and a sign that neither was as young as they used to be. He felt a sudden and protective surge of affection toward his boss. She was as lovely as the day he'd met her.

"Vaughn?"

Vaughn sighed. "It's Jamie." He recounted the scene he witnessed at his apartment.

Allison sat on the edge of his desk.

"Are you sure she hadn't simply fallen asleep while she was in there with him? They could have been watching television or something equally as innocent and just dozed off."

"She was in her pajamas, Allison, and she was holding him. Not like a nurse or a sister. Like a lover." The lover his brother could never have, Vaughn thought. And with that he knew why he felt so unsettled.

As though reading his mind, Allison's face softened. She said, "Hey, there are many ways to be someone's partner. Sex, in the typical manner, isn't the only way to be intimate, Vaughn. Just because...well, just because not everything works doesn't mean he can't satisfy a woman."

Vaughn was sure Allison was right, but he didn't want to see his brother get hurt.

Remembering the odd brown package, and grateful for a change in topic, Vaughn opened his top drawer and pulled the envelope from inside. "This was mixed in with yesterday's mail when I arrived this morning."

Allison looked alarmed. She snatched the envelope from his hand with a too-casual "cool" and stood to leave.

"Aren't you going to open it?"

Allison shrugged. "Later. It's probably just something from one of the group members. They're always leaving me articles and recipes."

Recipes? Vaughn raised his eyebrows, glad Allison didn't see the expression. She was already out the door, that envelope gripped in her hand. His boss needed recipes like he needed a bra. She rarely cooked—Jason did that. And when she did cook, everyone was grateful that she did it so infrequently. So either Allison had caught an unlikely case of the Becky Home-eckies or she was lying. Vaughn, who was not generally a betting man, would wager on the latter.

THREE

Allison tucked the envelope in the top drawer of her filing cabinet without opening it. She had an appointment in ten minutes, but that wasn't why she left the envelope intact. She was quite sure whatever was in there had something to do with Scott's death. Call it a hunch, women's intuition, a premonition, or just a good guess based on timing and the lack of postmark, but she could feel Scott's person on that envelope. More than that, though, she knew if she opened it now, Vaughn would corner her before her client arrived. He'd ask what had been in that envelope. Reluctant to lie to her friend, she'd either not answer or tell him outright it was none of his beeswax. Neither option seemed appealing.

Maybe he'd forget. But she'd seen the suspicious look in his eyes.

So Allison calmed her shaking hands, locked the cabinet and went out to reception. When Vaughn asked, she could honestly say she didn't know. Because she didn't.

Not for sure.

Raymond Obermeier was Allison's accountant, and he sat across from her a few hours later at The Corner Bakery, his brow furrowed in a full-face frown. He took care of her finances and the finances of her ailing family. When he said he'd wanted to discuss the affairs of Fred and Carol Chupalowski, her parents, Allison hadn't been too concerned. Her money was their money, and, frankly, they had so little of it left that she knew much of her own savings would eventually go toward their care.

"Allison, are you listening to me?"

"Of course."

"Then what did I just say to you?"

Allison leaned in. She was distracted, but she *had* heard him, and his tone as much as his words made her pay attention. Raymond was not your typical accountant. He had straight brown hair, broad shoulders and looked a lot like Captain America. But that wasn't why she liked him. She liked him because he was a straight shooter. Although right now she was having trouble believing what he had to say.

"She's been estranged for years. Why would she approach them now?"

Raymond shrugged. "I'm an accountant, not a psychologist."

Allison looked out the window, toward the parking lot. It was dusk and she was tired. It had been unusually cold for early November in Philly, but the chill she was feeling had less to do with the weather than with the mention of her sister, Amy. She hadn't heard a thing from Amy in over a decade.

November was a month for reappearances, it seemed.

"How much does she want?"

"Ten thousand dollars—"

"That's a lot."

"Let me finish." Raymond looked at her sternly. Raymond never looked at her sternly. "Ten thousand *cash*."

"What the hell? My parents don't have that kind of money. Why would she go to them and ask for that?"

Raymond raised his hand. "Again, accountant, not psychologist." He looked at her over adorable wire-framed glasses. "Or family therapist."

"Did she say why she needs the money? Where she's been? Anything at all about her life?"

"She said she was Carol's daughter and she needed money. She said, and I quote, 'It's a matter of life or death.'"

Allison sighed. Her sister had been dramatic as a teen. Was she still? Could Allison take that chance? Maybe there were medical bills or she was facing eviction or, God forbid, a loan shark was after her, threatening to kill if she didn't pay up. Amy may have cut them out of her life, but she was still blood. Allison liked to believe that meant something.

Allison stirred the coffee in front of her, which sat untouched. She crumpled a napkin, then stretched it straight, worrying the edges with her carefully-manicured fingers.

"You're stalling, Allison. Unlike you." Raymond leaned in and Allison could smell hazelnut on his breath. She found it funny that her strong, sexy accountant drank hazelnut-flavored coffee. "My advice? Say no now. I see this all the time. The reckless relative who can't manage their own money and uses guilt or threats—"

Allison sat up straighter. "Did she use guilt or threats?"

"No." Raymond threw up his hands. "Don't be so literal, Allison. I'm just saying that's the pattern. It starts with an innocuous request, and then the guilt and threats start. Before you know it, you and your parents are sucked dry." He sat back. "Take my advice. Say no now."

Allison considered his words. She looked down at her hands, stretched out before her. Her mind flitted to the brown envelope now sitting, open, in her glove compartment. Guilt and threats. She understood.

When Allison spoke, her voice was firm. "Give her two thousand. From *my* account. Tell her if she wants more, she needs to contact me directly."

Raymond, clearly sensing his client had made up her mind, nodded. He was wise enough to withhold further counsel. That was another thing Allison liked about him.

Allison shut the door to her car against a bitter, driving wind. She watched Raymond drive away in his old-model Miata, carefully restored, buffed and waxed, before reaching into the glove compartment and removing the envelope. She pulled open the clasp and carefully tugged the three papers from inside their resting place. She stared at them once again, feeling nauseous.

The first document was a picture, or, rather, a photocopy of a picture. It was of her and Scott in an embrace. They were nude, and the camera caught her in semi-profile. She could see the outline of one breast, the curve of her buttocks and the hollow behind one knee.

Scott's face was visible, and the bastard was staring right at the camera, or where the camera must have been. Allison recognized his townhouse, she recognized his bedroom, but she had never, ever consented to be photographed. Anger, shame, and something she recognized as slowly boiling rage filled her.

She flipped to the second picture. This was of the two of them at Thirtieth Street Station, just weeks ago. Scott was standing at the top of the stairs, beckoning to her. She was looking back. Her eyes were hooded with what looked like sadness, as though they were parting lovers. But in actuality, that had been concern and surprise on her face. Their encounter had been innocent, but someone had made it look tawdry. Why?

The last document was the most frightening. It was a plain piece of white paper, 9 ½ x 11. Someone had typed the words "SLUT" on it, above that was a perfectly round hole outlined in blood red marker. The meaning was not lost on Allison. A bullet hole. A threat. Crudely done, almost juvenile, but the effect was terrifying nonetheless. Shame, guilt, and threats. Only whoever sent this to her didn't want money. They wanted silence. But silence about what?

Allison arrived home to the scent of garlic and the sight of her ex-husband-now-boyfriend, Jason, and former mother-in-law, Mia, in the kitchen. Jason was stirring something red in a blue Dutch oven and Mia was slicing what looked like home baked bread. Allison worked her face into a smile and hugged them both.

"Dinner in fifteen, Allison?" Jason smiled. He still wore his suit pants, slim-tailored against athletic legs, but had traded his button down shirt and tie for a frayed Penn t-shirt. A black apron, the words "Men BBQ'ing" emblazoned on the front, was tied around his waist. Mia wore jeans and a red cotton cardigan, but the lipstick and subtle scent of Chanel said someone else was joining them. That, and the fourth place setting.

Thinking of the envelope and what she would say if he asked, Allison said, "Where's Vaughn?"

Mother and son looked at each other. "He's not coming," Mia said.

"Oh? Then who gets the fourth spot?"

Brutus, who had been following her around since she arrived, now stuck his nose firmly in her crotch, then stood back and barked. He wanted a treat. Now. Allison opened the cookie jar that held his dog biscuits and kept her eye on Mia. But it was Jason who spoke.

"I suggested Mom invite Svengetti over so we could meet him."

Mia said, "And he happened to be in town."

Happened, huh? Allison couldn't help the little niggle of relief—and guilt. No Vaughn meant no questions. "Of course. I'll go wash up."

"So, Allison, *you're* the Main Line's answer to Nancy Drew." Thomas Svengetti's joking tone and warm smile softened the words, but given the day's events, Allison had to control a shiver. Thomas Svengetti, a former federal agent for the IRS, had been involved when Allison's clients went missing the year before. He'd been Mia's contact though, and Allison had never met him in person. The man sitting across from her now was tall, trim and broad-shouldered. A thick head of graying brown hair and a trimmed salt and pepper beard softened an otherwise bony face. Inquisitive blue eyes probed her own.

Allison looked down at her salad and ran the tines of her fork across a narrow wedge of limp tomato. She smiled, but only because Svengetti expected her to. She said, "So what brings you to Philadelphia, Thomas?"

Svengetti smiled. "Mia."

Allison glanced at Mia with surprise. Was something going on between these two? Mia and Vaughn had been together for some time now. First friends, then more, they were the best kind of friends with benefits. It seemed out of character for Mia to do something so blatantly hurtful, and Allison felt a wave of protectiveness for her business manager and friend.

"Residual stuff for the Benini situation," Mia said quickly, referring to last year's missing client. "I'm helping Thomas tie up some loose ends."

Svengetti nodded.

"And I may have some questions for you, too, Allison. If that's okay."

"Of course," Allison said, relieved. The Benini affair was something she wanted to put behind her, but if her information could somehow help Tammy Edwards, her other former client who had gone missing last year, she'd do what she could.

Brutus nudged Allison's leg under the table. She grabbed a crouton from her plate and handed it to the dog, who gobbled it as though his last meal hadn't been twenty minutes ago. She wiped his slobber on her napkin, thinking how far they'd come. Just a few years ago, she'd been terrified of dogs. And just a few years ago, Brutus had been a stray.

"You're not supposed to give him table food," Jason said.

Allison dismissed him with a wave of her hand. She wasn't supposed to—hadn't the trainer said that?—but how could she resist that face? Her Boxer had a severe under bite and a big, jowly head, truly a face only a mother could love. Brutus thanked her with a slobbery kiss and an adoring gaze that made her smile.

Jason was about to say something else when the phone rang. Allison sprung out of her seat before Jason could beat her to it. She picked up the kitchen handheld, her gut tightening. But it was only Raymond Obermeier, her accountant.

Willing her pulse to slow down, Allison said, "You called to say you found some missing money and I'm now a millionaire?" The joke fell flat, even to her own ears.

"I'm afraid not."

His voice was tight, and Allison stood a little straighter. "What is it, Raymond?"

"Your sister, Amy. She wants to meet you."

"When?"

A pause. "Now."

FOUR

The Murray Motel was a one-story, u-shaped box with pink stucco siding and peeling white shutters. It sat on the outskirts of Norristown, surrounded by a half-empty parking lot and abutted by a derelict apartment complex on one side and a pawn shop on the other. The motel's office advertised clean rooms rented by the hour, night, week and month. A woman stood outside the office. Her four-inch heels and royal blue skirt, hiked up high on a skinny-flabby thigh, suggested she was looking for the hourly rental. She gave Allison and Jason a hazy, hopeful stare and then looked quickly away.

Allison felt Jason's grip on her arm tighten. "Are you sure this is the place?"

Allison nodded. "Room one-twenty-three."

Allison walked briskly. Each room had a small porch and one white plastic chair. Despite the bitter cold, they passed two male occupants sitting outside, cigarette smoke wafting from dark, gnarled fingers. One nodded at Allison; the other eyed them warily.

The room next to Amy's was dark. Sirens wailed in the distance. The air smelled of cigarettes and fuel. Allison squared her shoulders, and with a quick glance at Jason, knocked. It'd been nearly fifteen years since she'd seen her baby sister, fifteen years since Amy ran away from home, a seventeen-year-old with fire in her blood and lust in her heart. She'd disappeared with a boyfriend and was gone for two endless years. She showed up at twenty, while Allison was in graduate school, looking for a place to sleep and money, and then disappeared again, taking her parents' savings and her mother's engagement ring with her. Radio silence ever since.

Until now.

Allison raised her hand to knock again when the door flung open. Now gaunt and hollow-eyed, Amy's once thick, blond tresses had been replaced by a greasy mass of lifeless brown. Amy held her finger to her lips. She grabbed a coat from somewhere inside the darkened room and stepped outside.

"Baby's sleeping."

Baby? Alarmed, Allison looked to Jason and saw her concern reflected in his eyes. But if Amy noticed their apprehension, she didn't let on.

"She's five, but I still call her a baby." Amy smiled wistfully, and in that smile Allison saw the sister of her childhood: always rebellious, and a little regretful after the fact. "Name's Grace." Amy drew a cigarette out of the breast pocket of her coat. She held the pack out to Allison, then Jason, both of whom shook their heads. With a shrug, Amy lit up. She took a deep inhalation, letting the smoke out in concentric circles, and seemed intent on watching those rings disappear into the night.

"Grace's daddy's got religion. I figured if I named her Grace, he'd leave his wife and come with us." Another shrug. "Didn't work, though. He saw it as a sign from God that he should repent and confess to his wife. She forgave him, but made him swear never to see me or Gracie again."

Allison didn't know what to say. She had a niece. For five years now, she'd had a niece, and never had any idea. She thought of her parents, their joyless life and her mother's suffering. It would mean so much to them to have a grandchild to dote on. And Faye—did she know?

Jason said, "Amy, where are you living?"

Amy nodded toward the motel room. "For now."

"Come and stay with us. Bring the baby."

Allison looked at him, surprised and grateful. She nodded. "Yes, come with us. We have plenty of room." We...she and Jason weren't quite a "we." Still, it felt right.

Amy shook her head vehemently. "Sorry."

"Then why did you call?"

"You know why."

"Money."

"Don't sound so damn judgmental, Allison."

Allison looked at Amy. Maybe despite the child, nothing had changed. Same old Amy, thinking only of herself. "What do you need the money for?"

"Does it matter?"

"You asked Mom and Dad for money. They have nothing. *Nothing.*"

"I have nothing, Allison. *They* have a roof. *They* have food." Amy laughed and Allison saw a faint bruise along her jawline, a pink scar above her upper lip. "They have you."

Allison's mouth tightened into a hard line. If it wasn't for the little girl in room one-twenty-three, she would have headed for the car. But she had a niece. The news still stunned her, and she couldn't—wouldn't—walk away.

"How much do you need?"

"Ten thousand." Amy's chin jutted up. "Or more, if you have it."

"For what?" Jason asked.

Amy's head snapped in his direction. "Who is this, Allison? No ring, so I know he ain't your husband."

Allison felt Jason stiffen beside her. "Let me think about it," she said.

Amy's eyes widened. "You don't get it. I need it. Right away."

"Why?"

Amy looked down at her feet, bare except for black socks. "Give it to me and I'll go away."

Allison sighed. She looked around at the motel. The two men and the hooker were gone now, but the sense of hopelessness lingered. "What if I don't want you to go away?"

Amy scoffed. "You gotta be kidding."

"There's Grace. I've never even met her."

"And you never will." Amy's expression softened at the look of pain on Allison's face. "I'm sorry, Allison. I can't stay in one place long, you know that."

"All the more reason—"

But Amy shook her head again.

"Money, and I go away. No trouble."

"And otherwise?"

Amy pulled her shoulders back in a familiar gesture of defiance. "I'll go directly to Mom and Dad. They'll give it to me."

So that was the choice. Money or heartbreak for her parents.

Allison stepped back off the small stoop. Finding her voice, she said, "I'll have a decision tomorrow."

But her sister wasn't listening. From somewhere in the depths of her coat, her cell phone was ringing. That panicked look back again, she opened the door to her motel room. "What now?" Allison heard her say into the phone before the door closed behind her.

They were silent in the car for what felt like a millennium. Jason turned the radio on to WXPN and waited until he was back on the Pennsylvania Turnpike before saying anything.

"I'm so sorry," were his first words. "That must have been very painful."

But Allison couldn't respond through the tears. They choked her speech and blinded her sight. Jason reached over, found her hand, and held it.

By the next day, reason had returned. In the morning, Allison facilitated two client groups, one called "Returning to the Workforce," for clients who were looking to refresh their images and their careers after a long hiatus, and her recently divorced group. She forced herself to focus on her clients' issues and goals rather than her own problems, and that helped. By noon she knew what she needed to do.

"Your sister has a history of lying," Jason had said the night before. "We don't even know if Grace really exists, or if she's a handy tale to guilt you into handing over the cash."

As usual, he was right.

Allison dialed Amy's mobile number, the one Raymond had given her the day before. When no one picked up, she left a quick, cryptic message. As predicted, her phone rang thirty seconds later. It was Amy.

"Will you do it?"

"On three conditions," Allison said. "One, you tell me the truth about why you need it. Two, you never—and I mean never—ask Mom and Dad for money. Mom's sick, Amy. Very sick. And Dad's not all there."

"Yeah, yeah. I get it. What's the third?"

"I want to meet my niece."

"No."

"Then no money."

"Shit, I'll just go to Mom and Dad."

Allison tightened her grasp on the phone. "You're not listening. They're broke. I control the little money they have left. And Faye has nothing, either. Plus, Mom's dying. Amy, doesn't that matter at all to you?"

Amy was silent. "Broke?"

Some things never change, Allison thought. "Yes, broke."

Amy hissed a series of curses under her breath. "Meet me at four at the McDonald's right near my hotel room. Don't be late. And don't tell my daughter who you are."

"You don't get to set the conditions."

"Allison—"

"I want to see a birth certificate. And you need to tell Grace the truth about who I am."

Another pause, longer this time. "I hate all of you. Fine, fine. Four, Allison. And don't bring your boyfriend. Those eyes make me nervous."

FIVE

By four o'clock Tuesday, the sun sat low on the horizon. Allison had spent the afternoon trying hard not to think about the pictures of her and Scott that sat locked up in the file cabinet in her office. Instead, she used every break to research her sister: social media, paid sites, even criminal databases. From what she could tell, Amy had very little online presence and no record. That, she supposed, was a good thing. But the fact that she knew almost nothing about her sister made her heart and head ache. At three, she downed two migraine tablets and headed back to Norristown, avoiding Vaughn's questioning eyes as she walked out the door.

She arrived at McDonald's early. She bought a cup of coffee and chose a booth near the kids' play area from which she could see both entrances. At four-twelve, Amy showed up, a small child bouncing ahead of her, all perky smiles and deep dimples.

Amy saw her, but stopped by the counter and ordered ice cream. While the pair waited for their food, Allison watched them. She acknowledged the relief she felt because of the child's health and vigor. Grace stood next to her mother, bouncing on her toes, an expectant smile aimed at the woman behind the counter. When the clerk handed her a cone, she said "thank you" in a clear voice.

"Come on," Amy muttered.

The pair joined Allison at her table. Grace was bundled in a cheap purple coat and matching mittens. Her thick, dark hair had been coerced into two braids. Wayward strands stuck out at odd angles. The little girl looked at Allison with mild curiosity.

"You're Mommy's sister?"

"I am." Allison smiled. "How are you, Grace? It's nice to meet you."

The little girl looked at her matter-of-factly. "I'm good now. I have ice cream."

"I'm always better when I have ice cream, too."

Amy fussed with Grace's braids, smoothing the hair back from her daughter's face. She pulled something out of a satchel by her side and slid it toward Allison. Allison flipped it over. A birth certificate: Mother—Amy Denise Chapulowski; Father—Darren Lowe.

"Satisfied?"

"You can't stay where you are, Amy. Come stay with me. Just for a few days. I have room, and a dog. And..."

"And no."

"Why not?"

Amy stood and eased off her coat. Underneath she wore a turquoise acrylic sweater and a pair of jeans. She'd washed her hair, but it still hung lifeless down to her shoulders. Her eyes were black pits. The scar Allison had noticed last night was a garish pink in the light of day, and the bruise along her jaw was a livid purple.

"Who is he?" Allison asked.

Instinctively, Amy's hand shot to her face. She turned away. "Ten thousand, Allison. A new start. A new life for me and Grace."

Allison caught her sister's eye and pointed at the play area. The ice cream, now half eaten, lay on a napkin in front of Grace and the child was watching a group of kids play in the brightly-colored tubes with obvious interest.

Gently, Amy wiped Grace's mouth with a clean napkin. "Want to go play?"

"Yes!"

"Go, then. Stay where I can see you."

The two women watched as Grace wormed her way into the group with obvious ease. Amy said, "I did something right, huh?"

Allison smiled. "She's precious."

"She's smart and brave and exasperating. And the reason I left him."

"Darren?"

Amy shook her head. "Someone else. His name's unimportant.

He's not a nice guy, and I figured it was only a matter of time before he went after Gracie, too. I asked her father for help, but he told me to get the hell out of his face. Just like that, too. 'Get yourself and that bastard child out of my face.'" Amy ran a hand through her hair, scowling at the memory. "I had nowhere else to go."

Allison studied her sister. Amy's eyes darted from object to object, chewed-up nails tapped the tabletop. Allison wanted to believe her, wanted to believe that Amy had had the good sense to leave an abusive relationship before things turned worse. But her sister had always had a way of twisting the truth into something that suited her needs. Was she doing that now?

"What will you do with the money, Amy?"

"Get a car, some new clothes, find a decent apartment and a job. Me and Gracie, we'll head west. A friend told me about some openings in Chicago. Chicago should be far enough from him."

Allison turned her head and watched her niece. Grace was crawling through a plastic pipe on hands and knees, a look of intent focus on her features, features that were cute now but would be stunning when she got older.

"Do you want to leave Grace with me while you get settled?"

That look of alarm was back. One skinny hand shot out toward Allison, and then receded, finding a home in Amy's lap. "No. She stays with me."

Allison nodded. She had such mixed feelings: grief, rage and a tiny trickle of relief. Her sister was trouble, and Allison didn't need more trouble. But when she looked again at Grace, she realized the sadness and rage were winning. What kind of a life could Amy possibly give her daughter? And how far would ten thousand dollars get them? If she could help, she should.

Allison reached into her purse and pulled out a fat envelope. She passed the wad of hundreds across the table. Amy grabbed it. The money disappeared into her satchel.

"Get settled. Find a job. Then let me know how things are going. If you need something for Grace..." Allison's voice trailed off as she watched her niece playing. So much life in her eyes, so unlike her mother. Allison stood to go, choking back those damn tears again. "Well, just call me."

*   *   *

Later that night, Allison lay in bed next to Jason, her arm wrapped around his naked chest. He was asleep, and she listened to the gentle sound of his breathing, relishing the feel of his warm skin against her breasts. Ever since the client disappearances of last year, when Francesca Benini and Tammy "Swallow" Edwards went missing on the same day, she and Jason had reached some kind of truce. Before then, he talked constantly about marriage and kids. Now he rarely mentioned either. Nevertheless, Allison saw the longing in his eyes when they were around friends' babies or others spoke of marriage. Her ex-husband was getting sentimental as he aged. What was wrong with her?

Allison turned over, facing the window. She loved Jason. That much she was sure of. But what kind of mother would she make? She was endlessly busy, selfish, ambitious...and scared. As a kid, she'd never been anyone's little girl. Her father was an abusive, cold man, and her mother had constantly been ill, first with debilitating migraines and later with Alzheimer's. Allison had had to fend for herself from an early age. With a resentful older sister, Faye, and a delinquent younger sister, Allison had been the stereotypical middle child. And now the thought of raising a kid made her quake. What if she was unable to do any better than her parents had done?

Brutus let out a low, long snore from his spot at the foot of the bed. She reached down to pet him.

Around them, darkness pressed in, and with it, other thoughts. Allison considered the photos. Who had sent them? Scott, before he died—had he somehow scheduled their delivery? Someone else, someone with a vested interest in scaring her? Well, they had succeeded. Allison had no idea what to do. Ignore them, and risk that the same someone will send those pictures to Jason or make them public? Or try to figure out who sent them and why?

Neither option seemed practical—or palatable.

Allison turned over again, spooning Jason's body against her own. She traced her fingers down the length of his back, feeling the welts left earlier by her nails. Their lovemaking that night had been feverish, rough. Afterwards, Jason had looked at her with surprise. For that matter, she'd surprised herself. Her desire, she knew, had been rooted in need. A need for escape, or a need for possession? She wasn't sure.

Vaughn wanted to ask Jamie about Angela. But he couldn't. It was nearly seven-thirty in the morning, and when he left Jamie in Angela's hands, he'd seen the look that passed between them. It wasn't a sisterly-brotherly look, that was for sure.

Vaughn skipped the gym. Instead, he headed west, toward Mia's house. He'd called to let her know he was coming, and the sleepy-sultry sound of her voice had stirred something other than his conscience. He drove down the long, winding driveway toward her small bungalow, searching for Buddy, her dog. The acres of farmland on which her rustic stone home sat were quiet on this November morning. The clear sky and chill air felt good. Being out here in the country, he could almost feel his spirits lifting.

He let himself into Mia's house. After greeting Buddy, who knew him well, he slipped through the kitchen and into Mia's bedroom. She was there, in bed, reading a Donna Leon novel while propped against the pillows. Her long graying hair hung loose around her shoulders. She wore a men's flannel shirt, unbuttoned nearly to the navel, and the rise of her small breasts under the cotton material made him hard.

She smiled at him. Vaughn slipped off his clothes and climbed in bed with her, giving in to the passion that had clouded his mind. Mia was quieter than normal, and the sex was comfortable: languid and slow. Sex between friends. Best friends. Mia was older by twenty years, and had long made it clear that she wanted nothing from him but companionship and release.

Had he fallen in love somewhere along the way?

Had she?

He curled around her in the bed, taking in the minty smell of her hair and the honeysuckle tones of her skin. He wanted to stay there all day, but he couldn't. Work waited.

He toyed with telling Mia about Jamie, about his concerns related to Angela. He knew what she'd say, though: don't worry about him. Let him have his own life. You can't protect him from everything.

He'd been doing just that for so many years. How to let go?

*   *   *

Allison awoke with a start. She felt groggy and slightly nauseous. A migraine was digging its talons into her neck. What time had she finally fallen asleep? Three a.m.? Later? The bed was empty except for Brutus, who was staring at her expectantly from three inches away. When she yawned, he rewarded her with a slobbery kiss.

"Oh, Brutus," she murmured, wiping her mouth, and patted his head. She rolled out of bed before he could bestow more affection.

In her office, she opened the day's calendar. An eleven o'clock session with a state representative, a noon session with a local executive and a two o'clock seminar for sales representatives at Munroe Pharmaceutical Industries.

Allison showered and got dressed. The day outside was clear but cold, and she opted for an ivory-colored wool crepe pantsuit with matching Ferrigamo heels. An ivory, ice blue and cocoa scarf completed the outfit. Dressed and ready, she stared in the vanity mirror, tracing the faint lines emanating from the corners of her eyes and her mouth. She'd be thirty-four this coming spring. Thinking of Grace, of Jason, she wondered how much longer she could wait to decide the next steps in her life.

She heard her mobile phone buzzing from the next room. Quickly, she grabbed her make-up case and headed into her bedroom. She clicked the phone without checking the ID. She heard nothing at first, then the faint sounds of breathing.

"Who is this?"

More breathing, then silence. She heard trucks in the background followed by a loud *bang* that could have been a car backfiring—or a distant gunshot. She pulled the phone away from her face. Clearly, this call was meant to scare her. But she felt more enraged than afraid.

"Answer me, damn it. Who is this?"

Whoever it was hung up. Allison looked at the caller ID. As she suspected, an unknown number. Damn, she thought. Related to the picture? Or somehow connected to Amy?

She was betting on the former.

She toyed with calling the police. What would she say? *Someone prank called me—and oh, by the way, a former boyfriend was recently murdered and here are some pictures of the two of us someone sent me; these things may be connected.* No, she'd keep this call to herself. For now.

Allison grabbed her purse and headed downstairs. She'd feed and walk Brutus and then go to work. She had clients to attend to, and she wasn't about to let this get in the way of her career. Plus, there she could do some more research on Scott Fairweather. She was beginning to think Leah was right; his death was not a drug deal gone wrong.

But if that was the case, what was it? What had Scott been hiding?

Eleanor Davies was no stranger to fear. Mostly, however, it was the self-induced kind. Rock climbing, mountain biking, skydiving. Eleanor was a self-proclaimed adrenaline junkie. Some people felt out of control when faced with physically dangerous situations, but Eleanor felt time slow down and her senses sharpen. As a matter of fact, the only time Eleanor really felt *in* control was when she was doing something dangerous.

Right now, for instance, she felt distinctly out of control, and she was hating every second of it.

Eleanor grabbed a suitcase from her closet and threw it open. She tossed in clothes, barely thinking about what she'd need.

She had to get on the road.

She closed and fastened the suitcase and then ran into her bathroom. She gathered all of her toiletries and the few prescription medicines she had. In the dining room that doubled as her home office, she threw papers and files into a cloth shopping bag, leaving only the most innocuous things: a few pads of paper and a pile of store circulars.

Flipping off lights as she went along, Eleanor walked from room to room. Was she forgetting anything? I'll be back, she told herself, but only half believed it. Didn't matter. She had plenty of funds if she needed them.

She glanced at her watch. It was nearly two in the afternoon. If she waited any longer, she'd hit traffic on her route south, and she wanted to be past Baltimore before the heaviest rush-hour congestion.

On the way out the door, she stopped and put down her suitcase.

Her cat, Simon, was still outside, roaming the neighborhood. She called for him, but when he failed to come, she decided to leave him. He was a cat, after all. He could fend for himself.

SIX

By three, it had started to snow. Allison watched from her office window at First Impressions as the flakes first melted, then coated cars and sidewalk surfaces. The sky overhead was a morbid gray, with clouds fringed in ebony moving in from the west. Soon, the roads would be slippery, and with the first snow of the season came accidents.

Allison glanced at her computer screen. She'd been searching online for anything she could find about Scott and Leah Fairweather.

Eventually, Allison had a clearer picture of what Scott Fairweather had been up to in the years since they'd parted. He'd stayed at Mystic Toys long enough to do an ex-pat rotation in India, where he was credited with rejuvenating the company's branding of toys aimed at the female market. He'd left Mystic three years ago and was hired by another public company, Tenure Polk, a furniture manufacturer. He left Tenure nineteen months ago. His last employer was a company named Transitions, Inc. From what Allison could tell, Transitions owned a series of retail stores and managed the brand Transitions, which catered to teens with preppy tastes and rich parents.

On his LinkedIn profile, Scott was listed as the director of marketing for Transitions.

Allison stared at the papers spread out on her desk. She thought about Scott's job history. Three positions in four years. In today's market, changing jobs was usually the best way to make more money. Loyalty and tenure rarely paid, a sad truth. If Scott's salary had gone up with each job, he had been making a nice, fat six figure salary when he died, maybe more if he was receiving options. Plus, Leah had her

PhD. She was a chemist with a major pharmaceutical company, so together they would have been doing quite well.

A wife, a baby, plenty of cash...why drugs? Was it a clichéd story of power and pressure gone wrong? Dead. Two gunshot wounds to the head. North Philadelphia, in a neighborhood awash in violence, drugs and gang warfare. A victim of his own greed?

Allison gnawed on the end of her pen. All of this conjecture made a certain sense. She could see the Scott she knew getting caught up in a lifestyle, much the same way he got caught up in their affair. But why was her name in his calendar?

Allison changed her search terms. Leah's online presence was skimpy. Her LinkedIn profile said she'd been employed until about eight months ago. She had a Facebook account that was blocked to anyone other than friends. Otherwise, all Allison found were scholarly research papers, 5-K results and a blog post about natural childbirth.

Dead ends.

Allison tried the real estate angle. Could debt have somehow contributed to Scott's death? With Leah not working outside the home and a house that was under water, was it possible Scott had been motivated to sell drugs for money? But if his death really was drug-related, who the hell sent those pictures to Allison?

Allison went back to Scott and Leah's LinkedIn profiles. After changing her security setting to "anonymous," she made a list of the connections Leah and Scott shared. One in particular caught her attention. Shawn Fairweather, age 29, was listed as a freelance artist in Pennsylvania. A quick search turned up quite a bit of information on Shawn, more than she could digest right now. Allison found his address in the Manyunk neighborhood of Philadelphia and jotted it down.

She searched for other connections with Transitions listed as the employer. Two looked promising: Julie Fitzsimmons, Public Relations Lead at Transitions; and Eleanor Davies, Purchasing Director. She made note of their names and information.

Allison's phone rang. Vaughn. "Yes?"

"Someone here to see you."

"I don't have any appointments this afternoon."

"This gentleman doesn't need an appointment."

Allison closed her eyes. "Who is it, Vaughn?"

"Detective Jim Berry. Philadelphia police."

Allison met the detective in the client room rather than her office. Her dalliances with the investigating world had taught her not to give away anything, and meeting an official in your home or private office could provide them with personal data you'd rather not share. Although Allison's first thought when she heard that Berry was here was of Amy and her niece, Grace, she realized quickly that it had to be related to Scott Fairweather. She was right.

"I won't take up much of your time, Ms. Campbell," Berry said. "This is a formality. I just have a few questions."

The detective was a rotund man. His squat frame was clothed in crisp khaki pants, a blue and white striped button down and brown Oxfords. His hair, a thinning red, was combed back from his face, and wire-framed glasses and a thick but neatly-trimmed mustache lent him an academic air. He was soft-spoken and polite, but Allison heard steel in his voice. She sat across from him and nodded for him to go on.

"Did you know Scott Fairweather?"

"I did."

"When and in what capacity?"

"He was my client. And later, my boyfriend."

The detective must have caught the hesitation in her tone because he looked up from a laptop in which he'd been typing. "Was he your boyfriend while he was your client?"

"For a short period. Then I...I let him go as a client."

"Hmmm." Berry typed for a moment. Allison tried to read his expression, but it was inscrutable. "How long ago was this?"

"About four years ago."

"And since then?"

"Since then, nothing. I found out he was engaged. We broke it off. I never contacted him again." Which was true, she thought. She'd never contacted him...the encounter in Thirtieth Street Station was not *her* doing.

"Did you end the relationship or did he?"

"Does it matter, Detective?"

Berry smiled. "I get to ask the questions, Ms. Campbell. It's about the only fun part of being a police officer." He smiled. "Who dumped whom?"

Allison recounted the ordeal at Scott's townhouse. "Scott had little choice if he wanted to be married, but let me be clear, Detective. I would not have continued the relationship regardless. I don't date men who are in a relationship."

Berry stared at his screen for a moment. Without looking up, he said, "You were married during that period, Ms. Campbell. To a Jason Campbell."

Allison took a deep breath, let it out slowly. "Yes, I was still married. In name only, though. We were separated."

"So your husband knew about Scott." It was a statement, not a question.

"No."

"I see." Berry grabbed his wireless mouse and scrolled through whatever document he was working on. "Mr. Fairweather had your name in his appointment book, Allison. May I call you Allison?"

"Of course."

"Can you tell me about the nature of your appointment?"

"I have no idea why Scott wanted to see me."

He looked at her over his glasses. "How can that be?"

"Because I didn't have an appointment with him, Detective. As I said, I hadn't contacted him in years."

Berry sat back in his chair. "Yet you don't seem remotely surprised to hear that you were in his appointment book."

Allison put her hands out in front of her, palms up. "Because his wife, Leah Fairweather, called me right after his death."

"What did she want?"

"To accuse me of having an affair with her husband."

"And were you, Allison? Having an affair, I mean?"

Allison felt her patience thinning. "No. As I said—"

Berry waved one chunky hand. Allison saw a thick gold band on a fat, hairless finger. "Yes, yes. You hadn't contacted Scott in years." Berry took off his glasses, wiped at tired eyes, then pointed at Allison with his glasses. "Look, you're not dumb, I'm not dumb. Scott Fairweather had a reason for putting your name in that book. If the two of you had rekindled your affair, I could care less. Unless, of course, it gave you motivation for killing him, or it gave someone else—your boyfriend, his wife, whoever—reason to murder him. But if you were just screwing him and don't want the world to know, tell me now and save us both the headache."

Allison met his stare. She breathed in, slowly, just like she taught her clients to do. Focus on the breath, Allison, until you're calm, she told herself. In and out. When she felt her anger go from red hot to manageable, she said, "I was not having an affair with Scott Fairweather. Other than a chance encounter at Thirtieth Street Station a few weeks ago, I had not laid eyes on the man since our affair ended."

"At the train station?" Berry asked.

"Yes. If you want the date, I can give it to you. I was on my way to New York to deliver a speech. The event was publicized. You can find it online if you look."

"And Scott?"

"I have no idea. We didn't speak."

"Can you get me the date and some verification of your travel?"

"Of course."

Berry closed his computer and tucked it and the mouse into a laptop bag. He took his time. For such a large man, his movements were slow and graceful, almost feminine. He stood, slipped a wool, camel-colored coat on, and looked pointedly at Allison. "Get me that information while I wait in your reception area. And here." He handed her his card. "If your recollection of events changes, please call me."

"They won't."

Berry gave her a weary smile. "That's what they all say."

After Berry left, Allison retreated to her office. She didn't even bother logging back onto her computer. She knew any second Vaughn would come in to ask about the police presence in their offices. She could lie and tell him Berry was here for something related to her family, or the Benini and Edwards' disappearances—or a client, for that matter. But she didn't want to lie to him. She didn't want to lie to anyone. Not proactively sharing information was one thing, she told herself. Being dishonest was another.

Sure enough, about four minutes after Berry's unhurried departure, Vaughn knocked at her door. "It's like you're a damn refrigerator and trouble is a magnet." He softened his words with a smile. "Why was there a cop here this time?"

"The death of a former client."

Vaughn studied her. "Why talk to you?"

"He was killed near North Broad. Looks drug related. Berry is just asking questions of anyone who knew him."

Vaughn sat on the edge of her desk. His dark skin was shadowed in the vanishing daylight, his eyes hooded by disbelief. In an attempt to avoid the scrutiny of his gaze, Allison looked past him, out the window. The snow had picked up, and the beauty of the large, fat flakes against the window startled her. She realized how much Scott's death and the events after Leah's call had been weighing on her. She wanted to tell Vaughn, wanted the relief that would come with sharing this burden. But he had enough on his plate, and right now, telling him would only lead to questions. Questions she wasn't ready to face.

So Allison stood. She reached for her purse and the paper on which she'd written the list of Scott's LinkedIn connections. On it, Shawn Fairweather's address was scribbled in black ink. He didn't live far away. She turned the paper over and quickly shoved it into her purse.

"Allison, you know we've been through a lot."

"Vaughn, I need to get out of here before the roads get worse."

He shook his head slowly back and forth. "It's supposed to clear up in an hour. Now would be the worst time to leave."

"Jason and I have plans—"

Another shake of the head. "Nuh-uh. Nice try. Jason called to say he was working late. He'll meet you at your house around ten."

Allison grabbed her coat from the hanger behind the door. She could feel Vaughn watching her, but she wasn't ready to talk. Not until she knew more.

"Allison, the truth?"

"I told you the truth, Vaughn." Allison looked at her friend. "Detective Berry was here to ask me about a client. The client was killed near North Broad, an apparent drug deal."

"What does this have to do with you, Allison? You've not been yourself. You seem...skittish."

Allison gave him a half smile. "After all we've been through? Murder, attempted murder, disappearances? I think I have reason to be skittish." The lie was easy because it held so much truth.

Vaughn glanced away. "You're right. I'm sorry. I should have figured that." He held the door open for her. "Just be careful. The roads are slick."

SEVEN

Manyunk is hilly. Not a problem on a normal day, but Vaughn had been right. Now was the worst time to venture out in the snow. Allison fishtailed her way up the steep incline of Shawn's street, narrowly avoiding the cars parked bumper-to-bumper along the side.

Shawn's house was a narrow row home on a street of narrow row homes. Brick fascia, an iron porch railing, and newly-painted white trim marked his house, as did the soda can sculpture on the front porch, which used crumpled Coke, Pepsi, Mountain Dew and Sprite cans to spell out "Shawn" in giant letters. Allison climbed out of her vehicle and trudged up the snow-covered pathway to the front door. At least she knew she was in the right place.

A young woman answered the door. She had closely-cropped black hair and a silver nose ring, and her army fatigues made it half way down thick calves before they were met by a pair of black combat boots. She crinkled her nose when she saw Allison.

"Here for Shawn?"

Allison nodded. "Is he home?"

"Depends. Did you bring cash? He's two months behind on his half of the rent."

Allison, not sure what she was talking about, decided to play along. "Is he here?" She looked past the woman's shoulder into a stark black and white living area. A pit bull lay on the couch, snoozing away.

The woman glanced over her shoulder. "That's Crafty. He won't hurt you. Wait here. I'll get Shawn."

Allison eyed the dog, but Crafty didn't look inclined to wake up, much less attack. A few seconds later, a slender young man in jeans and a green Dead Milkmen t-shirt walked in the room. "Thanks Kelly," he said over his shoulder, but his voice trailed off when he saw Allison.

"Who are you?" he whispered.

"Cash!" Kelly called from somewhere in the back of the house.

Shawn at least had the courtesy to blush.

"I'd like to talk to you," Allison said. "About Scott Fairweather."

"My uncle?" Shawn hesitated, but after a contemplative glance in the direction of his roommate, he said, "Come to my rooms. We can talk in private."

His rooms were two bedrooms that opened into one another through a large archway. One room had been painted a deep violet, the other a jarring blue. The space was littered with art materials: paint cans, brushes, canvasses, jars of murky water and garbage. Allison saw more soda cans, bits of plywood, a tripod, twisted metal rods, an easel, even an old toaster. Despite the clutter, the rooms were mostly clean. They smelled of latex paint, marijuana and Clorox.

"Okay, I have no idea who you are," Shawn said. "But thanks for the quick getaway. Kelly's a nag, especially when it comes to money." He smiled, and Allison saw echoes of Scott. "So...I guess I should ask: why are you asking about Uncle Scott?"

Shawn looked young. He had an open, friendly face and a fresh rash of pimples that surrounded his mouth and colored his chin. He was tall like Scott, but thin to the point of emaciation.

"I'm sorry about his passing."

"Yeah, well. Are you the police?"

"No." Allison hesitated. "Scott and I were...old friends."

"Friends?"

Allison glanced down at her hands.

"Friends."

"I didn't know my uncle to have a lot of female...friends."

Allison looked at Shawn, holding his gaze. He stared at her steadily, but there was no real challenge in his eyes. Finally, she said, "Were you close to your uncle?"

Shawn shrugged. "I haven't seen him much recently. He and my dad had a miserable relationship." He smiled. "Adults tell kids to behave, and then they go and act like children."

"Yeah, adults are funny like that." Allison paused. "I know I sound like I'm prying, Shawn, but can you help me understand something? Your uncle...what was he like before he died?"

"I thought you said you were friends."

"Long ago."

"Maybe you can narrow down your question?"

Allison grappled with what to say. What did she hope to gain? Suddenly she felt silly. "I guess I just wanted to connect with someone who knew Scott. I remember him when he was at Mystic Toys. He seemed so ambitious. On the cusp of getting married—"

Shawn snorted. "That almost didn't happen."

"Oh." Allison bit her lip reflexively. "Well, it seems like he and Leah patched things up. They even had a baby."

"That would be Jessica. I haven't seen her yet." Shawn stood and walked toward the paint and feather canvas. He stood in front of it, back to her. "My family is messed up. But what family isn't, right? Uncle Scott and my dad haven't spoken in weeks. Leah, well—" he turned around again, "—she hates my dad. And, by extension, me and my mom. We may go to the funeral anyway. Even though Leah made it real clear she doesn't want us there."

Allison remembered the obituary. "When is the funeral?"

"Saturday. If they release the body. Closed casket. Two o'clock at Saint Andrews."

"Do the police have any idea who killed him, Shawn?"

"Hell if I know."

"I've heard that money or drugs could have been involved. That doesn't sound like the Scott I knew."

"Anything's possible." He waved his arm around the room. "Money, or the lack thereof, can make people desperate."

True, Allison thought, thinking of her own sister, Amy. Allison looked out the window, at the small yard beyond. The snow had tapered to flurries.

"Thanks for talking," she said. "Again, I'm sorry about your uncle. And about your family troubles. I understand how hard that can be."

Shawn nodded. "When I was a kid, I thought Uncle Scott was the bomb. He always had something big going on. Always. And even though I was young, he was always willing to let me in on it. You know how that made me feel? Like a man."

Allison smiled. That sounded like the Scott she remembered. "It's too bad you lost touch."

Another shift of the eyes. "Yeah, it'd been a while," Shawn mumbled. Only Allison didn't believe him.

EIGHT

Eleanor's TomTom said Savannah was just sixty-five miles away. She could make it. She'd just passed Walterboro, South Carolina. Her eyes felt lined with lead, and her heart was pounding from the three cups of black coffee she'd consumed between Baltimore and Fayetteville, but she really had no choice but to get more distance between her and Philadelphia. Ideally, she'd make it all the way to Amelia Island tonight, but her heavy eyelids meant that wasn't going to happen, caffeine or no caffeine.

Sixty miles now.

Eleanor stepped on the gas to get around an eighteen-wheeler. Keep it steady, she reminded herself. No more than five miles above the speed limit. Stay in the right lane. Be innocuous. At least that's how she figured it was done. She was happy for once that her Jeep Grand Cherokee was an unassuming navy blue. She wanted to blend.

She heard her cell phone buzz again just as she was easing back into the right lane. She glanced down at the Android, now on the passenger seat beside her. Same number as before. Damn it, she mumbled to herself. She toyed with turning the phone off, but she wanted to keep tabs on things.

A red Ferrari pulled up beside her, the light over its dash on. A handsome older man smiled at Eleanor before zooming past. She toyed with playing a game of cat and mouse—maybe it would end in company tonight, and she really kind of wanted some company—but she'd promised her sister she'd be in Florida tomorrow, and even more than she wanted company, she wanted to get to Ginny quickly.

It was after two in the morning when Eleanor finally arrived in Savannah. She made do with a Best Western right off the exit and pulled the Jeep into an open spot in a darkened corner of the parking lot before killing the ignition. She'd just stuffed her phone back into her purse when she noticed the red Ferrari in the parking lot, six cars down. The gentleman in the front seat was still sitting there, alone. She paused before getting out of the car. Coincidence? Possibly. There were only so many hotels off the exit, so he could have arrived first and gone straight to this spot. Or he could have been following her.

She had no choice, she had to keep going. She couldn't risk being tailed—by the police or otherwise. Eleanor turned on the ignition and pulled the car out of the lot. She didn't see Ferrari man follow her, but she wasn't taking any chances. With a double espresso and a shot of Five Hour Energy, she'd drive all night. Amelia Island, she thought, here I come.

It was early Saturday morning. The snow from earlier in the week had given way to sunny skies and cool, crisp days. Allison glanced outside. The blue sky overhead promised another beautiful autumn day, far too cheery to be funeral weather. Allison selected a plain black and cream print dress, black Mary Janes and a double string of pearls for the services. She'd pay her last respects and see who else arrived.

Before she left, Allison dialed Jason's number. He'd left Friday morning to interview a witness for a case he'd been assigned to and she wasn't expecting him home until this afternoon. When he didn't pick up, she left a message and turned off the phone. It was better he not be able to reach her. She'd be busy all day. After the funeral, she had a luncheon meeting for Delvar's new charity, Designs for the Future.

Downstairs, Allison found Brutus by the front door, chewing on her black Jimmy Choo. She said, "Brutus!" and he spit it out as though nothing had ever happened. She bent down to pick up the shoe and that's when she saw the envelope taped to the sidelights next to her door.

Jaw clenched, she opened the door, hand on Brutus's collar, and looked outside. No one was there. She tugged the envelope off the window, careful to get all of the tape off, too, and slammed the door shut. She ripped open the seal. Inside, she found an email dated almost four years ago.

Allison stared at the paper, memories flooding her mind. There was no doubt the email was hers. She remembered agonizing over the wording, feeling the excitement of a new infatuation and the pressing guilt of abandoning Jason. With a heavy heart, she read the words again now:

Dear Scott,

I've already spoken to your management team at Mystic Toys, so please don't try to change my mind. In light of our relationship and the events of the last few weeks, I am resigning as your consultant. I have provided Mystic with the names of other comparable consulting firms and have refunded their money 100%. I ask only that you not think poorly of me. This has never happened before. Perhaps it's my crumbling relationship with Jason or the promise of something new and exciting, but I don't think so. The feelings I have for you are real. Not well timed, but real. At some point, I need to tell Jason. Until I have the courage to do that, we should refrain from seeing each other.

With warmest regards,
Allison

Behind the email was another photograph. In it, she was resting her head against Scott's naked chest. A white satin sheet covered her lower torso. Her breasts were bare. It was a beautiful photograph: soft and sultry, with the early morning sunlight bathing her skin in a warm wash of gold. Scott was staring into the camera, a tiny, contented, knowing smile playing with the corners of his mouth.

He knew, Allison thought. These weren't photographs taken by a private detective who'd been hired by Leah, as Allison first assumed. No, these pictures were his. Allison squeezed her eyes shut. *The bastard had been photographing us all along.*

Allison rubbed her temples, giving in to the rage that colored her vision. Thank goodness Jason hadn't been here to find these. She stuffed the photo and email back in the envelope, more determined than before to get to that funeral and to the bottom of what had happened to Scott. She was more and more certain that his death and these pictures were connected. She just had to figure out how.

NINE

Saint Anthony's was filling quickly. Allison arrived early, after the viewing but before the funeral Mass. She chose a spot on the end of a long wooden pew, toward the back of the church, and watched the mourners as they arrived. She didn't recognize anyone until Shawn Fairweather entered the church. He walked behind a raven-haired woman and an older man. Although this man was heavier and shorter than Scott, he had Scott's square jaw and bright, intelligent blue eyes. Shawn and his family sat a few rows in front of Allison, their gazes affixed to the front of the church.

Five minutes before the service was set to begin, Leah Fairweather made her way down the long aisle, accompanied by her sister, Heather. Behind the two women, an older couple—Leah's parents?—walked slowly. An infant was cradled against the older woman's chest.

Watching the baby, Allison felt her anger wane. The infant slept, perfectly-round cheeks moving ever so slightly while she sucked on two fat, rosy fingers. The picture of innocence. Her life was forever changed, though. She would never know her father. It all seemed so hopelessly senseless.

Allison joined the mourners in the rituals of the Catholic Mass, taking some comfort in the familiarity of the words and the hymns, and the priest's voice, which was a soothing baritone. It all seemed so...normal.

At the end of the ceremony, after the priest performed the final benediction and the soloist sang "On Eagle's Wings," a great sob came from someone at the front of the church. Allison heard murmurings, then silence. A voice screamed, "Oh, God, how I hate you!"

It was Leah's voice, and she belted out her rage in the same pitch and tone as she'd used to accuse Allison just days before. Only this time, she had an audience. Another hush fell over the mourners before Leah's sister ushered her back up the aisle, toward the church's vestibule. Leah stopped feet from Allison. She raised one arm and pointed in Allison's direction. "You!"

Mortified, it took Allison a moment to realize Leah was pointing to Shawn and his family, not her.

Heather grabbed Leah's arm and pulled her gently toward the double-wooden doors. But not before Allison heard the words that Leah uttered under her breath. "Monster," she said. "*You* are a *monster*."

After the service, some guests milled about in the church's parking lot while others returned to their vehicles to follow the hearse to the cemetery. Allison watched as Leah and her family walked toward the waiting limousine. Leah seemed deflated and emotionless. Her sister held the baby now, and she cradled the little girl protectively, shielding her from onlookers as though she could also shield her from the pain that lie ahead.

Leah, who had been lingering behind her sister, increased her pace as she passed a small group of whispering mourners who'd congregated by the church's fence. The change in her gait was subtle, but Allison saw Leah glance their way and, with shoulders hunched forward, hurry toward the security of her family. The group, made up of three men and a woman, watched the family pass with rapt but solemn expressions.

The woman glanced down at the last second just as one of the men—short, dark-haired and wiry—reached for Leah's arm. Leah stopped. He held her forearm gently and said something into her ear. Leah nodded before moving on. After Leah passed, the woman in the group looked up and Allison got a good look at her face. She recognized her as Julie Fitzsimmons, one of Scott's work colleagues from the LinkedIn profiles, and made a mental note to talk to her at some point.

The hearse drove off, the limo and a parade of mourners behind it. Allison turned around and found Shawn Fairweather next to her. He still looked ruffled by the display back in the church. The older man was with him.

"Son, aren't you going to introduce me to your friend?" said the older man.

"I would if I knew her name." He smiled at Allison. "She is a friend—sorry, was a friend—of Uncle Scott."

"Allison Campbell." Allison held out her hand.

"Mark Fairweather," the man said. "Scott's brother." He gave Allison a slow once-over, lingering a moment too long on her face. A flash of recognition crossed his features. He recovered quickly, though, and asked, "How did you know Scott?"

"We worked together a few years ago."

"At Tenure Polk?"

Allison shook her head. "While he was at Mystic Toys."

"Ah," Mark said. He squinted as though he were trying to place her, but Allison got the feeling he knew quite well who she was. "Your name is familiar. Maybe I met you at one of Scott's work functions?"

Allison was about to respond when the raven-haired woman joined them. She placed her hand firmly on Mark's elbow. "We need to head to the cemetery," she said. She was younger than Allison thought originally, maybe thirty, and although her features were too harsh to be pretty, she possessed a striking beauty born of strong features and a direct, confident gaze.

"This is Nina, my wife."

Allison and Nina shook hands. Allison noticed precisely-manicured, slender fingers, a three-carat diamond ring and a very limp handshake.

Nina looked bored. She whispered something in her husband's ear.

He smiled indulgently. "Soon, my love," he said, patting her hand. "Allison was just telling us how she knew Scott. Weren't you, Allison?"

"Scott and I were seeing each other at one time. But then, you already know that, don't you?"

Mark gave her a tight-lipped smile. Shawn looked away. Nina laughed.

"Is *this* the woman?" Nina asked her husband.

Mark nodded. "One of them, anyway."

Nina smirked. "I didn't recognize her."

"You wouldn't," Mark said. "She's the one who got away."

Allison drove from the church to Delvar's luncheon with a stomach full of butterflies and a head full of questions. Around her, the crisp, fall air was blessedly dry and clear. Trees, their leaves a symphony of reds, golds and oranges, swayed in a gentle breeze. It was cool enough to be pleasant, but not cold enough to portend winter. A true autumn day, increasingly rare. But Allison was distracted. Her mind was on the Fairweather family. Leah's word for Mark Fairweather, *Monster*, stayed with her, as had the little scene after the funeral. Mark Fairweather knew who Allison was before he'd actually met her. It was not her name he recognized, but her face. Could *he* have sent the pictures?

And what about Nina's words: *Is this the woman?*

Is this *what* woman? If Shawn had recognized her initially, she would have known. It was just Mark. But how had he known of her? Scott...Scott must have told him. Perhaps Mark had even seen the pictures. Unthinkable, but a possibility she couldn't ignore.

Allison merged on to the Pennsylvania Turnpike and headed toward Allentown and the Grand Bistro, the venue Delvar had chosen for today's event. Allentown was close to her parents, so after the meeting, she would swing by and check on her family. Her mother, who had been struggling with Alzheimer's for years, had been steadily declining. Her father, a loud and abusive man during Allison's childhood, had devolved into an unruly child. Allison's older sister Faye, their caretaker, had finally agreed to let Allison hire help. But Allison was afraid the ten hours a day of nursing care still wasn't enough.

Stop dwelling, she thought to herself. Faye has things under control. And Jason would be home tonight. Even though he'd only been gone two days, Allison was looking forward to seeing him. Jason and Brutus. Her makeshift little family.

A large oak leaf fluttered across the roadway and landed on Allison's windshield. She watched it shimmy across the glass before it fell away.

TEN

The luncheon was a merry affair, or it would have been, had Allison been in the mood. Delvar presided over his Designs for the Future board of directors like a nervous bride meeting her future in-laws for the first time. He bounced from person to person, fussing over tiny details. Allison finally pulled him aside.

"Are you okay?"

He smiled. "Sweetheart, do I look okay?"

They were in a small alcove next to the restrooms. Delvar, as always, was dressed in dark colors: a European-cut suit and Giza cotton button down shirt, all in shades of gray.

"Why the nerves? You should be used to the spotlight by now."

Delvar looked down at his nails. The jagged edges contrasted to the neatly trimmed cuticles. "This is important," he said finally.

"And your work isn't?"

Delvar motioned toward the private room where twelve people and two reporters were gathered to discuss the new nonprofit. "When I'm designing, it's all on me. If I fail, I fail on my own terms. I know I can design circles around any one of those people in there. But this—" he shrugged "—this is bigger than me, Allison. Kids on the street who might not get a chance otherwise? I'm their hope. *We're* their hope."

Allison touched his arm. "And you're making their dreams a possibility."

Delvar shook his head. "You don't get it. When you gave me a chance, you were established. People listened to you. Me? I'm still a punk kid from a little city in Pennsylvania. Who the hell is going to listen to me? These folks? We have people from all sorts of companies in there. People who are educated, who've been around. I can't make

Designs for the Future happen on my own."

Allison smiled. "Not yet, anyway."

"Not yet, anyway," Delvar echoed. His stormy eyes held her own. "Maybe. But I need people to contribute real money. That's a risk for them. What if they see through me?"

Allison laughed. She hugged him to her. He was a boy, under all that designer bravado. Still a young kid on the streets making doll clothes with his mother's scraps. She pushed him back and, still holding on to his shoulders, looked into his eyes, round with surprise.

"Then let them see through you, Delvar. They will see exactly what I see, what I've always seen: a gifted, intelligent, kind and beautiful man." She smiled. "Now let's go start a nonprofit company and raise some funds."

Delvar finally smiled. "One condition. You sit with Beth Duvall. Her husband was one of those holier-than-thou types. Preached from the pulpit of his corner office, if you know what I mean. I'm not sure I'm ready for her."

"Deal." Allison led him back toward the dining area. She hadn't gone through the biographies of her fellow board members, but she would—eventually. "But only if you sneak me an extra brownie. It's really been a need-chocolate kind of day."

Allison's last stop was her parents' home. She pulled alongside the small one-story and walked to the front door with a heavy heart. She knew what she would find: her mother asleep in a chair, her gaunt form thinner than the last visit; her father watching some sports program with the television turned up way too loud; and Faye, sanctimonious Faye, busy being busy. They would all look to Allison to fix something: a broken sink, a clogged toilet, Faye's ongoing dispute with their mother's insurance company. Allison would do her best to make things right. That was her role. Despite being turned away by her father more than a decade ago, now that they needed her, she could hardly do the same.

But it didn't make coming home any easier.

Allison knocked once, twice. She knocked a third time more loudly. The bell was broken, had been for years, and probably no one could hear her over the television. When still no one answered, she began to worry. She fumbled with her purse and pulled out the key. She wiggled the lock to get the key in and finally pushed open the door. No one was in the living room. She heard sounds from below, in the small room that had once been their playroom. It'd been empty for years.

It took her a moment to realize what she'd been hearing. Laughter. Giggling.

"Faye?" Allison ran down the steps into the musty room. Only it wasn't musty. The carpet had been washed, the walls scrubbed, and the furniture, an old couch and a velour-covered blue recliner, vacuumed. The room smelled of Pine Sol and citrus. And there, in the twenty-by-fifteen space, was her family. Her mom sat on the recliner looking dazed but happy. Her father sat on one end of the couch, next to their nurse, Eloise. And Faye was kneeling on the floor, playing with a plastic dollhouse with Grace. When Allison walked in, the pair looked up at them.

"Aunt Allison!" Grace said. "Aunt Faye bought me this house. Do you like it?"

Allison glanced from the toy to her sister and back to Grace. She said, "I absolutely adore it."

"Get the girl another!" her father yelled. He watched his granddaughter play with the rapt attention he usually saved for football.

"Faye," Allison said, "can we talk?"

Faye placed a tiny plastic female doll next to the kitchen sink. A male doll was by the kitchen table, a tiny coffee cup in front of him.

Grace grabbed the male doll from the kitchen and tossed him casually to the side. "We don't need him, do we, Aunt Faye?"

Faye looked worried. She stood up, straightening neatly pressed dark indigo jeans. "Not today, perhaps," she said to the child. "For now, the mommy will be enough."

In the kitchen, Allison mulled over what to say. Why was Grace here? And where was Amy? And, for that matter, what had happened to the $10,000?

Before Allison said a word, her sister put a hand on her shoulder, much the way Allison had done to Delvar just hours ago.

"That's Amy's girl."

"I know. I met Amy, gave her money."

Faye nodded. "She told me."

"I don't understand...why is Grace here? Where's Amy?"

Faye took a long, hard look at Allison, clearly struggling with how to say something. This sort of self-censorship was new for Faye. She'd always been the first to hurl an accusation, and she loved to play the martyr role. But ever since Allison was injured a little more than a year ago, ever since the sisters' estrangement had climaxed and they both thought they would lose each other, Faye seemed to temper her interactions.

Faye said finally, "Amy isn't ready to be a mother."

"I know."

"I'm not sure you do." Faye sat down, and when she did so everything about her seemed to sag. "Your sister is a drug addict."

"I figured as much."

"Yet you gave her money."

"She said she was getting help. That she needed cash to start a new life."

"And you believed her?"

Allison crossed her arms in front of her chest. "I saw how she was with Grace. I thought...maybe. Okay, yes, I believed her."

"Oh, Allison." Faye looked at Allison with a twisted mix of love, affection and frustration. "Your baby sister is a hot mess. She's been living with a trucker who beats her every chance he gets. She only stays with him because he keeps the drugs coming."

"She told me about him—"

"She told you what she thought you'd want to hear."

"Did she come here looking for money, too?"

Faye nodded. "I knew she'd steal what little mom and dad had, so I turned her away." Faye blushed. It was her turn to look ashamed. "I had no idea about Grace."

"And then she came back here after I gave her the cash?"

Faye nodded. "She didn't want the child. At least not right now."

"So she could get settled first?" Allison said hopefully.

Faye just stared at her, eyebrows knitted into a frown. Allison was sure she, too, remembered a younger Amy—from the tempestuous little toddler to the precocious preteen to the delinquent who spent more time in detention than in class. Amy hadn't changed, that much was clear.

Allison sat down, hard. "She could have left Grace with me. I offered."

Faye's mouth turned upward in a mockery of a smile. "I'm not sure you're ready to be a mother, either."

When Allison started to speak, Faye raised her hand. "You can't just throw money at things and make them right. It doesn't work with drug-addicted sisters, and it doesn't work with children."

Allison swallowed. Was she right? Is that what Allison had done with Amy? "What now? How will you take care of Mom and Dad and Grace?"

"Oh, we'll manage." Faye smiled, and this time the expression was genuine. It wiped fifteen years off her features. "We kind of like having the little one. Mom seems more alert than I've seen her in years. And you can visit anytime you like."

ELEVEN

It was mid-afternoon before Eleanor arrived in Amelia Island. The homes along Magnolia Way, her sister's street, were sprawling one-story Florida-style houses with guest wings, cement lanais and tiny, screen-enclosed outdoor pools. Tropical flowers edged driveways, and palm trees, their giant fronds blowing in an escalating wind, offered welcome shade to over-fertilized lawns. Eleanor rolled down the window. Despite the proximity to the beach two blocks over, the neighborhood was silent.

Eleanor didn't care for Florida—it was too hot and humid—but her older sister, Ginny, loved it, and Eleanor respected, if not loved, Ginny. Ginny was recently divorced, but that didn't stop her from socializing and having fun. Ginny belonged to a wine club, two book clubs and a health club. She did yoga, line dancing and took a Pilates class on the beach, and that was in addition to her real estate practice. Her dance card was filled, and she never seemed bitter about the fact that her husband of twenty-five years had left her for another woman.

Of course, Ginny didn't know that in another relationship, Eleanor had been the other woman. She could never know that. Eleanor's saintly, good-natured older sister wouldn't approve. In spite of herself, Ginny's opinion mattered to her. It always had.

So when Eleanor called to say she was coming to spend an indefinite time in Ginny's well-appointed guest suite, she didn't mention Scott, his death or anything else that hinted at scandal. She'd just said she needed a break. And Ginny, always the giving one, had agreed—just as Eleanor had known she would.

Eleanor pulled the car into Ginny's empty driveway. The fact that it was empty didn't worry her; Eleanor kept her Lexus in the garage, away from the damaging sun. And anyway, Eleanor had the code. She punched it into the garage door opener now, and sure enough, Ginny's silver SUV sat in the spotless interior. Eleanor stepped around three blue-striped beach chairs and up the two steps to an entrance into the house. She felt for the key under an empty gas can, and there it was, just where Ginny said it would be.

She knocked before finally unlocking the door. Stepping into the mud room, she shivered. Her sister must have set the air conditioning at fifty degrees. The house was frigid.

The hairs on the back of her neck prickled. Ginny was always cold. *Always.*

Eleanor put her suitcase down and walked quietly through the hallway and into the open living room/dining room/kitchen area. No sign of her sister. Heart pounding, she told herself to take it easy. Ginny had fallen asleep without realizing how high she'd turned up the air. Wasn't her sister always doing silly things like that? Or maybe she was going through menopause. She was of that age.

But something deep in Eleanor's consciousness said it was neither forgetfulness nor hormones. Something bad had happened.

More quickly now, Eleanor made her way through a set of double doors that led to Ginny's bedroom. She took a deep breath, preparing herself for the worst. That room was empty, too. Forcing herself to stay calm, she opened the bathroom door. No Ginny.

She felt brave enough to call her sister's name. No answer. Maybe she's by the pool, she thought. On the way to the lanai, Eleanor checked the guest room and the guest bath: also empty. She was even more certain she'd find her sister somewhere outside. Maybe gabbing with a neighbor. Wasn't Ginny the talkative one? Eleanor smiled. Events of the last week had made her jumpy. What happened to the woman who'd once climbed the Matterhorn? Where were her nerves of steel?

Eleanor went back to the entry to get her suitcase. There, she noticed one room she hadn't checked: the laundry room. With a casual push, she opened the door. A scream caught in her throat. Her sister's petite body had been wedged into a cooler. The cooler, still partially filled with ice, had overflowed, spreading puddles on the floor. It sat under an air conditioning vent. Between the ice and the cold air, the sickening smell, noticeable in the closed laundry room, had been undetectable in the rest of the house.

Eleanor, too terrified to cry, backed out of the room.

She closed the door to her sister's laundry room and wiped the door handles with her shirt. Then she headed back into the garage, cleaning anything along the way that may have her prints. She had to get out of there. Calling the police was out of the question. Ginny was dead; there was nothing she could do about that.

Ginny was a warning. Someone was on to her, and she refused to be next.

Allison arrived to an empty house. After walking Brutus, she changed out of her funeral clothes and into black yoga pants and a pale pink t-shirt. She pulled her hair out of her face with a ponytail holder, and splashed cold water on her skin. She felt washed out, exhausted, and anxious. Very anxious. She headed for the kitchen, reached for her old friend, the peanut butter jar, and then, looking down into Brutus's dark, daring eyes, gave him the finger full she had meant for herself.

He was quite happy to help.

The two made their way upstairs to Allison's office. There, she unlocked her file cabinet and pulled the information she'd gleaned from LinkedIn. It only took her a moment to find the information on the woman from the funeral, Julie Fitzsimmons.

Allison jotted down the address for Transitions, Inc. in Valley Forge, Pennsylvania. Then she looked up Mark Fairweather. He lived close to her house. Perhaps he needed to arrange coffee with the grieving brother.

Jason arrived two hours later than he said he would. Allison was in the kitchen, drinking chamomile tea and looking at old photographs of their wedding. They both looked so happy, a whole world of normal wants and goals still ahead of them. What had happened? When she heard his key in the lock, she didn't move. He walked in to the kitchen to find her sitting quietly at the table, tears streaming down her face.

It wasn't the Scott issue. It wasn't even her sister Amy, exactly. It was all of it: the uncertainty about the future, the sadness for all that had happened in the past, and, perhaps most of all, the fear that anything good could be snatched away at a moment's notice. Maybe that was behind her reluctance to remarry Jason. If they kept things the status quo, she wasn't tempting fate. Marriage, and all that went with it, including the potential for happiness, would be a leap of faith.

Maybe she lacked faith.

Jason walked behind her. He looked at the pictures spread out before her, his tall, broad frame hunched over the table. One by one, he examined them, an inscrutable expression on his face. Finally he stood. He tilted Allison's head up and stared into her eyes. Without saying a word, he wiped the tears from her face, leaned down, and kissed her. It was a long, slow kiss, and Allison felt herself responding.

Jason took her hand, urging her out of the chair. They went upstairs in silence, the wedding photos still scattered on the table to be put away in the morning.

It was after midnight and Vaughn couldn't sleep. Angela was still here, despite the fact that her shift had ended two hours ago. Lying in his bed, he could hear them. Rather, he could hear Angela and then the silences punctuating her speech that meant Jamie was responding on the screen. He used a mouthpiece that caused his words to show up on a computer monitor. Although Jamie's vocal chords had been stolen along with his mobility when he took the bullet meant for Vaughn years ago, the device could speak for Jamie. But Jamie didn't like the tinny sound of its voice. More of a reminder of his loss than the words on the screen, he said.

So Angela stayed. How long, Vaughn didn't know. After another forty minutes of hearing their one-sided banter, he got up and went to his bathroom. He rummaged around, looking for something that would help him sleep. For the first time in years, he wanted a drink. A six pack would send him dreaming, as would a few shots of vodka. But he had made a pact long ago with himself, and so he made do with Benadryl, reluctantly swallowing the two pink capsules.

Back in his bedroom, he looked around. He'd confined himself to this apartment, years of penance for the actions that cost his brother use of his body. But now he felt trapped. And Mia? He felt her pulling away. If he asked her, she'd deny it. At least that's what he told himself. He was afraid if he did ask her...well, the asker had to be ready for the answer.

Lights out, brother, he said to himself. He felt the Benadryl start to kick in. He wanted the bliss of sleep. Tomorrow was a new day. Maybe he'd figure some shit out. Maybe he'd accept the fact that his friend and lover was moving on and his brother had a woman in his life. Maybe he'd make some decisions about his own future.

Or maybe he'd just keep going, trying hard to avoid anything that smelled like change. Because his last thoughts before drifting off were about change. It was coming, and there wasn't a damn thing he could do to stop it.

TWELVE

Mark Fairweather agreed to have lunch with Allison at eleven-thirty Monday morning. He named a meeting place, an Indian restaurant a few blocks from his law office in Center City. "Don't be late," he'd growled. "For me, time is money."

It was eight-forty in the morning. Allison had plenty of time ahead of her meeting with Mark to talk with Julie Fitzsimmons. Allison had seen the strange change that came over Leah when she passed Julie's group outside the church. The public relations executive might not know anything about Scott's death or the photos, but Allison hoped Julie could shed some light on Scott's career or his state of mind leading up to the day he was killed. A close coworker would notice changes in appearance or demeanor that may indicate drug use. While Allison couldn't say for sure whether Julie was a close co-worker, the fact that she'd attended his funeral said they at least knew each other. That would have to be a start.

The headquarters for Transitions, Inc. was in an industrial park near Valley Forge, not far from Allison's house. Allison drove north on Route 202 and then followed the GPS directions on her phone. The directions took her through a maze of broad streets lined with nondescript office buildings. She finally found Transitions, Inc. on a cul-de-sac at the back of the industrial park. Like many of the buildings in the park, the building that housed the company was a plain beige rectangle. Unlike many of the other buildings, though, Transitions seemed to be the sole occupant.

Allison parked in one of the spots marked for visitors. She noticed prime spaces for compact cars and, along the wall of the building, plug-in outlets for electric vehicles. A field of solar panels was positioned at the back of the building, far from the picnic tables and grills that lined a broad cement patio. A plaque near the building's entrance announced that Transitions, Inc. was pursuing its LEED certification. It strived to be a "green" company.

The interior of the building was clean, fresh and very modern. A receptionist sat surrounded by freshly-cut flowers. Allison announced herself and asked to see Julie Fitzsimmons.

"Do you have an appointment?" the woman asked. She was in her sixties and had the well-scrubbed, glowing complexion of a woman who'd recognized the benefits of a good diet and exercise long before it became trendy.

"I'm afraid not." Allison handed the woman her card. Taking note of the placard that identified the receptionist, Allison said, "But I think Ms. Fitzsimmons will agree to see me, Dottie. I'm here to talk about brand recognition and the changes Transitions is going through."

Dottie looked through emerald-green reading glasses that matched her sweater set. "First Impressions?" She looked skeptical. "Ms. Fitzsimmons doesn't generally see people without an appointment—"

"This isn't a sales call."

"And you're not a reporter?"

"No."

Dottie nodded, looking somewhat mollified. She dialed. After a few moments of unintelligible exchange, Dottie said, "If you're willing to wait until nine-thirty, Julie will see you then."

Allison was willing to wait and she told Dottie as much. She positioned herself in a bamboo chair and watched as Transitions employees made their way into the office. Despite the welcoming atmosphere, no one stopped to chat with Dottie and few people talked to one another. A busy Monday, or a corporate culture that hadn't quite caught up with its cheery image?

True to her word, at nine-thirty Julie Fitzsimmons fetched Allison from the waiting area. Up close, Allison got a better look at her. Dark red hair, almost auburn, had been carefully curled into a sleek shoulder-length bob. She had bright green eyes and a tall, slender body. As the head of public relations, Julie would be a good choice. Her open, friendly face was lovely enough to be interesting, but not so beautiful that others would find her threatening.

Allison glanced at her left hand. No wedding ring.

"Thank you for seeing me, Ms. Fitzsimmons," Allison said. "I was hoping we could chat." She handed the woman a business card. "Your company is undergoing some changes. Change is my specialty."

Julie tilted her head. "I'm not sure I understand."

Allison glanced around the waiting area. "Could we go somewhere private? Scott recommended I speak with you. Scott Fairweather."

Julie's face contorted. "Scott's...well, Scott's..."

"Passed. I know." Allison looked duly mournful. "I was at his funeral. You may have seen me there?"

"Maybe. Scott's death...well, it came as a shock." Julie took a deep breath, gave Allison a half smile, and then threw her hands up in the air. "Let's go to one of the conference rooms. I can give you about fifteen minutes. Will that do?"

"I appreciate your time."

In the conference room, Julie closed the door and offered Allison a seat. After settling in, Julie said, "What's the real reason you're here?" When Allison didn't respond, Julie continued. "I'm familiar with First Impressions. We've considered using you to help our sales crew in the new campaign. But Scott put the kibosh on the idea."

Allison tried to look like her professional ego was bruised, but couldn't. Her mind was spinning with how best to respond when Julie said, "Look, I know you and Scott dated once upon a time."

Seemed like everyone knew her business these days, everyone but the one man who should. Allison sat back in her chair. She kept her gaze steady, giving away nothing.

"Don't worry," Julie said. "Your secret's safe with me. We're like sisters in that regard." She shrugged. "The Slept with Scott Club."

"You and Scott?"

"For the better part of a year." Julie looked down at French-manicured fingernails. "He ended things about three weeks ago." She glanced up. "Okay, two weeks, six days and nine hours ago. Right after we'd slept together. Nice, huh?"

"Did he say why?"

Julie looked sharply at her, eyebrows arched. "He's married."

"He's been married for some time, Julie," Allison said gently. "That doesn't seem to have stopped him."

Julie looked away. Allison saw fine lines and dark circles, carefully hidden beneath expertly-applied concealer. Julie Fitzsimmons was burdened and tired, and no amount of spit and polish could completely hide that.

Finally Julie said, "The baby."

"Did you know about his wife and the baby?" Allison asked softly. "Before you became involved, that is."

Julie nodded. "In my role, image is everything. What will people say about the company? What could end up in the *New York Times* or *Wall Street Journal*? How do you spin this or that so that it has the right effect? Having an affair with a married man was hardly a smart thing to do. But I couldn't stop myself. Scott was so...*there*." She shrugged. "I should have known better."

"Things happen."

"Yes." Julie's lips twisted. "Things happen."

Allison was silent for a moment while she absorbed what Julie was telling her. Scott hadn't changed his ways. His affair with Allison may have been a first, but his risk-taking behavior hadn't ended there. "Did Scott seem different to you in the weeks leading up to his death?" she asked.

"Yes."

"Is it possible he was on something?"

"Do you mean drugs?" When Allison nodded, Julie shook her head vehemently back and forth. "No way. He did seem different...distracted and moody. But he would never have taken drugs. He was too concerned about his looks for that."

"You're sure?"

"Yes." Julie sat quietly. Allison heard the whir of the heating vents, the murmur of voices in the hallway. After a while, Julie shifted forward in her chair and glanced toward the door. "Someone has been sending me photos," she whispered.

Allison felt frozen in place.

"Photos of what?"

"Photos of...us. Scott and me." She looked away. "Photos I wouldn't want shared on the internet."

Julie's face twitched, her hands shook. She was scared. The tired eyes and burdened posture were not caused by guilt; they were caused by fear.

"Is someone threatening you, Julie? Letters, calls? Blackmail?"

Julie shook her head.

"Have you gone to the police?"

"No!" Julie covered her mouth with her hand. "I've said too much already."

Allison leaned forward. She toyed with whether or not to be candid with Julie and decided against it. Under the wrong circumstances, candor could get her killed. "Why tell me at all?"

"Have you ever had a relationship with a married man, Allison?"

"No. But I've done things…things I'm not proud of."

Julie smiled wanly. "It changes your life, and not for the better. Your friends who don't know become like strangers. There're so many things you keep hidden from them. And the friends who do know? Well, they're judging you. Whether they say so or not, your life is always on trial. As a result, you keep your circle small. You start to live for the moments you're with *him*. Your universe becomes so tiny. That's what happened to me.

"I'm telling you, Allison, because I have no one else to tell. When I confronted Scott about his reaction to hiring your firm, he told me your story. How you'd been lovers. How you were cheating on your husband and he on his fiancé."

"I wasn't—"

She held up her hand. "No need to make excuses with me. Just watch out. If I'm on her radar, you very well may be, too."

"*Her*? Scott's wife?"

Julie shook her head. She stood, newly composed. "Eleanor Davies."

That name rang a bell, too. Another woman from the social networking site. Another colleague. "You think she's behind the pictures?"

Julie smiled. "Oh, I'm sure of it. Here's the neat thing about Scott. He was a sex addict. He slept with women compulsively. I realized that too late. And Eleanor? She didn't want anyone else to have Scott. Not me, not his wife."

Allison thought about the photos. A lover may have had access to his private things. She may have wanted to warn off other women. But still, something didn't add up. "Scott's dead. Why send the photos now? What could Eleanor possibly gain?"

"She's crazy. Her actions don't have to make sense."

"Still—"

Julie shrugged. "I have to go. If you say we had this conversation, I'll deny it. But I don't think you will." She gave Allison a look that said they were part of a secret club, a club Allison wanted no part of. "If you get photos, just don't go to the police."

"Why?"

"It will stir up trouble for Transitions. And we can't take any more trouble."

"Eleanor works here, too, right?"

Julie nodded. Her hand was on the doorknob. She looked ready to flee.

"Then why not go to the source? Tell her to stop."

"Why, indeed?" Julie said. "Because Eleanor is gone. Left without notice. No one's heard from her since."

"Since when?"

"Since Scott's murder."

THIRTEEN

Eleanor's stash of cash was low. She'd spent last night in The Sweet Dreams Motel, a misnomer if ever there was one. It had been one of those mom and pop small motels in the Appalachian Mountains, a place where you could rent by the month if you wanted. And some folks clearly did. The mattress was saggy, the room smelled of mothballs and mildew, with an overcoat of Lysol that couldn't mask either, and ants were crawling around the bathroom floor. But Eleanor needed to pay cash, and they accepted cash with only a brief glance at her driver's license. No credit card required.

She'd pushed the rickety dresser in front of the door and slept fully clothed, thinking about her sister's body stuffed in that cooler.

She needed a gun. And a place to stay.

Now, after filling her tank at the cheapest station she could find, she sat in the shadows of the Quick Mart, eating mini blueberry pies (two for a dollar) and pondering her next move. Her phone was off— she'd seen many thrillers on the big screen and knew others could track her using her phone—and she was afraid to use a credit card or withdraw cash.

Eleanor counted out her last dollars: $61.72. Where was she going to go for $61.72? Her parents were dead, her sister was dead, and she had no friends. None she could trust with something this big, anyway.

She finished the last bite of Bonny Berry's Blueberry Pie, crumpled the wrapper, stuffed it into her trash sack and started the engine. She was in North Carolina, somewhere along Route 95. The sun was high in the sky, and clouds were nonexistent. It should have been a beautiful day. But she couldn't shake the grip of fear that had overtaken her normally fearless mind. Eleanor hated weakness. She had to stop running.

A car pulled into the lot. It only took Eleanor a second to realize it was a red Ferrari, like the one she'd seen a few nights ago. Could it be...? No, this driver was young and female. It took Eleanor a minute to calm her racing heart. She couldn't take anything at face value right now. Ginny's dead body told her that.

She pulled around to the back of the gas station, as far out of the Ferrari's line of sight as possible. When she was back on the road, she floored it, ignoring the squeal of her tires on blacktop.

With a sudden burst of inspiration, Eleanor knew where to go next. She would arrive unannounced and she would be anything but welcome, but she didn't much care. She turned on the GPS and put in the name of her general destination. Then she headed north.

Allison arrived at the Indian buffet a few minutes early. She took a seat at a small table in the back of the restaurant, far from the food and next to a wall of windows, and ignored the three emails from Vaughn wondering where the heck she was. The air was laced with the exotic smells of curry and ginger. Allison's stomach rumbled.

Mark arrived on time.

Allison saw him before he saw her. He glanced around. He wore a charcoal gray off-the-rack suit, a white shirt and red tie that sat left of center, and slightly scuffed black loafers. He nodded at the restaurant host and mumbled something at the same time that he spotted Allison in the corner. She waved.

"Glad you're punctual. Women are always late." He stood over the table, slightly out of breath. "Want to get some food first? I'm hungry and my schedule's packed."

Allison nodded. She rose and followed him to the buffet, marveling at the amount of food he managed to fit on his plate, including rice, chicken tikka, baighan bartha, braised goat and naan. Allison chose rice and a sampling of the vegetable dishes, then paused to get a hot cup of chai tea.

Back at the table, Mark dug in, attacking his food with the ferocity of a man who hadn't eaten in days. Allison watched him, cognizant of the time.

"Do you mind if I ask you some questions while you finish your lunch?"

Mark smiled. "Finish? This is just round one. I'm good for at least two, maybe three." He scooped up some chickpeas with a piece of limp naan. "Shoot. What do you want to know?"

Allison decided to be blunt. "I've read the news reports about Scott's murder. They all allude to drugs. Do you think there's anything to that?"

Mark looked up from his plate. "Why do you care?"

"Because he didn't seem the type."

Mark studied her. "My brother never did drugs. Scott was in great shape. He ran, lifted weights, and loved—I mean *loved*—indoor sports, if you know what I mean. And I think you do." He smiled, and Allison frowned. "Scott loved life," Mark continued between bites. "He loved pleasure, yes, but not the kind of pleasure you get from drugs. I don't think he would have done anything to jeopardize…things."

"Things?"

Mark took a sip of water, then waved to the waiter. "A pitcher for the table, amigo."

The waiter, who didn't look thrilled at being called Mark's amigo, nodded. He was back seconds later with water.

"Stuff's damn spicy today, don't you think?"

Allison voiced her agreement, although she hadn't touched her food. "What wouldn't your brother have jeopardized, Mark? Leah and the baby? His job?"

Mark put down his fork. He made a show of looking Allison in the eyes. "Sex. Yes, some drugs can enhance the experience, true, but others, especially the hard stuff, can kill the libido. Or even worse: they can make the equipment fail, if you know what I mean."

Allison knew exactly what he was saying. Clearly, subtlety was not Mark's specialty. She said, "So Scott would have been concerned about his ability to have…marital relations?"

Mark laughed. "Sure, whatever you want to call it. My brother liked the sins of the flesh. But then, you know that, don't you?" Mark flashed a lascivious smile that made Allison's stomach turn. She pushed her uneaten plate away and decided to ignore his comments, again—for now.

"Then why would someone want him dead?"

"Who the hell knows? Wrong place, wrong time? Pissed off someone's husband?"

Neither of those reasons rang true. "What can you tell me about Scott's role at Transitions?"

Mark swallowed the last of his meal, leaving only a forkful of rice. "Scott was the Director of Marketing. Fantastic job for him, all things considered."

"All things considered?"

"My brother got canned from his last job. Okay, not canned exactly, more like demoted. But it sure felt like being fired to Scott. You know how competitive he was."

"What happened?"

"What do you think? Got caught *in flagrante delicto* with an underling. In the boss's office. By the boss's secretary. My brother knew how to go down with a bang. Company honchos told him he had a choice. They could send him to the Montreal office as a copywriter or he could go quietly. His brand was ruined. He had no choice but to reinvent himself."

"So he became a spin doctor."

"With my help." Mark stood and glanced at his watch. "Let me get more grub. I need to be out of here in fifteen."

While Mark made his second trip to the buffet, Allison thought about what he'd said. She wasn't surprised. Disappointed, but not surprised. In her view, any man who would take photos without his partner's consent was of suspect moral character. And Mark's story corroborated Julie's characterization of Scott.

When Mark returned, plate again piled high, Allison asked, "Did Leah know?"

Mark placed a plate of naan in front of her. "Here, I got you some. Nice and hot." He sat down and picked up his fork. "Did Leah know why he left Tenure Polk?"

Allison nodded.

"No. All he told her was that they wanted to move him to Montreal. Leah hates the cold. Kind of ironic, frigid bitch that she is."

"You don't like her much?"

"More like she doesn't like me." He shrugged. "Still angry that I got a finder's fee for Scott's job."

Allison thought back to Scott's job history. The man she remembered was a gifted businessman: smart, strategic and smooth-talking. That Scott wouldn't have needed help. "What did you do for him, Mark?"

"I was drafting some separation agreements for Transition's current CFO. He mentioned that they needed an executive with a marketing background, preferably someone with international experience. After Scott's role at Mystic and his dealings in India, he seemed like a shoe-in. I played matchmaker. They hit it off."

"But Leah wasn't pleased?"

"She was pissed that I got $10,000 out of the deal. She thought I should have turned the cash over to Scott."

Mark looked down at his plate while he talked, sopping up the last remnants of chicken tikka masala with a piece of naan, so Allison couldn't see his eyes. Allison wondered whether this was the reason for the falling out Shawn had mentioned. She got the feeling Mark wasn't being fully honest, though. Getting a finder's fee for a corporate hiring seemed fair. There had to be more to the story.

But she wasn't going to get that out of him now. Mark threw his napkin on his plate and pulled his wallet from his jacket pocket. He started to pull cash from within when Allison held up her hand.

"I asked you. My treat."

Mark smiled. "I never let a pretty girl pay for lunch." That lascivious smile again. "I like when they owe me."

"I'm afraid I don't come that cheaply."

"But you do have a price."

Allison shook her head. "Afraid not." But maybe that was the answer. If Leah was upset about a finder's fee, perhaps money *was* at the root of everything. "Could Scott's death have been related to money problems?" she asked. "Maybe Scott was selling drugs, not taking them."

Mark stood. "Doubtful. As far as I knew, they had plenty of cash. Or that's how Scott made it seem. Maybe he liked the thrill of selling drugs, but I doubt it. Too messy. He liked his messes more—"

"Yes, I know. Of the physical variety."

"Exactly."

"How about the spin doctor bit, Mark? What did Transitions need Scott for?"

"No way. You want more information, you show me your price. I don't come that cheaply, Ms. Campbell."

Allison laughed, but only because it seemed more productive to treat his words as a joke.

"Tell you what," Mark said. "Call me next week. A nice dinner, a bottle of good French wine, and we can talk about Transitions. I can't break client confidentiality, of course." He winked. "But with the right...enticements...I can tell you a few things."

No way. "Sounds good."

Encouraged, Mark smiled. "Scott said you were a tigress in the bedroom. Show me that side of yourself and, well, I may even forget that Brad Halloway is a client at all."

Allison would have been offended if she hadn't felt so dazed. Brad Halloway: another blast from her past. Not a boyfriend this time, thank God. Not even a client, exactly. But someone she could contact for information about Scott. Someone she could trust. Outside the restaurant, she thanked a confused-looking Mark and turned in the direction of her car.

Mark called, "How about next week?"

"No way," Allison called over her shoulder, echoing his earlier comment. "How about never?"

FOURTEEN

Allison didn't go right home. She texted Vaughn to say she was doing some research for her book, said a silent prayer of forgiveness for the lie, and looked up Eleanor Davies' address on her phone. Maybe she'd get lucky and the woman would be back at home.

Eleanor lived in a townhome community on the outskirts of the Main Line. Situated on a field that had once been farmland, Harvest Hills was awash in stucco and middle-class perkiness. Identical townhomes, each with a deck and small wooden balcony, lined wide, black-topped streets. A small playground graced every other throughway, although Allison saw no kids. Allison eventually found Eleanor's house at 629 Apple Orchard Way and parked outside. Eleanor's parking spot was numbered and vacant. A gray tabby sat outside 629, looking miserable.

Allison stepped around the cat and rang the bell three times. No one answered. The shades to a large picture window had been drawn. No newspapers sat outside the door.

The cat meant that Eleanor couldn't have gone far. No one leaves without their pet, at least not willingly. She bent down and stroked the feline. He stood, arched his back and meowed loudly. Allison watched him watching her as she headed back toward the car. The cat let out another insistent meow and then, apparently resigned to his fate, curled back up on the doormat. Allison got back in her car and drove away.

The cat continued to bother her. This one looked healthy and well groomed, as though he'd spent a pleasant enough life chasing mice and sleeping in front of a fire, but when she petted him, he seemed cold, really cold, as though he hadn't been inside for a while. Cold, and a little too hungry for affection. Weren't cats supposed to be standoffish? And the meowing. The little guy had clearly been trying to tell her something, or at least he was demanding something of her. What if Eleanor hadn't let him in because she couldn't? What if Eleanor was dead?

Allison pulled abruptly into a Wawa, turned around and headed back toward Harvest Hills. While she wove in and out of traffic, she asked her Bluetooth to dial 4-1-1. The operator connected her directly to the administrative office for the townhome community. A receptionist answered, and after a hasty exchange, told Allison they couldn't let her into Eleanor's house.

"But I'm her sister," Allison said.

"Oh, I'm sorry. We're not landlords. We're simply the management office."

"Surely you have a key on file."

"Only if work needs to be done, and right now there is no work order for number 629. I'm afraid if you're that concerned, you'll need to call the police."

Frustrated, Allison dialed the phone number she'd found listed for Eleanor, but no one answered. Once again, she pulled up in front of Eleanor's house and stared at the façade, willing it to give her some clue.

Voyeuristic photos, a dead man, sordid affairs...and now a missing mistress?

Allison turned her head just in time to catch movement in the townhome next to Eleanor's. She didn't see a car parked in the spot for house number 627, but that didn't mean no one was home. On impulse, she walked up to the door and rang the bell. After a few seconds, an older woman opened the door. She peered at Allison through the few inches afforded by the chain lock.

"Can I help you?"

Allison decided to stick with the sister line. Allison recalled what Julie had said about the life of a mistress. She'd bet her wages that Eleanor Davies was a private person. The neighbors would probably not recognize Eleanor's family members, if they even knew what family she had.

"I was wondering if you've seen Eleanor lately. She's not answering my calls, and I see her cat outside. I'm her sister."

"Thank goodness!" The woman unlocked the chain hastily and opened the door wide. She had a head of short, bristly white hair, kind eyes and enough wrinkles to suggest a hearty sense of humor. Allison took an instant liking to her. She felt bad for lying, her second lie of the day.

"Her sister, Ginny?" She looked relieved. "I am so glad you drove up here from Amelia Island. Eleanor told me how busy you are, with your real estate business and all. I haven't seen your sister in almost a week. And that cat...well, Simon has been showing up at my house every evening for a snack. This is unlike Eleanor. Very unlike her."

"Do you happen to have a key? I'd like to check on her."

"Oh no!" The woman's face colored. "You don't think something has happened to her? I just figured...well, I figured she'd taken off with that beau of hers. Paris, Sonoma. Wherever young people go these days."

"Beau? You mean Scott?"

The woman smiled. "I never know their names. I just see them pull up in front of Eleanor's house. Sometimes they don't even get out. This one gets out, though. He's her most recent beau. Nice car, too. Your sister has good taste in men." The woman became suddenly quiet. She looked pensive, as though considering something, before saying, "Come in, Ginny. Let me see if I still have her back door key. Your sister is a very private woman, but I don't have to tell you that."

Allison followed the woman into a wide foyer. Beyond the foyer, Allison could see a beige-carpeted living room on one side and a small dining room on the other. The furniture was surprisingly contemporary, with sage and plum fabrics and black accents. The kitchen and a narrow hallway lay beyond the dining room and the woman headed in that direction.

"Wait here a second," she called. "Let me check my junk drawer. If I still have that back door key, that's where it will be." She returned a second later with a triumphant grin. "Your sister went backpacking in the Adirondacks a few months back. Alone. You should talk to her about that. Anyway, she asked me to feed Simon. He can't come in here because I'm allergic, but I went over there and took care of him." She gave a fond smile. "Nice cat, that one. I didn't mind."

"Would you mind letting me in Eleanor's house, Mrs...."

"Ms., not missus. Elizabeth Duncan. I've never been married, Ginny. You can just call me Liz."

"Okay, Liz." Allison smiled. "Can we check on Eleanor?"

"Take the key, but bring it back, okay? I wouldn't feel right, with your sister being so private and all."

Allison promised to come right back and return the key. She followed Liz's directions and went out the back door. Next door, Allison fumbled with the key, all the while hoping there was no alarm system. She hadn't seen a decal, but you never knew.

But when the door opened into a small kitchen, no alarm sounded. Allison walked through the kitchen and into the living room and dining room, her pulse racing and the key out in front of her, an ineffective weapon.

Quietly, she made her way upstairs, the hairs on the back of her neck standing upright. This was creepy, and felt a lot like breaking and entering. What would Jason say? She pushed that thought away and kept going.

The upstairs was empty. The clothes strewn around Eleanor's room, and the absence of toiletries in the bathroom said Eleanor had left in a rush. That and the cat. If Eleanor Davies left her cat behind, she'd clearly left in a hurry. Why? Had she been involved in Scott's murder? Was she behind the photos as Julie suspected? Or had someone done something to Eleanor, too?

Allison was on her way back downstairs when she heard Liz calling.

"Ginny? Ginny! Is everything okay?"

"Yes, coming!" Allison took one last glance around. Eleanor's California king was dressed in sumptuous silk and cotton bedding. A large mirror faced the bed from one end of the room. Birth control pills sat on the bedside table.

Odd, Allison thought. She has a love nest and left her pills behind.

"Ginny!"

"Coming!"

Allison wanted to explore further, but she couldn't risk tipping off the neighbor. As she re-entered the downstairs hallway, she spotted the cat carrier tucked next to a closet, the door open, as though Eleanor had tried to take the cat but changed her mind at the last minute.

Liz was standing by the stairs. "You had me worried! Any luck?"

"I think I know where she is," Allison said. She sighed for effect. "That woman is always gallivanting off to somewhere."

Liz pointed to the cat carrier. "Are you taking Simon with you?"

Allison hadn't planned to, but now that she thought about it, having Eleanor's cat would give her some connection to Eleanor if and when she returned. Plus, she felt bad for Simon. He seemed so forlorn.

"Yes, I'll take Simon. If Eleanor returns, just tell her where he is."

"I will," Liz said. "Will you be local?"

"I'm staying with friends. Just give her this number." Allison rattled off her own cell phone. Then she handed the older woman the key. "Thank you for feeding Simon."

"No problem," Liz replied. "We single ladies need to stick together."

By the time Allison returned home, Jason was there. Happily, she walked into his outstretched arms and gave him a hug.

"I love you," she said.

Jason looked surprised. He kissed her.

"I love you, too. What's going on, though? You look exhausted."

Allison couldn't very well tell him about Scott or her unofficial investigation, although she desperately wanted to. But unburdening herself would only cause him angst. He didn't know about her affair with Scott, and she wasn't ready to tell him.

Plus, after all they'd been through with Maggie McBride and then the disappearances of two clients last year, even the mention of another murder would have him concerned. She couldn't risk that. Not until she knew more.

A few more days, she told herself. Then, if no more photos show up, I'll go to the police and let them handle it.

"I have a surprise," Allison said.

"You're pregnant?"

Allison could see he regretted the words even before they fully left his mouth. He'd said it as a joke, she knew—they certainly weren't trying—but it felt like a slap across the face.

"No, but guess who is living with my parents?" When he shrugged, she told him about Grace.

"Amy left her daughter with your folks? No offense, Al, but are they able to care for that little girl?"

"Faye's there," Allison said quickly. "And you have to see them dote on her. She's breathed new life into that household."

"That's what kids do," Jason said.

They stared at one another until Allison broke the silence. She said lightly, "How about that surprise?"

Jason ran his hands down her side, lingering at her waist. "I have a surprise for you, too. But it will take a few minutes—"

Gently, Allison took his hand from her body and held it in front of her. "This won't wait." She led him to her car, where Simon sat in his carrier, meowing loudly.

"A cat? That's the surprise?" He peeked in the carrier at a set of wide feline eyes. Simon meowed again. "Have you gone mad? What about Brutus? And what about the fact that you don't like animals all that much?"

Allison took the carrier out of the back. "People change. And besides, he needed a place to stay."

"But what about Brutus?"

"I stopped by the vet. She said give them time to adjust slowly. She thinks they'll be fine."

But Jason looked skeptical. "A cat, Al? Really? Where did you get him?"

"His name is Simon. A friend of a client had to go away. They were desperate. It should only be temporary." All true statements, Allison thought. Please don't dig, Jason.

Jason didn't dig. Instead, he looked from the cat to her and back again. A small smile crept across his face. "A cat, huh. Well, people *can* change."

Allison knew cats weren't the only thing on his mind. Cats...dogs...*babies*. But she wasn't in a position to argue. She took the cat inside, still in his carrier, and let a very excited Brutus sniff the cage. Then she put the cat in the laundry room and let Jason take her to bed.

* * *

Mia awoke with a start. She heard something outside. Or, more precisely, Buddy heard something outside. The mutt was standing by the window, head cocked. He barked once, twice—his mean bark—then let out a long, slow growl. Mia slipped out of bed and pulled on her robe. Her pulse pounding, she felt her way along the walls, toward the kitchen, cursing herself for not having a flashlight. She didn't want to put on her bedroom light for fear an intruder, if there was an intruder, would be able to see in. An older woman alone broadcast vulnerability.

She fumbled around in a drawer next to the stove and eventually pulled out a small flashlight. Her eyes now adjusted to the dim light, she headed back to her bedroom and looked outside. She saw nothing. It was hard for someone to sneak up on her given her location. The long gravel driveway was like a first alert, the sound of wheels on gravel unmistakable.

Unless an intruder parked along the road and walked.

Buddy growled again, and then, after a minute of listening, seemed satisfied that whatever danger had been lurking outside the bungalow had passed. The dog jumped back on her bed and lay down with a loud huff.

"Sure, wake me up and then fall right back to sleep," Mia muttered. But the damage was done. Her clock read 3:48, but sleep wouldn't return for the rest of the night. It wasn't just the scare. Once she was awake these days, sleep eluded her. You're getting old, she told herself. And then quickly another part of her brain said: you're only as old as you allow yourself to be.

Not yet willing to let go of the cover of darkness, Mia decided to read by candlelight in the living room. She lit three large, vanilla soy candles on the side table and settled into the couch with a worn copy of *Lonesome Dove*. But seconds after she sat, she realized she was chilly. She stood and stretched and then started to reach for a coverlet from the chair opposite the couch. That was when she heard the noise. Someone or something was scratching against the front door.

Mia reacted quickly. She sprinted for the kitchen and grabbed the phone and a butcher knife. A reawakened Buddy heard the noise, too, and he charged out into the living room, all deep barks and growls. Mia was about to call 9-1-1 when she stopped and peeked out the window. Night was absolute in this part of Pennsylvania and she couldn't imagine anyone getting around without a flashlight. Sure enough, she saw a light bobbing in the distance, back toward the road.

So there had been an intruder. Thinking of the year before and her run-in with the Russian mafia, Mia thought calling the police would probably be warranted. But she'd fought hard to be independent, and if they came out here for what turned out to be nothing, she didn't want to end up on their "crazy old woman" list. No way *that* was going to happen.

So knife in one hand and a jumpy Buddy by her side, Mia opened the front door, every silly horror movie running through her head. No one was there. She let out her breath, unaware she'd even been holding it.

Limp with relief, she was about to close the door when a flash of white caught her eye. She bent to find an envelope taped to the bottom of her door.

Carefully, she pulled the masking tape away from her door's surface. Stomach now a raging river of anxiety, Mia thought of the mafia. She thought of her ex-husband. She thought of all the terrible things a middle-of-the-night visitor and a white envelope could mean.

She opened it. Her breath caught, her temples pounded.

This, she had not thought of. Her son's ex-wife-turned-lover, Mia's mentee, in an intimate embrace. With a man who was clearly not Jason.

FIFTEEN

Allison awoke Tuesday morning to the feelings of sun on her face and weight on her chest. After an initial moment of panic, she remembered that this was Simon, the mysterious Eleanor's cat, and that he was staying with her temporarily. But he had been locked in the laundry room overnight. Why was he here now? And why was he staring at her so intently?

Then she saw the culprit. On the other side of the bed lay Brutus. He was staring hungrily at the cat. She wasn't sure whether his expression said "Yum! A tasty new treat!" or "Play with me!" Either way, the cat was having none of it.

"Don't escape and then run to me for safety," she said to Simon. That was all it took. Next thing she knew, Brutus was upon her, his great, wet tongue washing the sleep from her face. The displaced cat groomed himself from his new perch on Jason's pillow.

Jason. Where was he?

Allison rolled Brutus off her with a gentle nudge and a "good boy" and grabbed her nightgown from the floor. Last night, Jason had seemed insatiable. Allison had chalked it up to her own distant behavior. But it occurred to her that maybe it was more than that. Maybe something was going on with him, and she'd been too busy playing detective to realize it. She made a mental note to stop by his workplace at lunch. Talk to him. Draw him out.

The doorbell rang six times in quick succession.

"For Lord's sake," she mumbled. She slipped on jeans and a t-shirt and ran down the steps, Brutus behind her. Through the sidelights, she saw Mia. Her former mother-in-law looked terrible: no make-up, hair askew, and dressed in dirty sweats. What had happened?

Quickly, Allison unlocked the door. Mia charged inside waving a white envelope.

"I told him to *trust* you," Mia said, her voice so tightly controlled it was barely audible. "I told him to give you *space*. Last year, when you were in the middle of that Benini mess, I counseled him to let you do what you needed to do. I didn't think what you needed to do was another *man*."

"I can explain—"

"How could you, Allison? How could you do this to Jason?"

Mia waved the contents of the envelope in front of Allison's face. It was a 4x6 shot of Allison and Scott. He was behind her; both their faces were visible. Nothing was left to the imagination. Allison wanted to crawl beneath the table and stay there—permanently.

"It's not want you think."

"Really?" Mia's voice was raised now. "Really, Allison? I think I know sex when I see it. I'm kind of like the Supreme Court in that way."

Allison tried to take Mia's arm, but Mia shook her off. So Allison walked out of the foyer and into the kitchen. She put water on for tea and waited until Mia calmed down and joined her. She would, eventually. Allison fed Brutus, who looked confused by the yelling, and the cat, who looked nonplussed. Then she splashed cold water on her face in the kitchen sink and took two Excedrin from the cabinet. She'd inherited migraines from her mother. One was threatening now.

When the water was just at a boil, Allison poured two cups of chamomile tea, Mia's drink of choice.

"Tea's ready," she called.

It was another minute before Mia joined her. She still looked angry, but she had pulled herself together enough to sit down.

"Where did you get that picture, Mia?"

"Does it matter?"

"Of course it matters. You know me better than this. I am not cheating on your son."

"Not now...or not ever?"

Allison stared at Mia, her brain searching for a way to explain. Her excuses sounded lame, even to herself. Mia was thinking the worst, and she couldn't leave like this or the relationship they'd both worked so hard to rebuild would be destroyed.

"Wait here," Allison said. "Please."

When she returned, she found Mia standing by the kitchen window, looking outside. The anger had been replaced by a washed-out calm. For the first time since her daughter Bridget was killed, Mia looked even older than her years. Allison knew Jason meant everything to Mia. While she should resent the way Mia came barging in here, accusations flying, she envied her passion. Mia's love for her son was boundless. Was it *that* kind of commitment, the gut-wrenching, take-a-bullet-for-you unconditional love that good parenting requires, that Allison was so afraid of?

Mia said, "I'm sorry. I shouldn't have stormed in that way."

"Understandable, all things considered." Allison spread her own photos, along with the envelopes, on the table. She chose not to share the email; despite her nudity in the pictures, the words felt too personal.

"Because I don't think you've found a new career in porn, I'm assuming you're being blackmailed?"

"Not exactly."

Allison told Mia the gory details of the last weeks, beginning with the call from Leah. She left out little; it was too late for that. It was a relief to share this with someone.

"So you dated him *after* your divorce?"

"No," Allison said. This was the part she'd dreaded and she knew Mia would ask. "After we separated, but before the divorce."

"Does Jason know?"

"Not yet."

"Don't tell him." Mia looked at her sternly. "It's in the past. Your relationship with this man meant nothing, right?" When Allison nodded, Mia said, "Then it means nothing to you and Jason now."

"Jason has a right to know."

Mia looked uncomfortable. She sat, stirred her tea, and then pushed the cup away.

"Wait a few days, okay? Take some time to think this through." She looked up, brow furrowed. "Do you know who could be sending these pictures, Allison?"

Allison shook her head.

"The timing makes me think it's related to Scott's murder. First my name in his calendar, then his death and now the pictures. Clearly, something's going on. I have no idea what or why I seem to be part of it."

"This woman...the one who disappeared, maybe she knows something?"

"Maybe," Allison said. "I don't know."

"You need to be careful."

But it wasn't safety on Allison's mind. "Mia, you and I—" Allison hated the need in her voice, but Mia had been a mother to her, more so than her own mom. "We—"

"I'm worried about you, but we are fine. I have to remember I can't control everything. The young me wanted things a certain way. The older I get, the more I realize just what an illusion control is. What is the old Hebrew saying? Man plans and God laughs."

True, Allison thought. She hugged Mia and watched her get ready to leave, Eleanor's cat snaking his way through her legs.

Vaughn stared at the photo. It was Allison, all right. Naked as the day she was born and in the embrace of a man very much not her Jason. Vaughn put the photo down and rubbed his eyes. It was like seeing his sister naked, if he'd had a sister. He felt rage bubbling up, fueled by the tension of the last few weeks. Whoever had sent this to him meant business. The envelope was clean. It'd been delivered with yesterday's mail.

He remembered the envelope that arrived at First Impressions the week before. Maybe this explained why Allison had seemed so reserved since Delvar's reception. He'd have to show this to Allison. She wouldn't like it, but if she was in some sort of trouble, he could help. And if she was having an affair, and the very thought seemed too crazy to be true, she should know she's being watched.

Vaughn closed the door behind him, leaving Jamie in Angela's capable hands. Today wasn't looking promising. His mind again drifted to the booze that would erase everything. But only for the short term, Vaughn reminded himself. Stay strong.

He reopened the door and grabbed the gym bag he kept in the foyer. An hour of sweat at the boxing gym would help. Right now, it was the only real weapon against the urges that threatened to undo him.

Allison finished up with her recently divorced group at 11:38, eight minutes behind schedule. She had a three o'clock appointment with Midge Majors, a recent graduate of the recently divorced group and one of her favorite clients, and a four o'clock appointment with three sales executives from a local pharmaceutical company. Other than that, Vaughn had penciled in time to write the speech she was giving the following week.

Allison said goodbye to her group clients and walked back into her office. Vaughn had been awfully icy this morning, and at eleven-thirty he promptly disappeared. She wasn't sure what was up with him. It seemed to her everyone and everything in her life were suddenly topsy-turvy.

She picked up her mobile and checked for messages. She'd called Jason three times this morning to see if they could meet for lunch and each time his administrative assistant told her he was busy. This time, she called his cell. Still no answer. She left a cheery voicemail suggesting they meet for dinner and hung up.

Next, Allison did a search for Brad Halloway. She found his work number on the corporate page of Transitions. She dialed and got his assistant, Frank, a gentleman with a crisp, formal tone and very careful diction. He made it clear that Mr. Halloway had no time for unscheduled visitors.

"Brad knows me," Allison said. "Please. Just tell him Allison Campbell called and ask that he call me back."

Frank grudgingly agreed. It was clear that he took his role as gatekeeper seriously.

Nine minutes later, Allison's office phone rang. She jumped, hoping it was Jason, but the voice on the other line was one she hadn't heard in some time.

"Allison Campbell, so good to hear from you. It's been much too long."

"Thank you for calling me back so promptly. I wasn't sure Frank was going to give you my message."

Brad laughed. "Frank's a good egg. Tell me, my dear, how is our friend Delvar?"

Allison filled him in on Delvar's recent success and the nonprofit he'd started. Back when she first took an interest in nurturing Delvar's talent, in his last year of design school, Allison had been frustrated with the lack of opportunity for young Hispanic men. Antonia, Brad's wife, an ardent philanthropist, had been a client for a short period. Through Antonia, Allison met Brad, who at the time was Comptroller for Mango, a clothing manufacturer that specialized in clothes for teens. He'd agreed to get Delvar an internship at his company. Delvar's talent was noticed by Mango's management and his career took off. Allison had been forever grateful to Brad Halloway for going out of his way for a stranger.

Allison said, "Paris, Milan, Tokyo...Delvar's seen more of the world than I have."

Another chuckle from Brad. "That's what happens with kids. You help them grow wings and then watch them fly away. If you're lucky, they visit the nest once in a while."

"True," Allison said, warming to the idea of Delvar as a sort of surrogate son. "But Delvar isn't the reason I called you. I was wondering whether you have some time to meet. About a former client of mine who used to work for your company."

"Someone we let go?"

"To the contrary. Someone who died." She paused. "Scott Fairweather."

"I see." Brad was silent for a moment, leaving Allison to wonder if she had somehow overstepped her bounds. Finally, he said, "I have some time this afternoon, but I don't want to meet here. How about the Starbucks in the King of Prussia Mall? Say two-thirty?"

"Perfect. Thank you."

"Don't thank me yet, Allison. I didn't know Scott very well, and frankly, I'm not sure why you're barking up this particular tree. But you and I have been friends for a long time, so I'm happy to talk with you."

Allison thanked him and hung up. She had a few minutes before she needed to leave. She decided to brush up on her knowledge of

Transitions. Whatever spin doctoring Scott was doing for the company could be related. Even if it wasn't, she wanted to sound knowledgeable when she spoke to Brad. Beyond helping her with Delvar, Brad Halloway had said he would spread the word about First Impressions at a time when Allison needed to find corporate clients—and he did. He was one of those rare gems in the business world: a man who kept his word.

SIXTEEN

Brad Halloway had aged. The last time Allison saw him, he'd been graying around the edges, but his posture had been military-straight and his physique that of an athlete. In his mid-sixties, the Brad who sat before her had slumped shoulders, mottled skin and a paunch that said perhaps he'd traded golf and weight lifting for wine and cheese. But he smiled broadly when he saw Allison and, after a quick hug and an introduction to his colleague, Bic Friedman, motioned for her to pull out the chair across from him.

Friedman greeted Allison with a tepid nod and apprising glance. He was a smallish, hawk-nosed man with a runner's build and intense, intelligent eyes. Allison recognized him from Scott's funeral. He'd been standing with Julie Fitzsimmons.

"I'll leave you two to your business," Bic said. "Brad, I'll see you when you get back in the office."

Brad watched Friedman leave. When the other man was back out into the mall, he turned to Allison. "Would you like some coffee? Maybe a bite to eat?"

Allison assured him she was fine. "It's good to see you, Brad."

He nodded. "You look wonderful, Allison. As always." He raised a cup of coffee to his lips, took a small sip and said, "You want to talk about Scott Fairweather."

"You knew him?"

"I helped him get his job."

"I was sorry to hear that he'd died. And under such gruesome circumstances."

Brad nodded. "His Transitions family was devastated, as you can imagine. But I'm confused what that has to do with you or First Impressions, Allison. You said he was a former client. Was Scott working with you before he died?"

"No. He hadn't been a client in several years, since he worked for Mystic Toys."

Brad pressed his lips together in a slight frown. "Yes, Scott jumped around a bit. Talented fellow, though."

"I heard drugs may have been involved." Allison paused to let that sink in, but Brad didn't look surprised. "I guess I'm trying to reconcile the man I knew with a man who would jeopardize everything by getting involved with drugs."

"Yes, it's hard to imagine, isn't it? But unfortunately, those rumors seem to be true."

"You saw changes in his behavior?"

Brad looked thoughtful. "I'm sharing this because I trust you won't share it, Allison. Scott's life had taken a turn. In his last months, he had become paranoid and self-centered. People noticed absences at work, spotty performance. Sometimes he wouldn't show up at all."

"Did Transitions send him to get professional help?"

"That's not our way." Brad coughed, a smoker's cough that lasted a full minute. Allison waited it out, cognizant of the other customers who were now watching Brad. Finally, he regained his breath and his composure. "Sorry. I've been struggling with some type of cold. Had the flu and it lingered. Now this." He sipped coffee and sat back in his chair. "By the way, Antonia sends her regards."

Allison smiled. Brad's wife was a petite brunette, soft spoken and kind. She'd been diagnosed with multiple sclerosis the year before she came to First Impressions. Despite her illness, Antonia had been determined to maintain her job as a public relations specialist for the airline industry. Unfortunately, the demands of the job exacerbated the progressing disease, and she found herself unable to keep up. Allison had helped her through that period, and eventually, with the help of a career counselor Allison hired, Antonia found a job she loved. Allison hadn't seen her in years.

"How is Antonia?" Allison asked.

Brad's eyes clouded. "She was doing well for a period, but recently she seems to have taken a turn for the worse. Stress isn't good for her."

Brad didn't say more and Allison didn't pry. She remembered the Halloways as being generous people, but very private.

"Is there anything else you can tell me about Scott?"

"Why, Allison? Why the questions? He may have been a client once, but...well, frankly, why do you care?"

"I don't know," Allison said. And there was some truth to that. It was those damn photos. She knew she could simply turn the photos over to Detective Berry and let the police handle it. But that seemed risky—what if the photos leaked?—and personal. She felt compelled to find out what she could before deciding her next move.

"Allison, I think you're making a big—"

But Allison didn't want to hear it. "After talking with Scott's wife, Leah, I'm just not convinced the Scott I knew would get involved in something so risky. I'm a student of human nature, you know that as well as anyone, and it doesn't ring true to me." Allison shrugged. "I hate the thought that I could have been so wrong about someone."

"Well, you may just have to accept being wrong on this one. We took Scott on as Marketing Director almost two years ago. He looked promising. He'd turned things around at Mystic, was doing great things at Tenure Polk. He had international experience. Just the kind of guy we needed at the time."

"At the time?"

Brad looked thoughtful, as though debating how much to tell her. Finally, he said, "When you think of Transitions' clothing lines, what comes to mind?"

Allison considered his question. She wasn't too familiar with the brand.

"Socially conscious, appeals to the younger market."

"Do you remember Diamond Brands' environmental scandal a few years back?"

"When the company was having clothes manufactured in China and the chemicals they were using were polluting the streams there?"

"That's the one. Transitions was owned by Diamond Brands and was at the heart of the scandal. Ted Diamond, the head of Diamond Brands, decided to give Transitions, and by association, Diamond Brands, a fresh start by spinning the company off and refreshing the brand as socially conscious. You know, made in the USA, pesticide-free cottons, donates to the right charities, all that jazz."

"That was Scott's job, to reinvent the company's image?"

Brad nodded. He coughed again, his whole body shaking with the effort. When he regained his breath, he said, "He did a good job, in the beginning, anyway. Placed ads in the right magazines, got some good media attention, trained everyone on what to say and how to say it. He launched a pretty streamlined corporate makeover. No one seems to remember the old Transitions."

"Quite a success story, then," Allison said. "Considering how recently this all occurred."

"It was." Another shadow passed over Brad's face. "I'm afraid the company's not doing so well now, though. We're over budget and under-capitalized."

"How could Scott be blamed for that? Those sound like financial problems." Problems a CFO would be held accountable for, Allison thought, not a marketing executive.

"They're problems we inherited because of the spin-off. It wasn't Scott's job to raise capital or control expenses, but it was his job to sell clothes."

"And pressure was mounting."

"Yes. Scott wasn't meeting his stated goals. This meant reduced bonuses, smaller raises. His wife quit her job during a rough pregnancy. It was all on him and he buckled."

"Drugs."

Brad frowned. "And women."

Eleanor Davies. Allison noticed the disgust on Brad's face. As a man with militaristic bearing and a strong belief in the importance of character, he would disapprove of Scott's choices. Would he let that disapproval cloud his judgment? Could he be wrong about Scott?

Allison said, "Thank you. This makes more sense now." But did it? It was all so neat. Scott gets into drugs, has affairs, makes bad choices, maybe owes someone money he can't pay. Gets killed in the process.

But why was her name in his appointment book?

What could he possibly have wanted to tell her that day at the train station?

And who the hell was sending her and her family these pictures?

The pictures. With mounting horror, Allison realized that if Mia had received an envelope, it was likely Jason had, too. Her unreturned calls—so unlike her boyfriend. She stood, suddenly queasy and lightheaded.

"I have an appointment, Brad. I have to go."

Brad rose. He hugged her, giving no indication that he thought her sudden haste odd. "Allison, don't waste your time on this. The man you knew was not the man who died on that city street. Nothing can change that now."

Allison kissed him, making no promises. "Give Antonia my love," she said. His eyes darkened, but agreed.

From the mall parking lot, Allison tried Jason's numbers again. No answer on his mobile. His admin gave Allison a half-baked excuse about meetings.

He's avoiding me, Allison thought. She needed to explain. Could explain, if he gave her an opportunity. She should have told him. That was the price of dishonesty. Had she told him about Scott years ago...but it was too late now.

Only her appointment with Midge Majors kept her from driving to Philly to stake out his office. She needed to get back to First Impressions for their session. She wasn't expecting Vaughn to be sitting in her office when she arrived.

He had an envelope in front of him. The pictures were spread on the desk. Allison felt her face turn crimson. Mia was bad enough. For Vaughn to see her like that...unthinkable.

"Do you have something you need to get off your chest?" Vaughn said softly.

"It's not what you think."

"What do I think, Allison?"

"You think I'm having an affair."

Vaughn shook his head. "I had that man's face scanned into a database. I know his name is Scott Fairweather. I also know he's dead. Any affair would have been in the past tense."

"He was a client."

"I don't remember him."

The quiet steel of Vaughn's voice was maddening. She could deal with anger or judgment, but this was something new.

"Are you being blackmailed, Allison?"

"I don't know."

Allison pulled up a chair and sat across from Vaughn, her desk between them. One by one, she placed the photos back into the envelope. She wanted to scream. This was an invasion of her privacy, an act of harassment. Sending *her* pictures was bad enough. How soon before whoever this was sent photos to the media? And damn Scott for taking the pictures in the first place. Maybe he really was into drugs. A man unethical enough to take sexual photos without permission would surely stoop to other acts. Selling or buying drugs didn't seem that far out of the realm of possibilities.

Allison looked up. Vaughn was staring at her, his lips twisted into a half snarl. "Who is doing this to you, Allison?"

"I don't know that, either."

"Can you tell me something? Anything?"

She heard the frustration in his voice. And protectiveness. With a sigh, Allison repeated the story, beginning with her separation from Jason and ending with her discussion with Mia and the fact that Jason wasn't returning her calls. She felt the hot sting of tears on her face and realized she'd been holding them in for days.

"Why didn't you come to me?"

"And put you in a position where you would have to withhold information from Mia? I didn't want to burden you, or anyone, with this, at least until I knew more."

"And do you know more?"

Allison ran through what she'd learned from Julie and Brad. "Brad seems convinced that Scott was using and maybe even dealing. That pressure and money woes got to him."

"Wouldn't he know? He hired the guy."

"Yes, but you have to know Brad. He's old-school when it comes to family and commitment. He takes his responsibilities seriously. The fact that Scott was having affairs would have been enough to send Brad over the edge. But poor job performance? Scott put work first. I just don't know that Brad's capable of being fully objective given the circumstances."

"Hmmm." Vaughn ran a strong hand through his dark, closely-cropped hair. His voice had loosened and the anger and frustration in his eyes had dissipated. Allison recognized problem-solving mode, a much more comfortable place for Vaughn. "What's your next move?"

"I need to find this Eleanor woman. I get the sense that she's involved, but she seems to have disappeared."

"Jamie may be able to help. Why don't you give me the information you have and I'll see what he can do?"

Allison nodded, relieved. Jamie was a genius when it came to computer work. She said, "I have a file in my desk. I'll give it to you. Also, do you think Jamie could do some research on Transitions? The company was spun off from Diamond Brands some time ago. I vaguely remember the circumstances, but anything about that time period, or about the company's financials, would help."

Vaughn nodded. "Sure thing." He stood and walked to where Allison was now standing. He held out his arms. After a moment of hesitation, Allison responded, wrapping her arms around him. He held her tightly. Allison gave in to the warmth and strength of his friendship. The tears came, hot and unwelcome. She and Vaughn stayed like that for several minutes. When her sobs had stopped, Vaughn leaned down and kissed the top of her head.

"You're not alone," he whispered.

He was right, and she was glad.

SEVENTEEN

Dunne Pond, located about six miles off the coast of Maine, ninety minutes south of Acadia National Park, was a smallish body of water nestled in the hills, amid forests of pine and spruce trees. On this November afternoon, the sun was already beginning to set and the roads leading west were barren. Eleanor squinted, on the lookout for Dunne Pond Road. About a half mile down the paved highway, she saw a small wooden sign marking a dirt road. She braked and made the turn.

Her stomach growled. She pulled a Cliff Bar from her bag and unwrapped it, unsure whether she'd be welcome and when her next meal would be. Edit that, she thought. She certainly wouldn't be welcome, but that was to be expected. She just hoped she'd be allowed to stay. In the days since leaving Florida she'd traded her Jeep for a used black Civic and taken the cash as living money. She knew the transaction would be registered with the Commonwealth but she didn't care. Black Civics were common, and by the time her pursuers caught on, she'd be far from Pennsylvania.

The car wasn't happy about the unpaved road but it chugged along. About two and a half miles down Dunne Pond Road, Eleanor spotted the entrance to a dirt driveway nearly hidden by tree branches. She remembered the spot vaguely because last time she was here—admittedly ages ago—it had been across from a small sign for Dunne Pond Resort and the sign was still there. She made a right and followed the driveway about a hundred yards to where it dead-ended, next to a small Maine camp, a fancy name for a plain, rustic cabin. The cabin, bounded by trees and brambles, was dark. No cars were parked in front of the house. That was okay. Eleanor tucked the small Civic in a spot next to a decrepit picnic table that clearly hadn't seen a cookout in years. She could wait.

By ten o'clock that night, Allison was frantic. Where was Jason? He still hadn't returned a single call, and he didn't come to her house after work. Following her appointments, Allison set off to his apartment in Paoli. She opened the front door with her key but he wasn't there either. A call to Mia confirmed Jason hadn't gone to see his mother.

He'd gotten photos. She just knew it.

She considered waiting at his house for him to return but she honestly didn't know whether he would go there or to her place in Villanova. She wrote him a note saying they needed to talk and asking him not to think the worst. Then she went home.

Since then, she'd sat in the living room with Brutus and the cat, a navy blue flannel blanket wrapped around her legs, a box of tissues next to her. She was trying to read *The Birth of Venus,* but as much as she loved the book, her mind kept wandering. Finally, at ten minutes before midnight, she was just dozing in her chair when she heard the front door slam open. Jason stormed inside.

He walked to where she was sitting and stood over her, his face red. In a Tokyo second, she took in his rumpled white dress shirt, the five o'clock shadow on his face and the lingering scent of beer. She tensed, ready for a barrage of questions—justified, perhaps. But they didn't come.

Allison watched a slideshow of emotions cross Jason's face. First mild anger, then confusion, then something akin to tenderness. As suddenly as he'd stormed in, he dropped down onto one knee before her.

"Marry me, Allison."

Completely confused, Allison said, "What?"

"Marry me."

Allison stared, wide-eyed, his words penetrating. After a moment, she said, "Yes. Yes!"

He tilted his head back, smiling. "Really?"

"Really."

"I don't have a ring..."

"I don't care."

He grinned, a boyish, goofy smile that made her heart soar, then sink. "I have to tell you something, Jason."

"I know."

"Did you get...pictures?"

"A copy of an old email. But it was enough." He leaned in and kissed her. "I don't care."

"About Scott?"

He nodded.

"I don't understand how you know—"

"Vaughn." He kissed her again. "He explained everything."

"Vaughn?"

"I called him when I found the envelope taped to my door. I was so angry. He said he could explain. We went to Sal's for a few drinks—okay, I had a beer and Vaughn had Coke—and he told me what happened. I know Scott was in the past. I understand."

Allison looked down. Her fingertips were kneading the blanket as though of their own volition. "Scott and I had an affair."

"You and I were separated. I'm sure both of us did things during that period that we aren't proud of now."

Allison left it at that. She was sure he was right, and she certainly didn't want to think about him with other women. Allison stood, facing Jason. He smelled of stale beer and greasy food and his familiar spicy aftershave. "The marriage proposal...it wasn't the booze talking, I hope."

"No. Although the beer may have given me the courage to ask." He pulled her close and stroked her hair. "Did you really mean 'yes'?"

"I can't think of anything I want more." She looked up, meeting his gaze. "But—"

Jason took a step back. "No 'buts,' Al."

"I have to be completely honest first. Did Vaughn tell you I've been looking into Scott's death?"

"No, but I figured as much."

"With the Benini family and Tammy Edwards, you were upset—"

Jason held up a hand. "I want to marry *you. All* of you, including the crazy, reckless, determined side. Anyway, who wants a boring marriage full of evenings at home, neighborhood barbeques and Sunday night football? I'd much rather have satanic murders, Russian mafia and missing elderly women any day."

"Jason Campbell, you will make a very good husband."

"But only if I help you with your research?"

Allison smiled. "Only if you hold me tight."

Allison was awakened at three forty-six by the insistent buzz of her mobile. She reached toward the bedside table to silence it before it woke up Jason and saw her sister Amy's number flashing on the screen. Quickly, she slid out of bed and grabbed her robe off a chair. She padded down the hallway toward her office and closed the door behind her while she answered.

"They took her," her sister slurred into the phone. "And they won't give her back."

"Amy, where are you?"

"They stole her from me!"

"Amy! You're not making sense. Where are you?" Allison paced the floor in her office. Her sister sounded intoxicated—or worse, high. Her voice was low and guttural, and her words were slip-sliding into one another. Allison spoke firmly and calmly in an effort to make her focus. "Tell me where you are."

"They took her!"

"Who is 'they,' Amy?"

"Faye. *Them*!"

"Faye took Grace?"

"Yes!" Amy let out a high-pitched wail. "I want my baby back."

"Okay, okay. Where are you?"

"No."

"Amy, I can't help you if you don't cooperate. Tell me where you are and I can come and get you."

Amy started to sob. "I just want to see her," she whispered. "Faye won't let me see her."

"Did you go there tonight?"

"Yes."

"And they turned you away?"

"Yes. No."

No doubt because Amy was a mess, Allison thought, frustrated. "Let me pick you up, Amy."

"Knew you wouldn't help." She hung up.

Allison called the number four times but Amy didn't pick up. She tried Faye, but no one answered. After that, she went back to bed. Sleep never came.

EIGHTEEN

Allison spent most of Wednesday vacillating between euphoria and a strong case of the what-the-hell-am-I-doings. For the third time in three minutes, she straightened the files on her office desk. First Impressions was quiet this morning, and the lack of noise meant too much time in her own head. Almost everyone close to her had now seen the photographs. That thought was disturbing enough, but the possibility that the photos would be sent beyond her inner circle was terrifying.

The most logical explanation was that someone thought Scott had told her something, that he meant to meet with her and pass along some critical piece of information. Whoever was behind the photos, and Scott's death, thought she held damning evidence. Of what? And if they were so sure she knew something, why not blackmail her rather than simply send pictures? She reminded herself that Scott was *dead*. Murdered—that fact was undisputed. If the photos and his death were connected, she could be on someone's hit list.

But if Scott's death *was* drug-related like Brad Halloway suspected, why would whoever did it care two hillbillies about Allison's affair with Scott four years ago?

Allison's phone buzzed. "Judge Lint is here for your session."

"Be right there," Allison said. She stood up, placing the client files in her drawer as she did so. She hated feeling powerless, and right now, that's exactly how she felt: powerless and frustrated. What was her next step? The police? But then she'd have to turn over the photos. Not something she was ready to do.

And whoever was sending them was banking on that.

*   *   *

Judge Lint had been one of Allison's original clients. A sixty-seven-year-old Third Circuit judge with a severe fear of public speaking and a secret shoe fetish, Judge Lint had been using Allison as his secret weapon for remaining on the bench. Together, they practiced the relaxation skills and cognitive therapy techniques that kept the judge from hyperventilating on the stand. Lint came twice a week religiously. Allison could only reschedule under the direst of circumstances.

She hadn't felt that her current circumstances qualified as dire.

"Belly breaths, Judge," she said now. "Breathe from here." She pointed to her diaphragm. "Not here." She motioned toward her chest. They were in the client room, a briefing room strategically decorated in soft shades of peach and brown and designed for client comfort. Some years ago, she had purchased a small version of a judge's stand, and before each session, Vaughn carried it in and set it up. The judge did better if he had props.

"I'm...I'm trying." Sweat poured down his face and he wiped his brow with a pristine handkerchief. He pulled his shoulders back and plucked at a rubber band on his wrist that Allison had given him to combat obsessive thoughts.

"Take your time. Continue when you're ready."

"As I was saying, historically the Third Circuit has taken the following stance on witness protection."

The judge continued his speech about protections offered witnesses in federal cases. He always prepared lengthy discourses on subjects relevant to his cases, an effort he saw as killing the two proverbial birds with one stone. Allison rarely listened to the substance, preferring instead to focus on his breathing, body language and any signs of panic or discomfort. But this time, she perked up.

Witness protection. Federal crimes. *Witnesses.*

The woman in North Philly whom Leah mentioned, the one who was a possible witness to Scott's murder.

"In 2007," Judge Lint continued, "in Wilson versus Moran, the Third Circuit held..."

Allison watched her client's mouth move. Her professional self continued to monitor his vitals, but her mind was far away. Venturing into Philly to speak with a witness seemed a little extreme, even for her. But there was a lot at stake.

When the judge paused to take a breath, Allison said, "Judge Lint, is there anything under the law that prohibits a citizen, not someone accused in a case, from talking to a witness about what he or she may have seen?"

Judge Lint looked momentarily startled.

"For purposes of intimidation?"

"No, simply to better understand what may have happened."

"Like a friend or relative asking questions of a potential witness?"

"Sure. Like that."

The judge shook his head.

"Not unless there's a gag order in place. A witness is generally free to speak to whom he or she wants, and the media, strangers and friends are free to ask questions, unless of course they are trying to intimidate a witness. Are you sure that's not the case in your hypothetical?"

"Quite sure. Thank you for the information."

Judge Lint looked at Allison over the top of his black-rimmed bifocals.

"Allison, in all the years we have worked together, you have never stopped to ask me a question about the topic du jour. Are you sure you're okay?"

"I'm fine, Judge. I was just curious."

"Well, I like your inquisitiveness."

Allison smiled. She'd always been so focused on the mechanics of the judge's speeches, not the content. She'd have to show more interest in the future.

"No way, Allison. Are you crazy?" Vaughn slammed his hand down on his desk. "There is no way you can go sauntering into that section of Philly."

"And why not?"

He looked at her over his glasses.

"Really? Do I need to tell you the reasons?"

Allison grabbed her coat off the hook. It wasn't even one o'clock.

She had plenty of daylight. Outside, the sun was shining. A perfect day for a trip into the city.

"I'll be fine."

"Allison—"

She stopped short of the door and looked at him. After her session with Judge Lint, Allison had done an internet search and found the name of the witness who claimed to see the boys running away from the scene of the crime. Edith Myers, fourteenth block of Light Street. Allison understood Vaughn's hesitance, but it occurred to her that maybe this woman would talk to her, woman to woman, if she went down there. She had to try.

"Let me at least go with you."

Allison started to protest. Her mind spun for a reason, and she realized that maybe having Vaughn there wouldn't be such a bad idea, not so much for protection but because he had been born and raised in Philadelphia.

He would know his way around, and he might provide more of an entrée to a conversation with the neighbors. She was an outsider. People would be suspicious of an outsider, especially if trouble really was afoot.

"Fine," she said. "But only because I adore you for helping me patch things up with Jason."

Vaughn smiled. She loved the way his eyes smiled, too. Not for the first time, Allison wished life had worked out differently for Vaughn. He'd make an amazing father and husband. That wasn't in the cards with Mia. But who was she to judge their relationship? They seemed to work, and that was all that mattered.

"Didn't take much convincing, Allison," Vaughn said. "Jason wanted to believe the best."

"Still, it would have been hard for him not to jump to conclusions."

Vaughn nodded. "He's an easygoing guy. But just because he doesn't demand attention doesn't mean his needs aren't important."

Allison felt her face redden. "Did he say that?"

"No, no. Strictly my observation. Jason's willing to be the wind beneath your wings, to quote that sappy song from the eighties. With people like Jason, it's easy to take things for granted. Forget the photos. I'm talking stuff bigger than that."

"Like marriage?"

"Like showing Jason he's a priority in your life. Whatever that takes." Vaughn shrugged. "Look, what the hell do I know about relationships? And this is coming from me, not Jason. He's an awesome guy, Allison. Don't lose him."

As they put their coats on and headed outside, Allison almost told Vaughn about their engagement. *Almost.* But something held her back. Maybe she needed time to adjust to the thought. Or maybe she was afraid that sharing the news and giving in to the happiness would mean it would be snatched away.

NINETEEN

After three hours of waiting, no one showed up. Eleanor thought about breaking in. It would have been easy enough to do, but she figured that wouldn't be the best way to start her new relationship with her deceased father's former live-in. So she packed up and paid cash at one of those tiny motels along the Maine coast. She'd registered as Doris Long, shelled out four twenties, and cursed the real Doris Long for not being home.

At noon on Wednesday, she was making her third trip to Dunne Pond. For a reclusive nut job, Doris sure was out a lot.

Third time's a charm, she thought. This time, an old Subaru station wagon was sitting in the driveway, its white paint and undercarriage dotted with rust. Before she'd opened her car door, Eleanor saw a round face peering through the window in the house. She climbed out of the Civic and heard dogs barking.

The front door of the small cabin slammed open and Doris's two German Shepherds ran toward her, barking madly. Eleanor climbed back in the car and rolled down the window. She had expected this. In fact, she was relieved to see the dogs. They'd offer protection.

"Doris!" She yelled out the window. "Damn it, Doris, it's just me! Eleanor!"

The dogs kept barking. Eleanor was certain Doris could hear her, though. She'd seen the front window open. "Doris!"

Eleanor looked around the interior of her car for a treat...anything to calm the beasts. She was reaching for a Power Bar when the front door opened again and Doris came outside. She looked angry, but then, Doris Long always looked angry.

"What do you want?"

"Nice to see you, too, Doris."

"Nice is a word I save for people I like."

Eleanor took a deep breath. She needed Doris now. With no access to her funds and cash running low, she needed a place to hideout, somewhere she could think and plan. Doris couldn't know the truth. It would scare her. No, correct that: Doris wasn't a woman who scared easily. It was probably more accurate to say it would be a nuisance. Doris Long hated a nuisance, like her boyfriend's children. Eleanor would have to appeal to Doris's very greedy nature.

"Doris, I know we've never been close, but—"

"This oughta be good." Doris took a few steps closer, gnarled hands on sturdy hips. She wore a white Polo knock-off, tucked severely into blue elastic-waistband hiking pants. Her cropped hair was a steely gray that framed a round face and beady, distrusting brown eyes. Those eyes squinted in Eleanor's direction.

"I have a proposition. It involves money," Eleanor said quickly.

Doris made a tsk, tsk noise. "Are you here alone?"

Eleanor nodded.

A storm cloud wafted across the sky and the sudden shadow darkened Doris's woody corner of the world. Doris looked up, moving her squint from Eleanor's face to the cloud and back again. "I guess you can come in."

Eleanor eyed the dogs. "Will they attack?"

"Brick and Mortar?" Doris asked stonily. "All bark, and that's when I'm lucky. I tried training them to attack. Attack with kisses, maybe."

Eleanor got out of the car warily, but all the dogs did was wag their tails and look at her expectantly.

"Oh, for gawd's sake," Doris huffed at the dogs. She took a hard look at Eleanor. "You've aged. Too much sun. Still doing all that rock climbing and other nonsense?" She waved her hand. "Never mind. Don't want to know." She walked toward the cabin. Over her shoulder, she said, "Come on in. Let's hear about this proposition."

*   *   *

Edith Myers lived in well-maintained brownstone in North Philly. Her house had fresh green paint on the windowsills, potted plants and two wrought-iron chairs on the small front porch, and a cross that had been nailed to the front door, as though to ward off evil. Allison figured the bars on the windows were also for that purpose. Sadly, the houses on either side of Edith's were crumbling, once-stately testaments to neighborhood blight and skyrocketing crime rates.

Edith's doorbell didn't work. Vaughn knocked, but no one answered. He tried again, more insistently this time, and they heard the frantic yipping of a small dog. Finally, the door opened violently, catching on the chain. An angry face peered out, eyeing them up and down.

"Not talking to no more reporters."

She started to slam the door again, but Vaughn inserted his foot in the doorway. "Mrs. Myers, we're not reporters," he said quietly.

"Then who are you?"

"May we talk for a few minutes?"

The woman's eyes widened. "Who are you? Police? Duane's not here."

"We're not police," Vaughn said. He looked at Allison.

"Mrs. Myers, my name is Allison Campbell." She held out a business card through the door and the woman snatched it. "I just want to talk to you about the man who was murdered nearby a few weeks ago."

"And which man would that be?"

There was no reproach in the woman's voice, but Allison felt a jolt of shame. The murder of a well-to-do white man in this neighborhood might be big news, but she reminded herself that men—kids, mostly— were murdered here on a regular basis. The world paid scant attention.

Allison said, "I'm sorry Mrs. Myers. You are Mrs. Myers, right?" A faint nod, but enough. "I want to talk about Scott Fairweather."

"What's it to you?"

"I don't think those kids did it," Allison said. "And if they did, I don't think they were acting alone."

*   *   *

"Exactly how are you involved, Ms. Campbell?" Edith Myers asked. Once she heard the reason for their visit, she'd let them inside her house—insisted they come in, really—and ushered them to a small parlor off the front entrance. Like the house's exterior, the inside was clean and neat. Floral wallpaper and a vinyl kitchen floor, visible from the parlor, dated the décor, but everything about the place said this was the headquarters of a woman bound and determined to fight the decline of her neighborhood. Edith herself seemed to be out of a different period. She wore a prim floral shirtwaist dress in shades of lavender and ivory. Her silver hair had been plaited and the plaits pulled into a neat bun on her head, a striking contrast to her ebony skin. She was painfully thin, and when she sat, Allison saw dark bruises on her arm.

"I knew Scott," Allison said. "And please, call me Allison."

"Allison, I don't think I can tell you anything I haven't already told the police." Edith's hands flitted before she busied them by stroking her dog's back. The dog was some kind of miniature poodle mix, and had finally stopped barking. "I didn't really see anything anyway."

Vaughn said, "But the papers said you saw a group of teenagers running away from the scene."

"And that's the truth."

"Hmmm." Vaughn tilted his head. "Did you actually see the kids with the body, Mrs. Myers?"

"No. By the time I got there, they had run."

"So it's possible they had stumbled upon the body, too?"

"Are you calling me a liar, Mr. Vaughn?"

"Not at all," Vaughn said. "I'm just trying to figure out whether these boys may really be innocent."

Edith stood, placing the dog on the floor. She pointed a shaking finger at Vaughn.

"These boys are not innocent. Make no mistake. I know these boys. They're the reason I can't go out at night, why folks are afraid to leave their houses in the day sometimes." She shook her head, emphasizing each word. "They may look like babies on the outside, but they were done being babies long ago."

"I'm sorry, Mrs. Myers. I didn't mean to suggest—"

She waved her hand at him. "Don't be sorry. You wouldn't understand what it's like around here. It used to be so pretty. Church-going folks, nice houses, not much crime. Nowadays these kids run wild. They have guns." She shook her head again, saying to no one in particular, "Children with guns."

"So the boys who you saw near the victim...they've caused trouble around here before?" Allison asked.

Edith looked down at her dog, who had curled up next to her feet. "Hold-ups, harassing folks near their own homes, breaking in, selling drugs to children. When I saw them by that body, I knew they hadn't just happened upon it." She looked up just long enough to glare at Vaughn. "I told the police: that man was buying what they were selling."

"And you didn't see anyone else in the area?" Allison asked.

"No one who could have done that."

"Were the kids carrying guns?" Vaughn asked.

Edith shook her head. "I didn't get close enough to see. I saw the body, I saw those boys, and I called the police. I have learned my lesson many times over, Mr. Vaughn. I mind my own business."

"Yet you called the police," Vaughn said softly.

Edith looked up and met his gaze. Allison saw stubbornness in those eyes. That was the grit that had allowed Edith Myers to remain in one of Philly's worst neighborhoods.

Just then, the front door opened and a young man sauntered inside. He was tall and broad-shouldered, with a handsome, chiseled face and cold eyes. He stopped short when he saw Allison and Vaughn.

"Who the hell are they?"

"Watch your mouth, Duane."

"Stop talking to reporters."

"They're not news people."

"Then who did you let in here, Gram?" His voice was low and menacing. "Did you even ask them who they were?"

"Of course I did. Who they are is none of your concern."

Edith sat back down in an attempt to seem calm, but it wasn't working. Allison watched Edith's hands shake. She felt bad for causing Edith trouble.

Allison stood. "Thank you for your hospitality, Mrs. Myers."

"It was no problem. I was just going to suggest some tea." The older woman glanced in Duane's direction. "Maybe my grandson would like some, too. Once he finds those manners he seems to have misplaced."

Duane took a step toward his grandmother just as Vaughn stood up, blocking his way. "Come outside with me, Duane," Vaughn said. His voice was low, matching the menacing tone Duane had used with his grandmother. "I would love to talk to you for a few minutes."

Allison watched as the boy looked from his grandmother to Vaughn and back again. He seemed to be around nineteen or twenty, and while he was tall and heavy, Vaughn was taller and much fitter. Vaughn clenched his fists in an unspoken threat. Allison saw the telltale vein pulsing on the side of Vaughn's forehead. He wasn't just looking for information. Vaughn was angry.

After a silent minute, Duane muttered *shit, man* under his breath and followed Vaughn outside.

"He used to be such a good boy," Edith said after he was gone. "Good grades, good manners. I've done what I could for him."

"Bad crowd?"

Edith looked at Allison for a long time before answering. Finally she said, "There ain't nothing else but bad crowds, Ms. Campbell. Around here, even the good ones don't have a chance. And nobody cares." She sighed, and Allison heard the echoes of heartbreak in that simple sound. "Children with guns, killing each other. What kind of world we living in when no one seems to care?"

TWENTY

Vaughn was quiet as they drove back toward the Main Line, and Allison, aware that he was likely battling his own demons, gave him space. Vaughn had grown up in West Philly, in a neighborhood not unlike the one they had just visited, and she knew memories from his youth cut deep. When they reached the highway, though, she couldn't stand the silence any longer.

"What did you say to Edith's grandson?"

Vaughn stared straight ahead. He was driving, jaw clenched, knuckles tight-fisted around the steering wheel.

"I told him if he wants to be a man, he needs to cut the crap. Real men don't hurt women."

"Edith's arm?"

Vaughn nodded. "Yeah, those were fingerprints. That boy has an anger management problem."

"I hope he doesn't think she said something. I'd hate to see him take it out on her after we left."

"I don't think that will happen."

Allison tensed.

"What did you do?"

"I spoke in a language he could understand." Vaughn turned to look at her and the darkness in his gaze made her shudder. "I made it clear that it's not nice to hurt people weaker than you."

His tone was closed. Allison trusted her colleague enough to know he wouldn't have really hurt the kid, but she also knew his sense of justice, and his intolerance for stupid, sometimes outweighed reason.

Vaughn occasionally let anger get the best of him as well.

"Found out something interesting about the murder, though," Vaughn said. "Funny how the boy was willing to talk after a few minutes of intense discussion."

"What did he say?"

"Those kids? The ones who were seen running away from the scene of the crime? Bad news. Threats, drugs, rape, gang violence…says they even killed a man over a pair of sneakers."

"That's in line with what the grandmother said."

"Yep. Kid also says they always carry, but this time, they had nothing."

"So?"

"So, they tossed the gun that killed Scott. The cops didn't find the murder weapon on any of them."

"Was the weapon ever found?"

"I don't know. But I suspect if it was, it was clean."

Allison was thoughtful for a moment. "So Duane backed up his grandmother's story. The boys could have killed Scott over drugs or drug-related money."

"Sounds that way."

"But you don't believe they did it?"

Vaughn was quiet while he pulled the BMW around a Honda doing sixty-one in the passing lane. "I don't believe the *kid*. He was lying to me."

"About the boys?"

Vaughn glanced at Allison. "That's just it, I don't know. I just can't shake the feeling that Duane was lying about something."

Vaughn hadn't been completely truthful with Allison, and he was feeling bad about that now. After he dropped Allison off at First Impressions, he headed home. He told her he wanted to talk with Jamie to see what his brother had turned up about Transitions. He also wanted to run some searches of his own on Edith and her grandson, Duane. Something about them didn't sit right with him. Maybe they were just scared, but his gut told him there was more.

Vaughn found Jamie in his room, at his desk, reviewing

something on his computer monitors. Jamie owned two computers and four monitors, not including the one by his bed that displayed the words he spoke into his mouthpiece. Like the voice system, his desk and computer set-up were also controlled with a mouthpiece. Jamie was manipulating it now to change the view on his screen to a different window. He smiled as Vaughn walked into the room.

"Making progress?" Vaughn asked.

Jamie smiled again. He looked bright and alert, and had a fire in his eyes Vaughn hadn't seen in a while. Mrs. T was here today, Vaughn's favorite nurse-caretaker, and the house smelled of cinnamon and apples, perfect for a cool fall day.

But Vaughn knew the happiness reflected in his twin's face had nothing to do with pie. Angela was the reason for that glow, and who was he to interfere? Even if the thought of his brother getting hurt scared him way more than some thug kid from the streets of Philly.

Jamie wheeled his electric chair over to his bed and spoke into the mouthpiece. Immediately, the screen lit up and words appeared.

I'M LOOKING INTO SCOTT'S ROLE AT TRANSITIONS. EVERYTHING ALLISON TURNED UP LOOKS ACCURATE.

"Transitions is the company spun-off by Diamond, right?"

RIGHT. THE FOUNDER OF DIAMOND BRANDS, TED DIAMOND, WANTED TO CREATE A SOCIALLY AND ENVIRONMENTALLY-CONSCIOUS BRAND.

"In line with what Halloway told Allison."

CORRECT. TRANSITIONS, ALONG WITH A NUMBER OF OTHER RETAILERS, WAS HIT HARD BY THE MEDIA WHEN IT WAS DISCOVERED THAT THEIR FACTORIES IN CHINA WERE CAUSING POLLUTION.

"How bad was it?"

THE FULL EXTENT OF THE DAMAGE WAS NEVER ESTABLISHED. Jamie jutted his chin in the direction of his desk. ENLARGE THE SECOND WINDOW.

Vaughn did. What confronted him was a series of photographs, each one more disturbing than the next. Black river water, dead fish on the river bank, a young boy, no more than ten or eleven years old, his young face drawn and thin, his body covered in red sores.

The news outlet, an online paper called *The People's Voice*, ran the photos along with a headline that said, "Environmental abuses in seven factories owned by Diamond Brands."

"That's pretty damning," Vaughn said, his gaze lingering on the young boy's haunted eyes.

DIAMOND ACCEPTED BLAME FOR THE DUMPING, BUT CAREFULLY SHIFTED THE FOCUS TO LAX CHINESE LAWS AND POINTED TO THE OTHER COMPANIES ALSO ACCUSED OF THE VIOLATIONS.

"And then Diamond spun off Transitions, as a way to show how socially forward the company really is?"

MAYBE, Jamie said. He looked troubled. OR MAYBE TED DIAMOND SIMPLY WANTED TO DISTANCE HIMSELF FROM THE MESS AND DUMPING TRANSITIONS WAS THE QUICKEST AND EASIEST WAY TO DO SO.

Allison arrived home to the hungry kisses of an ecstatic Brutus and the insistent meows of his new best friend, Simon. Brutus wanted affection; both wanted food.

Allison smiled. "In a minute, you two." She placed her purse and keys in the foyer and slipped off her black Ferrigamos. Jason was coming for dinner tonight, and she wanted to put her culinary skills to work. After a quick study of the contents of her refrigerator, she settled on pasta with olive oil and garlic, steamed broccoli and champagne. No one would credit her for being a great cook, but she did know how to appreciate good champagne. She placed it in the refrigerator and glanced at the clock. She had at least two hours before Jason arrived. Time to check out a few things, including the whereabouts of Eleanor Davies.

Upstairs in her home office, Allison pulled out her growing file. She started with Eleanor's cell phone number. As expected, no answer. She left a message and asked Eleanor to call her back. Then she turned on her computer and started searching.

Eleanor Davies had to have friends, relatives, someone whom she might turn to in a crisis. Eleanor's neighbor had mentioned her sister, Ginny. She didn't have a last name or an address, other than Amelia Island, and she didn't even know if Ginny was her given name or simply a nickname. Nevertheless, finding references to Ginny Davies online was easy enough, and a few more minutes of searching found Ginny Littman, once again called Ginny Davies following her divorce, in Fernandina Beach, Florida.

Allison stared at the screen. A phone number was moot. The woman was dead, found murdered in her home. The date put it just days after Scott was killed.

First Scott, now Eleanor's sister. Two previous amateur investigations had underscored that there were no such thing as coincidences. But why Ginny and not Eleanor? Unless someone had mistaken Ginny for Eleanor. Someone who didn't know what Eleanor looked like.

Allison stared at Eleanor's LinkedIn photograph and Ginny's picture on her real estate website. The two sisters looked very much alike. A friend or colleague could tell them apart, but possibly not a hit man who was going by a photograph.

This begged so many questions. If someone killed Ginny thinking it was Eleanor, why? Was it the same person who killed Scott? Or was it revenge for Scott's killing? Was Eleanor the murderer? Had she also killed her sister?

Allison reached for her mobile phone. She found a list of living relatives in Ginny's obituary. The parents were dead, but the father had a niece in Tennessee and a sister who lived in Detroit. The niece refused to speak with Allison, so Allison dialed the aunt's number. When a woman answered, Allison described herself as an old school chum and asked for help in locating Eleanor.

"Oh, dear," the woman said. "I haven't seen Eleanor in years."

"Do you have any idea where I can find her? We're planning a reunion and would love for Eleanor to come."

The woman was silent for a moment.

"Are you sure you have the right Eleanor?" she said finally. "My niece isn't really the social type."

"Eleanor Davies," Allison said firmly. "Has a sister Ginny. Originally from Pittsburgh."

"That's her all right." The woman sighed. "I wish I could help you, I really do. I always worried about Elle and wanted her to have some girl friends to hang around with. A reunion sounds real nice, and it's nice of you to go to all this trouble looking for her."

"Of course," Allison said, pushing aside a pang of guilt. "Do you have any idea where I might try other than her home? Ginny's not responding, and I don't know of any other relatives."

"Oh dear," the woman said. "I'm afraid Ginny has passed. A terrible, terrible thing. I would imagine that's where Elle is now, down in Florida, attending to the arrangements. I wish I could go. Their father would want that." She sighed again. "But these days, it's all I can do to stay on my feet. The doctors have me on three different painkillers, but nothing seems to be helping."

"Thanks, Mrs.—"

"Travis. My husband's long passed, but I have kept his name, as it should be. I don't believe in these new ideas of morality. Living together, extramarital affairs. It's not good for kids. I told that to Elle's father, but he didn't listen. Up there with that Long woman for all those years. That's why Eleanor could never settle down. A mother who left home, a father who lived in sin. What do you expect?" She paused. "At least Ginny tried her hand at marriage."

But Allison had zoomed in on Mrs. Travis's earlier statement. That Long woman. A longtime companion? Someone who wouldn't show up on official records, but a family connection nonetheless?

"Mrs. Travis, is it possible Ms. Long would know where Eleanor is? I hadn't thought of asking her before."

The woman laughed. "Oh, hardly. Have you met Doris? There is no love lost between those two. Elle was a feisty teen and an even feistier twenty-something. And Doris Long has the social skills of a gnat. I wouldn't bother looking there."

"Where is 'there,' Mrs. Travis?"

But Mrs. Travis couldn't remember. "Once Lenny hooked up with that woman, I lost contact with my brother. He and Doris came to a wedding or two, but that was it. I just know from conversations with Elle and Ginny that she is as tough as rawhide. Loves her guns, though. Try some gun enthusiast clubs, if you're bent on finding Elle. But don't get your hopes up. Eleanor may just have to sit out of this reunion. Won't be the first time, I'm sure."

TWENTY-ONE

By six o'clock in the evening, Eleanor got tired of waiting for Doris Long to leave the house. That woman was *always* there, fussing over the dogs, Brick and Mortar, whom she professed to hate, or watching television. Old reruns of *I Love Lucy* and *The Bob Newhart Show*. The television-watching wouldn't be so bad except that the television was in the living room, which also happened to be Eleanor's bedroom.

And Doris smoked. The house reeked of cigarette smoke, and a haze of gray blanketed everything. For Eleanor, used to the outdoors, it was a boring, pointless, sexless life, and she couldn't understand the appeal.

But she didn't have to. She just needed to withstand it for a little while.

Eleanor sat outside on the small front landing and stared into the woods. She was wearing a parka begrudgingly borrowed from Doris, and she wrapped it around her tightly to ward off frigid Maine air. The parka, like everything else, smelled of cigarettes and neglect, and it struck Eleanor that she missed her home. Thanksgiving was quickly approaching, and the thought of spending it here, with Doris, was almost unfathomable. She hadn't spent a holiday in the same room with Doris since she was twenty-two.

Something in the woods moved and Eleanor followed the sounds. It was already dark, and she squinted to see. Nothing, maybe a deer. Good to be paranoid, she thought, and stood, letting go of the edges of her parka.

Eleanor peeked through the window. Doris was still wide awake, sitting on the couch/bed, a cigarette in one hand and a Diet Coke in the other. Eleanor glanced at her watch: six-fourteen. If nothing had changed in forty-six minutes, Doris would switch to beer and the evening news. Fox Television, her favorite. If the right wing pundits didn't get her too riled up, she might just drink enough beer to fall asleep early. And if the beer didn't do the trick, Eleanor had no qualms about slipping her a few sleeping pills to help things along.

An owl hooted somewhere in the distance and Eleanor jumped. Dusk was settling into night, and before long she'd be getting sleepy. She felt like a caged animal, restless and discontent. A thought struck her: it would be so easy to do away with Doris. Then she could stay here indefinitely without having to deal with dogs and smoke and stupid television shows. She pushed the thought away, tempting as it was. Doris was a necessary evil.

Nah, she just needed to hold on a while longer. Things would die down and then she could flee.

Jason arrived at seven-twelve bearing a file folder and a bouquet of deep purple irises, Allison's favorite flowers. He handed her the bouquet and pressed against her with a warm kiss, long and slow. Allison placed the flowers on the small table in the foyer. She took Jason's face in her hands and leaned in to kiss him while her fingers reached for his suit jacket. Slowly, she pulled the jacket off him. She unbuttoned his blue dress shirt, lingering at each button to stroke the muscular chest beneath. Jason moaned. Gently, he pulled Allison's dress over her head so that she stood in the foyer in panties, heels and a bra.

"That's better," he murmured. He opened his eyes and gave her a languid, hungry look. He took her hand and moved it downward. "Here, or upstairs?" he whispered.

Allison smiled. She reached for the hallway light switch and flipped the lights off. In the soft glow from the kitchen, she could still make out the shadows of his face. His breath, warm and real, tickled her neck.

"Here."

Jason pressed her against the foyer wall and kissed her again. His mouth moved from her collarbone to her breast, and she felt a moan escape her own lips.

A picture flashed before her: her face, captured unwittingly on camera, in a sultry state of ecstasy. But this is different, she told herself. This is Jason. Things would be all right.

Jason moved to the skin on her stomach with butterfly kisses that sent her senses soaring.

Things *would* be all right. At least for a little while.

Allison and Jason lay on the living room floor, a down blanket underneath them and another on top. Allison's head rested on the crook of Jason's arm while he traced lazy circles on her belly. Jason's hand traveled from her belly to her thigh. He kissed the top of her head. "Have you given any thought to a date?"

Allison looked at him, surprised.

"You want another wedding?"

"Maybe not the whole bridal-party-gala-event thing, but I'd like to do something special."

"I was thinking small and catered. Close friends, family, that sort of thing."

Jason smiled. "Or we could elope. Hawaii? The Aegean? Maybe France?"

"Your mother would kill us."

"Mia can come, too."

Allison mock-hit him. "Then it's not eloping. It's a destination wedding."

Jason laughed. Allison loved the sound of his laugh. She loved having him here, with her. She wanted to believe they could make this work, that the second time would be different. Time had a way of easing pain until it was a distant memory. Allison was worried that all of that pain, the reasons they'd divorced in the first place, would come back to haunt their marriage. But she knew Jason wanted this, and deep down, she wanted it, too.

Jason snuggled in closer, his breathing becoming more regular. She felt his fingertips on her belly again. This time, he spread his hand flat, gently kneading the area around her belly button as he dozed off.

It seemed an unconscious act, sweet and intimate, and it stabbed at Allison as sad, too.

Allison matched her breathing to Jason's. She felt the cat, Simon, padding over to where they lay, and soon he was on top of the blanket, at the foot of their improvised bed. Where Simon was, Brutus would soon be, and sure enough, her noisy love of a dog plopped down next to the cat. Allison smiled, contentment washing over her like a warm summer wave. Her little family. Makeshift or not, this felt right.

Brutus picked his head up and growled.

"What's up, boy?" Allison said. She pushed herself up, onto her elbow, and listened. She heard the heater come on and Jason's rhythmic breathing, but otherwise nothing.

Brutus growled again. Outside, a car door slammed, and an engine revved as a car pulled out of the driveway.

Damn, Allison thought. Another photo. Maybe this time she could catch the person in the act.

Allison was just starting to stand, pulling the blanket from beneath the animals, when Brutus shot up like a bullet. He ran toward the front door, barking madly. Allison heard pounding and screaming. Quickly, she wrapped the blanket around her nude body and covered Jason, who had snapped awake, with the other. This wasn't the photo stalker.

"Who's here?" Jason asked.

"I don't know."

Allison went from one room to the next, gathering clothes. She tossed Jason's suit pants and shirt to him and slipped her dress over her head. At the door, she turned on the outside light and looked through the window. She couldn't see anyone.

Another knock. Another scream.

Allison opened the door. Jason reached the front entrance just as she did so, and they looked down at the heap that was her sister, Amy.

Amy looked up from the ground. "Help me."

Allison opened the screen door. She took one of Amy's arms and Jason took the other. Together, they lifted Amy up and inside the house, placing her in the kitchen, on one of the chairs. She was a mess. Tears had tracked mascara down sunken cheeks and over a blossoming bruise. Fingerprint marks tattooed her wrists and the pale skin under her chin. Her black tank top was torn, showing a lacy pink bra that struck Allison as both wanton and heartbreakingly innocent.

But that was her sister: the reckless child who never grew up.

"Help me," her sister slurred. Allison flipped over her arms and looked for track marks. To her relief, there were none.

"She's drunk," Jason said. "Booze, and maybe pills." He ground coffee while he talked. "Where's your Excedrin?"

"In the cabinet."

"She's going to need it."

Allison knelt in front of Amy. Gently, she pointed to the bruise. "Who did this to you?"

Amy closed her eyes, shook her head.

"Amy, if we're going to help you, you need to tell us."

"Grace. Help me," Amy whispered.

Allison had so many questions, but a long look at her sister said none of them would be answered. Amy needed help. More help than they could give her.

"Can you stay with her for a few minutes?" Allison asked Jason.

"Where are you going?"

Allison stood. "Upstairs to get her some clean clothes and to call Mason House, the private rehab I sometimes refer clients to."

Jason looked at Amy and shook his head. She'd slumped over in her seat and her chin touched her chest. A thin line of drool was trickling from her mouth and across her cheek. "Do you think she'll go?"

Allison shoved aside her own doubts. "If she wants her daughter back, she really has no choice."

TWENTY-TWO

Allison spent the rest of the week getting her sister Amy settled at Mason Rehab Center. A physical exam showed no serious injuries, but it had been clear to staff, and to Allison, that someone had roughed Amy up before sticking her in a cab and sending her off. From the bits and pieces Allison had been able to pull together from Amy's disjointed story, that someone was an old boyfriend. Amy had slept with him, and after several nights of popping amphetamines and binge drinking, he'd become jealous. They'd fought. Amy was lucky to still be alive.

Unfortunately, Allison thought, Amy didn't see it that way. She wanted out of rehab. It was only the social worker's warnings about her daughter that kept her there.

"Will she stay?" Mia asked. Allison was at Mia's farm. Outside, the mid-November air held the sharp promise of snow. A gray sky, low and ominous, pressed down, blocking the mid-day sun. Allison had gone to Mia for counsel and escape. Sitting in Mia's kitchen by the old Aga stove, chamomile tea in hand and Buddy by her feet, Allison felt some degree of solace.

"I don't know," Allison said. "Right now, she's a mess. They won't let me see her or talk to her, but staff say she's emotionally labile and demonstrates 'spurts of violence.'" Allison looked down at her teacup, an antique china painted with a rim of delicate flowers, and sighed. "It's my fault." The words were said without a trace of self-pity, only resignation.

Faye had been right. She should have never given that money to Amy. It was guilt money, done for her own benefit, not her sister's.

With her background and experience, she of all people should have known better.

"You can't make choices for your sister," Mia said. "We each have a journey. There are bumps along the way. We can do our best to cushion those bumps for the ones we love, but at the end of the day, the road is the road."

"And sometimes smoothing does more harm than good." Allison finished the thought for her friend. Mia's husband, Jason's father, had been a raging alcoholic. Mia's daughter Bridget had died after he crashed the car in which they'd been driving. His blood alcohol level had been twice the legal limit. Mia still wore her pain like a Purple Heart.

They sat in silence for a moment. Through the kitchen window, Allison watched the first snowflakes fall from the sky. They held so much promise.

"About Thanksgiving," Allison said finally. "We have some issues."

She and Jason had planned to announce their engagement to both families on Thanksgiving, but now with Amy in rehab and little Grace staying at her parents', Allison wasn't sure what to do. Jason had suggested dinner out, but that just didn't seem very homey.

Mia tilted her head and waited for more. Allison explained her current family situation. "So I'd like to be with them on Thanksgiving. I was just hoping we could all be together."

"Bring them here."

Allison hadn't thought of that. The bungalow in which Mia lived was lovely, lots of hardwood and field stone, but small. As she looked around, though, she realized the cavernous living room, with its full-length fireplace and bank of windows overlooking the yard, would be a nice place to enjoy some family time. And there would be plenty of room to place extra tables and seats.

Mia said, "We can rearrange the living room to hold two tables. We'll still have the couches and chairs for your parents to sit. And your niece will love the animals."

True, Allison thought. And her mother would, too.

Mia stood and glanced out the window. "Snow already. And it's only November." She turned. "It'll be a motley crew. Vaughn and

Jamie. Maybe Angela. Your family." She shrugged. "But isn't that what Thanksgiving is about? Family. We should all be thankful for the people in our lives."

Allison nodded. She thought of Leah and Scott and their little girl, now fatherless. She thought of Grace, no father and a mother who couldn't seem to get her act together. But perhaps some family was better than no family.

Allison stood and brought her teacup to the sink. As much as she loved the comfort and peace of Mia's cottage, she had work to do. First up: find Eleanor Davies.

Mia leaned over and hugged her suddenly. "Be careful."

"I will."

Mia's gaze held her own for a long moment. She wiped a stray hair back from Allison's eyes in a motherly gesture. "Children bring pain and grief and frustration," she said. "But they also bring incredible joy. Don't be so afraid of happiness, Allison."

Allison looked at her, unsure where this advice had come from. Advice that was, as usual when it came to Mia, right on the mark.

"I'll see you later?"

Mia nodded. "I'm picking Vaughn up for dinner. He and I still have to talk."

"Maybe you should take your own advice about happiness," Allison said. "And just accept it."

Mia looked thoughtful, and a little forlorn. "You know, I think maybe I am."

Doris Long was appearing more and more like a figment of Eleanor's aunt's imagination. Allison found almost forty-two thousand references to "Doris Long" online, but only one that may have been related to Eleanor's father's partner: a mention of a speaker at a gun show in Texas three years ago. The topic? Gun rights.

Based on Eleanor's aunt's description, this Doris Long felt like the right woman. Only additional searches turned up nothing, and a call to the organizer of the gun event was met with a distrustful, grunting, "We don't talk to officials."

No matter how much Allison applied her powers of woo, insisting that she was nothing other than a long-lost friend, the man at the other end of the line wasn't buying it.

And so after two and a half hours of searching, Allison came up empty.

It was Saturday afternoon. The morning's snow had stopped and an indolent sun was peeking its way through the cloud cover. Inside, Brutus was asleep by Allison's desk. Simon sat a few feet away, busily grooming his fur with long, lazy strokes.

Allison wanted a nap.

But that wasn't in the cards. Jason was at the office, finalizing some notes for an upcoming trial, and Vaughn was with Jamie. Allison considered stopping by their apartment, but she didn't feel like company right now.

She felt like getting answers.

Allison shut her laptop and packed it in her bag. In her bedroom, she pulled a pair of brown leather boots on over her jeans and traded her silk t-shirt for a dark green wool fisherman's sweater and a green, gray and maroon scarf. She patted Brutus, who was looking at her woefully.

"Back in a few hours, boy," she said, and bent down to give him a few strokes behind the ears. "Watch the house and the cat while I'm gone."

Simon eyed her warily. He obviously had no intention of being presided over by a dog.

It took her nearly an hour to make it to Leah's house. When she arrived, there were no cars in the driveway. Disappointed, she decided to wait. A half hour later, Leah arrived alone.

She started to get out of her car. When she saw Allison, she slid back behind the wheel. Allison jogged over and stood so that Leah couldn't close the car door. "Please," she said. "Just a few minutes."

Leah fumbled for her keys. She refused to meet Allison's eyes. "I have nothing to say to you."

"Leah, I told you. Scott and I hadn't seen each other in years."

Leah got the key in the ignition. She started the engine. "Move out of my way."

Allison stood firm. "I want what you want: the truth."

Leah gripped the wheel, knuckles white. "Go. Away."

"Leah, does the name Eleanor Davies ring any bells?"

Leah didn't answer. Drawn face pinched into an angry frown, she grabbed her purse and started digging. She pulled out her cell phone. "I'm calling the police."

Allison took a deep breath. "Be reasonable, Leah. You called me in the first place, remember? I'm trying to figure out what happened to Scott."

Leah looked at Allison sharply, eyes narrowed, nostrils flared. Allison saw bruised hollows under her cheeks, flat, greasy hair under a brown wool cap. "Two months ago, I was a happy stay-at-home mom with a young child and a devoted husband. Today, I'm the widow of a drug-dealing pervert. Tell me, Allison, how am I not being reasonable?"

"I'm not the enemy."

"It doesn't matter," Leah said. She seemed to deflate before Allison's eyes. "None of it matters now."

"It all matters. Don't you want to know the truth?"

Leah had put the phone down, but she started the engine to the car. "I've been living a lie for so long," she said. "I'm not sure I would recognize it anyway."

Allison sat in her Volvo for another twenty minutes, thinking. *Perverted drug-dealer.* Allison knew about Julie, and Julie had told her about Eleanor. Did Leah know, too?

Could an irate wife have arranged the death of her own husband?

Of course she could have. Allison knew firsthand that anger and jealousy honored no gender boundaries. But what would Leah have to gain? Revenge? Insurance money?

A death benefit from Transitions?

How could she find out if Scott's family was owed benefits? Leah certainly wasn't going to tell her.

Grudgingly, she dialed another number. Mark Fairweather picked up right away.

"Change your mind?" he asked.

Allison remembered their last encounter. Ignoring him, she said, "I just have a few questions."

"My time is not free, sunshine."

Allison took a deep breath.

"What do you suggest?"

"You, naked, maybe somewhere with a hot tub."

"Really? That's the best you could come up with?"

Mark laughed. "You're in luck. The wife is home this weekend and she wouldn't appreciate me having a snack before mealtime, if you get what I mean. So what do you want this time? Still obsessing over my brother?"

"Did Scott have an insurance policy, Mark?"

"As in could the little lady have benefitted from his death? Sure, he could have."

"But you don't know for sure?"

Mark was quiet for a moment. Allison heard talking in the background. When he came back, his tone was more serious. "What's with all the questions, Allison? They seem extreme for a...*friend*."

Allison took her time answering.

"I just can't accept Scott's death. I can't accept that it was drug-related." Because he was looking for me, Allison thought. And that wouldn't make sense. But she kept those statements to herself. "Didn't you handle Scott's estate?"

"What estate? Look, Allison, save yourself some trouble. My brother had nothing other than a basic life insurance policy that is rendered void if the deceased dies at his own hand or is killed in the course of an illegal act. So if Scotty was dealing, Leah gets nothing. If you're thinking my sister-in-law set the whole thing up to cash in, I'm telling you that's not what happened. I hate the bitch, but I don't think she killed Scott. At least not for money."

"What about other agreements? Maybe a benefit or severance provision with Transitions that would be triggered by his death?"

"That I wouldn't know anything about."

"I thought you brokered the agreement between Scott and Transitions."

"The original one, yes. But there was no death clause. If something was negotiated later, Scott didn't tell me."

"How about—"

"I'm done talking, sunshine. You want more, you gotta pay."

In money or something else? Didn't matter. Allison had what she wanted. "Thanks, Mark."

"I'd say anytime, but I wouldn't mean it."

TWENTY-THREE

Sunday morning brought sheets of icy rain and a raging migraine. Allison woke to Jason's arms wrapped protectively around her. She slowly opened her eyes. Light stabbed at her, but not before she saw Jason staring down at her face. Grinning, he kissed her nose. She smiled through the haze.

"Morning, sleepyhead."

"Mmm...morning."

"Headache?"

"Pressure changes always do it."

Jason slipped out of the warmth and came back with her magic pill and a glass of water. Allison sat up and swallowed. She said, "Give me thirty minutes and I'll make you breakfast."

Jason shook his head. He'd already slipped his pajama bottoms off and was heading toward the bathroom. "Have to be at the office. Still have a few hours of prep to do for Tuesday's trial."

Allison watched him, wishing the headache would disappear so she could send him off the right way. Standing there naked, sleep still clouding his eyes, his hair playfully mussed, he looked delicious. She tried to lift her head off the pillow again. *Yowza.* Not yet.

"When will you be home?" she asked instead.

"I'll head back to my place before dinner. Want me to come over here later?"

"Yes," Allison said, surprising herself. "I want you to come home."

Jason paused by the bathroom door. "What are you saying, Allison?"

"I'm saying move in."

"Before we get married?"

He sounded bewildered, and Allison laughed. "Are you worried about how it will look? Because I think that ship has long since sailed."

Jason walked back to the bed. He leaned over and kissed her forehead. "If it's what you want."

Allison smiled. "It's exactly what I want."

Vaughn woke up with a start, momentarily confused about where he was. He looked around, blinked, and, heart pounding, felt Mia in the bed next to him.

"You were having a bad dream," she said softly. She ran her hand along his shoulder, stopping to rub his neck. "Are you okay?"

Vaughn grunted. He sat up and rubbed his eyes. The room was warm. "What time is it?"

"Early."

Vaughn didn't respond. His pulse was slowing, but the remnants of the dream stayed with him. In it, he'd been running to save someone and he couldn't run fast enough, no matter how hard he tried. His legs had become heavy, his breathing ragged, and still he wasn't fast enough. He sank back against the pillows.

"Oh, man, I hope I didn't wake you up."

Mia trailed her nails down his arm. "I couldn't sleep anyway."

He turned over, facing her. Despite the isolation of her little farm, the shades were drawn and the room was dark. He could make out the outline of her face, but he couldn't see her features. He reached out a hand and, gently, traced the line of her jaw.

"When did this happen?" he asked.

"You fell asleep. Angela is with Jamie, so I let you go—"

"Not that," he said. "This. Us. When did things change?"

He felt Mia tense beside him. "What do you mean?"

"You're different. I can feel it, Mia. It's like you're pulling away. It's been this way for a while." He let his hand fall from her face to her shoulder and then traced his fingers along the curve of arm. She was all hard angles and straight lines, but he loved that about her.

When she didn't respond, Vaughn moved his hand back to her face. It was wet. He ran his thumb along her cheekbones and down to her mouth. She kissed his finger.

"You're crying," he said. It came out as an accusation. Abruptly, he rolled out of bed and walked to the window. He lifted the shade. When he turned, he saw Mia standing behind him, hair cascading down her shoulders in the morning light, a look of devastation on her beautiful face.

"Why?" he managed. "Just tell me that."

She shook her head slowly, back and forth. He knew he was pushing her, but he'd been living with this feeling, this *knowing*, for so long. He wanted her to say it.

"Why?" he demanded again.

"Our friendship means more to me than anything." Mia's eyes were round, beseeching. "I don't want to be a burden. And someday I will be. You're young, Vaughn. You can have children if you want, a full life. It's not too late for you." She reached out and touched his face, felt the scar he'd had since childhood. "You act like life is over and you're just biding your time. Stop. Live."

"I want you."

"You want to retreat. I've become your refuge."

"No, that's not true." He stared at her, angry now. "How can you say that?"

But Mia only smiled. She looked so goddamn ethereal, standing there in her white nightgown, her hair flowing down her shoulders, her eyes wide, wet and pleading. He hated her then. No, he hated himself.

He moved toward the door. Her arm shot out. She grabbed his wrist. "Not like this," she whispered. "Don't go away angry."

But he shook her off. And then he left.

Two hours later, he was sitting on the edge of his bed, staring at his dresser. More precisely, he was staring at the six-pack he'd purchased on his way home. He was about to give in when there was a soft knock on the door.

"Vaughn?" It was Angela's voice. "Are you okay?"

He realized he couldn't talk. He swallowed, wiped at his eyes and grunted.

The doorknob turned. "Can I come in? We're worried about you."

Before he could answer, the door cracked open. "Vaughn?"

He took a deep breath. "I'm okay."

Angela opened the door fully and stood in the glow of the hallway. She was a beautiful woman, with glossy black hair, pale mocha skin and almond-shaped brown eyes. But more than that, she was kind. The look she was giving him now, so full of concern, made his heart ache.

"I said I'm fine," he blurted, hating the bitterness in his voice. None of this was Angela's fault.

They stared at one another for a moment. Vaughn rubbed his face, massaging his temples with sweaty hands. He realized he was shaking. Angela's gaze traveled from his hands to his face to the six-pack. She moved into the room.

"You don't always have to be the strong one," she said.

Vaughn looked down at the floor, spine rigid. He felt her hand on his shoulder, then he watched out of the corner of his eye as she walked to the dresser.

"Can I have this?" she asked softly without turning around.

When Vaughn didn't respond, she picked up the six-pack. "I'm going to take your silence as a yes."

When she left, Vaughn felt his body go limp. His hands, still shaking, found his pillow. He pummeled it once, twice, then held it to his face and let the torrent come.

LOOK AT THIS, read Jamie's screen. His brother stared at him for what felt like an eon. WHAT'S THE MATTER?

"Nothing." Vaughn avoided looking at Jamie. He'd washed his face, had some coffee, and now he had himself together—or so he believed. Since they'd been kids, Jamie had been able to see right through him, though.

Jamie was quiet. Vaughn was the first to speak.

"What did you find?"

YOU'RE NOT GOING TO TELL ME.

Vaughn rubbed his chin. Two days' worth of black stubble made him look worse, he knew. He needed to shave. He said, "What did you find, Jamie?"

FINE, HAVE IT YOUR WAY. YOU ARE A STUBBORN SON-OF-

A-YOU-KNOW-WHAT. He paused. LIKE I TOLD YOU BEFORE, DIAMOND BRANDS WAS FOUNDED BY TED DIAMOND. HE WAS A CONTROVERSIAL FIGURE IN HIS TIME. ALIGNED WITH THE RELIGIOUS RIGHT. PRO-GUN. TOOK PRIDE IN A "MADE IN THE USA" TAG-LINE, ANTI-UNION, PAID A FAIR WAGE. TRUTHFULLY, SEEMED TO BE A PRETTY UPSTANDING GUY, A FEW OF HIS POLITICAL CONNECTIONS ASIDE.

"If he was so upstanding, what happened in China?"

I'M GETTING THERE. DIAMOND BRANDS STARTED SMALL. TED DIAMOND AND HIS FIRST WIFE LILY BEGAN WITH A SINGLE SHOP CALLED LILY. SPECIALIZED IN CLOTHING, BAGS AND JEWELRY FOR WOMEN IN THE UPPER ECHELONS OF SOCIETY. IN 1992, THEY ADDED BARLEY & ROW, AN UPPER-CRUST MENSWEAR SHOP. HEARD OF IT?

Vaughn nodded. They had one in nearby Wayne, although he had never shopped there. "And Transitions is the third brand?"

WAS THE THIRD BRAND. THE ENVIRONMENTAL STUFF WAS JUST THE TIP OF THE PYRAMID. THERE WERE ALSO ALLEGATIONS OF CHILD LABOR LAW VIOLATIONS. NOT JUST HYPE, EITHER. SUBSTANTIATED ACCOUNTS OF KIDS WORKING LONG HOURS IN SQUALID CONDITIONS IN INDIA AND CHINA.

"Kids as in how old?"

Jamie's face darkened. AS YOUNG AS SIX.

Vaughn let that sink in. "Didn't make Diamond look so good."

TED DIAMOND CLAIMED HE HAD NO KNOWLEDGE OF THE ABUSES. IN FACT, HE WAS SO CONVINCING THAT THE MEDIA LOST INTEREST. HARD TO CRUCIFY A GUY WHO IS BOTH DEVASTATED AND REMORSEFUL. HE—ALONG WITH SOME PRETTY POWERFUL DOLLARS, I IMAGINE—MANAGED TO SWEEP MOST OF IT UNDER THE RUG.

"Except for the river dumping."

THERE, THEY HAD MORE PROOF. IT WAS IMPOSSIBLE TO DENY WHAT HAD HAPPENED, WHETHER OR NOT DIAMOND HAD KNOWN ABOUT IT. PLUS, IT SEEMED THE LESSER OF THE EVILS.

Vaughn thought about Transitions. It was an upscale shop for teens and pre-teens, a preppy, more conservative version of

Abercrombie & Fitch. "It's hard to sell clothes for kids that have been made by kids." Vaughn stood. "Is Transitions still owned by Diamond Brands."

DIAMOND BRANDS OWNS A CONTROLLING SHARE AND THE DIAMOND FAMILY OWNS A GOOD STAKE, TOO. BUT TOGETHER, THEY OWN LESS THAN HALF THE COMPANY.

"So the Diamond family retained ownership interest in Transitions, but also sought to distance themselves from the scandal." Vaughn paced the room. "And you think this has some direct connection to Scott Fairweather's murder?"

I DON'T KNOW. THAT'S JUST IT. SCOTT WAS BROUGHT ON BOARD TO HELP WITH THE TRANSITION OF TRANSITIONS. A HUGE JOB FOR ANYONE.

Vaughn paused by Jamie's screen. "What if someone wanted him to fail?"

AS IN...?

"As in someone who had something to gain if the company didn't make it."

I HAD THE SAME THOUGHT. BUT WITH A PUBLIC COMPANY, NO ONE WINS IF THE COMPANY FAILS.

"Maybe a foreign contractor? Someone who lost business because of the new image?" Even as he said the words, Vaughn knew they sounded far-fetched. He ran his hand through his hair, thinking. "I know who might have an idea, though, if I can get an audience."

TED DIAMOND?

Vaughn nodded.

TED DIAMOND PASSED AWAY OVER A YEAR AGO.

Vaughn's head snapped up. "Murder?"

HEART ATTACK. HE WAS GOLFING WHEN HIS TICKER GAVE OUT ON HIM. MEDICS TRIED TO RESCUSITATE HIM, BUT IT DIDN'T WORK.

"So who's running the business now?"

Jamie sighed. He said, THAT I DON'T KNOW. THERE'S A NEW CEO, BUT HE'S NOT RELATED TO THE FAMILY. OWNERSHIP HAS BEEN RETAINED BY THE DIAMOND FAMILY, BUT THEY'RE NOT INVOLVED WITH THE DAY-TO-DAY.

Vaughn stared at the screen, then turned toward his brother.

Jamie's eyes were bright. It was obvious he loved this stuff, especially the puzzle aspect of digging into other people's lives. "A guy like that?" Vaughn asked. "No kid to run the family business?"

Jamie smiled. NO SON, AT LEAST. TED DIAMOND AND HIS FIRST WIFE, LILY, HAD A DAUGHTER. AMELIE DIAMOND.

"First wife?"

DIAMOND REMARRIED A FEW YEARS AGO. FROM WHAT I COULD TELL, SECOND WIFE IS NOT INVOLVED IN THE BUSINESS, EITHER. CAME INTO THE MARRIAGE WITH HER OWN MONEY.

"How about the daughter? She doesn't work for Diamond?"

NO, SHE DOESN'T WORK AT ALL, AT LEAST NOT IN THE CONVENTIONAL SENSE. AMELIE DIAMOND IS A BUDDHIST NUN. SHE'S BEEN ESTRANGED FROM HER FAMILY FOR YEARS. HER FATHER DISOWNED HER WHEN SHE CONVERTED TO BUDDHISM. FROM WHAT I READ, SHE DIDN'T EVEN ATTEND HIS FUNERAL.

"Is she nearby?"

PHILADELPHIA. SHE WORKS AS THE SPIRITUAL DIRECTOR OF THE BUDDHIST CENTER ON NINTH AND LOMBARD.

"A far cry from Tibet."

Jamie frowned. A FAR CRY FROM EVERYTHING SHE KNEW GROWING UP.

TWENTY-FOUR

At one o'clock Sunday afternoon, Allison was out the door when her mobile rang. It was Mia.

"You okay?" Allison asked. She climbed into the Volvo, phone cradled against her shoulder, and snapped her seatbelt in place. "You don't sound like yourself."

"Restless, I guess. What are you doing this afternoon?"

"Heading to Chadds Ford."

"Wine tasting?"

"Ha. Hardly. An old friend lives there. Brad Halloway. Remember him?"

"The man who helped Delvar?"

"That's him." Allison pulled out onto her street and meandered her way toward Route 30. Halloway had sounded happy to hear from her. In fact, he invited her down to his house to have afternoon tea with him and she'd accepted. "Want to join me?"

"Is this a social call?"

"Not exactly. Halloway works at Transitions. He knew Scott. I already met with him once, but I have a few more questions. So what do you say? An afternoon of picking people's minds about a murder? For old time's sake?"

Only Mia didn't laugh. Concerned, Allison said, "Hey, are you going to tell me what's going on?"

Mia didn't answer right away. Finally, she said, "I'll come with you. How about if I meet you halfway? At the Starbucks off 202, near the stables? I'll fill you in then."

Allison agreed. She hung up and pondered the call. Mia hadn't sounded upset, exactly, just melancholy. Allison thought of Vaughn, of Mia's little comments about their relationship. She was afraid she knew what Mia was going to tell her. She was afraid for her friend Vaughn, because she knew how devastated he would be.

Mia slid into the car next to Allison and placed a tan leather bag on the floor. She was wearing charcoal gray pants and a soft cream wrap sweater. Her hair had been pulled into a neat chignon, but her skin looked pale and her eyes were swollen and red.

Allison said, "You're not so great at hiding things. Vaughn?"

Mia didn't respond at first. She sat with her head turned toward the window, and when she twisted toward Allison, her face was a mask of pain.

"I love him, Allison. You know that. I will always love him."

"But?"

"I don't need to tell you all the reasons it won't work in the long run."

"None of that is new. The age difference, what you both have been through. Why now?"

"I'm not getting any younger."

"Neither is he."

"Exactly."

Allison let it go. She started the car and pulled out onto the road. Mia would share in her own time. Allison had learned long ago that people tell themselves what they need to in order to get through each day. If Mia was telling herself this was best for Vaughn, there was a reason—perhaps one that Mia wasn't ready to face right now.

"So what do I need to know about the Halloways?" Mia asked. Her tone said "new topic."

Allison gave Mia a quick update on their unofficial investigation into Fairweather's murder, including the missing Eleanor Davies, Eleanor's sister's murder and the mysterious Doris Long.

"So you think Halloway may know where Eleanor is?" Mia sounded unconvinced.

"I'm hopeful."

"I know you're grateful to Halloway for helping with Delvar, but he doesn't seem like the type of guy who would get down and dirty with the staff, if you know what I mean."

Allison looked at her. "You don't like Brad?"

"I only know him from the few times we met at Delvar's functions. I can't say I ever warmed up to him." Mia smiled. "But don't go by me. After Edward, I can't say I see myself as a great judge of male character."

"There's Vaughn." Allison regretted the words the second they were out of her mouth.

"There's no disputing Vaughn's character," Mia said. She smiled again, but this time there was a wistful glaze to her expression. "My judgment, on the other hand, remains questionable."

Allison hadn't been to the Halloways' home for years. The couple had moved since she'd last visited, and their new home was a large, ornate one-story. Tucked into a cul-de-sac in an upscale neighborhood of newer homes, the Halloway house had been designed in the French country tradition: stone façade, a complicated roof line and large divided-light windows. The only nod to his wife's medical issues was a concrete wheelchair ramp that led from the wide driveway to the front entry.

Brad had done well for himself, Allison thought. If anyone deserved it, he did.

Brad greeted them at the front door. He hugged Allison, shook Mia's hand and looked genuinely happy to see them both. "Come in, my dears," he said.

The inside of the house matched the promise of the exterior. A large entryway gave way to a great room/kitchen combination. Off to the left was a formal dining room. To the right, glass doors looked into a home office lined with bookshelves. Next to the office was a hallway. All the passageways were wide, and the hallway was lined with railings to accommodate Antonia's needs. The home spoke of loving attention, professional designers and excellent house cleaners. Everything sparkled; nothing seemed out of place.

"Is Antonia here?" Allison asked.

Brad smiled apologetically. "I'm afraid she's not feeling well today."

"I'm sorry to hear that," Allison said. And she was. Allison genuinely adored Antonia Halloway. She was one of those rare individuals who seemed to view her lot in life as a blessing, not a curse, and, in doing so, was an inspiration to others. "Perhaps I can visit her another time?"

"She would love that."

Allison and Mia followed Brad through the great room and into a glass-enclosed sunporch. "Have a seat," he said.

Allison chose a mission-style oak chair and Mia sank into a loveseat. The room was filled with plants: African violets, amaryllis, aloe, begonias and many others that Allison couldn't name.

"This is lovely," Mia said.

Brad smiled. "It's my wife's. Antonia struggles these days. This room cheers her up." He stroked the petals on a white orchid. "Especially the orchids. She loves that they survive indoors when outside it is so cold and desolate."

Mia smiled. "I can understand that."

Brad pressed a buzzer by the door. Within seconds, a young woman showed up. Red-headed and heavily freckled, she had the attentive, anxious demeanor of someone new to her job.

"Yes, Mr. Halloway?"

"Can you fetch us some tea, Adriana?" He glanced at Mia. "Chamomile, if I remember correctly?"

Mia nodded. "Thank you."

"And for you, Allison?"

"Chamomile is perfect."

"Make that one green and two chamomiles," Brad said. "And perhaps a plate of the biscotti you made yesterday?"

"Of course."

After she'd left the room, Brad sat on another Mission chair. He looked tired, and Allison felt bad for bothering him at his home.

"We won't take much of your time, Brad."

"It's no bother, Allison. Believe me, I'm happy to see you. We don't get as much company as we used to. It's hard. People feel uncomfortable." He shrugged. "I try to be understanding, but sometimes I get frustrated with her old friends. Even our children."

Adriana returned with a tray. She set the tray down and then reached into her pocket and pulled out a vial of pills.

"It's time, Mr. Halloway."

Almost brusquely, Halloway took the vial, opened it and swallowed a pill with the glass of water. He handed Adriana the pills and glass with a disgusted grimace.

"Don't let anyone fool you, Allison. It's terrible getting old."

Mia said, "I suppose it beats the alternative."

Brad smiled. "Not always." He stirred sugar into his tea but didn't pick up the cup. "How can I help you ladies?"

"Does the name Eleanor Davies ring a bell?"

"Of course. She works for Transitions. Why do you ask?"

"I'm trying to find her. She seems to have disappeared."

"Is this still about Scott?"

Allison nodded.

Brad studied her. He reached for a plate and a biscotti and took a moment arranging a napkin on his lap. Mia was sipping her tea, eyes on Brad. The tension in the room was suddenly thick, although Allison wasn't sure why.

Finally, Brad said, "I've known you for years, Allison, and I can tell that you're hiding something now. Why is that?"

Allison was slow to respond, choosing her words carefully. Why was she being so reticent? Embarrassment, she realized. Divulging much more meant telling Brad, a man she looked up to and respected, that she'd had an affair with Scott.

"I knew Scott as a client and as a...paramour," Allison said, struggling to get the word out. "We hadn't seen each other in years, but the day he died, he had my name in his appointment book." Allison looked up at Brad. "I want to know why."

"That sounds like a matter for the police."

"The police know, but they don't seem concerned." And then there're the photos, Allison thought, but chose to leave that detail out. "Anyway, I think Eleanor is the key. Scott and Eleanor were...close. She may know what happened to Scott in the weeks leading up to his death, why he wanted to get in touch with me."

"You have no idea?" Brad said.

"None."

"Perhaps it was something simple, Allison. A work referral or a speaking request."

"I don't think so."

Brad stood. His biscotti and tea remained untouched. Allison hated the way his disapproval made her feel. Unclean, ashamed. He's not your father, Allison reminded herself. You have no need to please him.

From across the coffee table, Mia caught her eye. Her look said, *caution.*

"Allison, at a company like ours, there are always rumors. Keep that in mind while I share what I know. Rumors are just that, gossip, not necessarily truths." He paused. "There were certain...*rumors*...about Scott in the last weeks. One was that he and Eleanor were lovers. Another even less palatable rumor—unsubstantiated, mind you—was that he was stealing from the company."

"Embezzling?" Allison looked up, surprised.

Brad nodded. "As I told you before, some believed he was in debt. Fast lifestyle, new child, a spouse who'd quit her job." He looked at Allison apologetically, "And mistresses. These things added up financially. Throw in possible drug affiliations, and, well, you have a train wreck." Brad frowned. "Scott Fairweather was a train wreck."

"Did the autopsy show drugs in his system?"

"Not that I know of, but frankly, I didn't ask."

"How do you explain Eleanor's disappearance?" Mia asked.

Brad turned toward Mia. "I'm afraid I can't."

Mia said, "If she's missing, aren't you worried that she's a victim, too?"

"Eleanor Davies is a headstrong, highly independent woman. She knew she was playing with fire, I'm sure, and for all we know she was part of his drug lifestyle. So yes, Mia, to answer your question, foul play could be involved. We—Transitions, that is—are concerned for her safety. So much so that we have alerted the authorities investigating Scott's death."

"Where do you think she could be?" Allison asked.

Brad walked toward the sunroom window. He looked out onto the well-kept front yard, hands on his hips. When he turned around, he said, "I think Eleanor is embarrassed and probably a little scared. Scott had a duty to Transitions, and sleeping with the purchasing director is hardly the right thing to do. But even more so, he had a duty to his wife and that new baby. He should have been ashamed of his conduct. And Eleanor...she should have known better. No one wins in that situation. Eleanor lost her dignity and Scott, his family and, ultimately, his life."

Brad spoke these words with such conviction that both Allison and Mia looked up, startled by the sudden harshness in his voice. Before either could respond, though, the doors into the sunroom swung open and the nurse wheeled Antonia Halloway into the room.

Antonia's body was a twisted husk. She sat in just a corner of the chair, a thick fleece blanket on her lap. Bony shoulders were encased in a soft chartreuse wool sweater. Most telling of all, though, were her hands. What had been long, graceful fingers were now claws, arched stiffly in her lap, the nails clipped short so as not to scratch unintentionally. Antonia's beautiful face was all hollows and jutting bones, made more horrific by brightly inquisitive, empathetic eyes.

"Hel-ll-o All-i-sss-son." Antonia struggled to get the words out.

Allison rushed to her side and gave her a gentle kiss on the cheek. "Antonia, so good to see you."

"You didn't tell me we had guests," Antonia said slowly.

Brad look chagrined. "You were resting, darling. As you should be now."

Antonia's icy look said otherwise.

Brad sighed. To Allison, he said, "Sit with Antonia and me and enjoy your tea. Adriana, fetch Mrs. Halloway a cup of tea. Not too hot, please. And perhaps some fresh tea for the rest of us. I'm afraid it's gotten cold."

Brad said these last words in a way that told Allison it was the topic, not just the time passed, that had made the tea cold.

TWENTY-FIVE

Back in the car, Mia seemed pensive.

"What did you think?" Allison asked.

"I may have misjudged him. His wife, Antonia?" Mia shook her head. "Such courage. And he is so tender with her."

Allison sighed. "I know. They have always been very much in love."

Allison pulled out of the Holloways' street. The day had turned sharply colder and she pushed buttons on the car's control panel to turn up the heat. She realized, though, that the chill she was feeling had nothing to do with the fall weather.

"Brad doesn't quite seem himself."

"His wife is ill. Very ill."

"I know," Allison said. She felt the weight of those words and the sympathy she had for Antonia. "But something's not right with him. That cough...I'm worried about Brad. And as for Scott, it's obvious Brad didn't care for him."

Mia chewed at her bottom lip, looking out at the passing landscape. "Has it occurred to you, Allison, that Brad's right? Perhaps Scott had simply made some very bad choices in life and those choices finally caught up with him." She glanced over at Allison. "Of anyone, you should know that Scott wasn't a nice person. He had issues."

"How do you explain the pictures?"

"Maybe Scott arranged to have them sent before his death. Maybe, just maybe, he intended to blackmail you and that's why your name was in his book."

"But they were sent after he died."

"He could have an accomplice. Perhaps Eleanor."

Allison glanced at Mia. "Perhaps."

"It would fit with Brad's depiction of Scott."

And it would. In debt, multiple mistresses, work pressures. He hadn't exactly shown himself to be a man who adhered to a high ethical standard. Blackmailing her for money seemed right up his alley.

"In fact," Mia said, "maybe Eleanor and Scott were blackmailing others, too...others who weren't as nice as you. She could have run to save her own life."

Maybe, Allison thought. "If only we could find Eleanor."

"Then what, Allison? What if you do find her?

"Then I go to the police."

"I think you should let this go," Mia said. "Talk to the police now. Tell them everything. Let the pieces fall where they may." She reached out and touched Allison's arm. "This one's not for you to solve."

"The police already know about my name in Scott's calendar. They questioned me. And Brad said Transitions told them about Eleanor. The only thing I can add is the photos, both the ones sent to me and Julie. I can't break her confidence, and so far, the press has not received those pictures of me. Sometimes things have a way of leaking once the police are involved."

"You could be obstructing an investigation."

Allison had thought of that. "I don't think so. Nothing concrete connects the pictures and Scott's death. Jason would have told me to hand them over if he'd believed I was breaking the law."

Mia didn't look convinced. "I think you should drop this. Take Brad's word as gospel and move on. But I know you better than that."

Allison smiled. "I need to find Eleanor, Mia. If she can't shed some light on this, then I may have no choice but to give up."

Mia sighed. "If that's the case, I may be able to help you."

Surprised, Allison looked at her. "How?"

But Mia wasn't telling. "Just drop me off at my car. I'll let you know when and if I find something."

The Tibetan Buddhist Center took up two three-story brick row homes on the corner of Lombard Street, not far from Pennsylvania Hospital.

Vaughn was surprised at the location. He'd envisioned Buddhist monasteries to be high in the mountains in Tibet, not deep in Philly. But a small red and gold sign identified this as the right place.

The entryway, a plain red wooden door, was unlocked despite the bars on the first- and second-floor windows. Inside was another door made of glass and bars. The vestibule in between was warm and sparsely furnished. There were benches, one on either side of the five-by-five space, and a small table with pamphlets about Buddhism, addiction and abuse. A single carved Buddha sat beside the pamphlets along with a bell. Vaughn picked up the bell. It was large and heavy in his hands. He rang it. Several minutes later, a woman's face appeared, framed by the glass pane of the inner door. She smiled warmly when she saw him and opened the door.

"How may I help you?" she asked. She was small-framed and portly, with a round, pleasant face. Her head had been shaved and was covered with a fine, black stubble. Her robes, orange and crimson, rippled when she moved. "I'm afraid the morning meditations have concluded."

"My name is Christopher Vaughn." Vaughn held out a card, which she took. "I'm here to see Amelie Diamond."

"I'm Amelie." A shadow passed across her face. "Is something wrong?"

"No, no. I just want to talk with you."

The woman studied him, unmoving. After a few seconds, she ushered him inside. The front room was simply furnished, with white-painted walls, and colorful, ornate wall hangings depicting images of Buddha. The room smelled faintly of incense. Amelie re-locked the inner door and turned to Vaughn.

"I'm no longer Amelie. I haven't been for years. My name is Tenzin Jinpa Choden." She smiled. "Am I right to assume you don't want to talk about the spiritual center or Buddhism?"

Vaughn gave her an apologetic nod. "Actually, I'm here to ask about your father's company, Diamond Brands."

"I'm afraid you've wasted a trip, then. I have nothing to do with Diamond."

"If you don't mind, it won't take long."

"I guess that depends on the nature of your questions. My father has been dead for more than a year. I don't interact with my family, and I have disavowed any interest in the company."

Amelie—Tenzin Jinpa—said all of this in a preternaturally calm way, giving off an aura of tranquility and compassion. Yet Vaughn sensed the slightest edge to her words. Had he hit a nerve? An hour of internet research had told him little about the only child of Ted and Lily Diamond. Born in Allentown, Pennsylvania, raised on the Philadelphia Main Line, educated at exclusive private schools and then, later, Brown University, she had been given everything needed to have a strong start in life. And then at age twenty-seven, she'd disavowed her inheritance and converted to Buddhism. Now she was a nun. Why had she turned her back on her family and the family business?

Vaughn decided to be forthright. "A man was murdered. A man who had been hired by Transitions to lead the new socially-conscious marketing campaign for the spun-off brand. I didn't grow up on the Main Line, Ms. Choden, and I know when I'm being played. I'm pretty sure something isn't as it seems." When Tenzin Jinpa started to speak, Vaughn raised a hand to stop her. "I'm not saying your father's business is at the root. I'm just trying to understand some history. How Diamond Brands could have gotten embroiled in such a mess overseas, and why Scott Fairweather was chosen to lead the new marketing charge."

Tenzin Jinpa was a small woman, but she held Vaughn's gaze with a firmness that surprised him. "And your role?" she asked. "Police? Private detective?"

"None of the above," Vaughn said. "I'm just looking for the truth."

"To what end?"

"Justice." Vaughn leaned in, using his height to his advantage. "Some kids are getting blamed for this murder, Ms. Chodin. Kids who probably didn't have any shot at a good life. The kind of kids you don't meet at preppy private schools and Ivy League universities." He looked at her, letting the words sink in. "I just want the truth."

Tenzin Jinpa turned suddenly, her robes swirling around her body, and motioned for him to follow. They walked through a white hallway to another door, painted red, and entered a small chamber. The floors were lacquered oak, the walls white. A mural of Buddha painted with splashes of gold, red, crimson and blue hung from a bar at the back of the room. Tenzin Jinpa closed the door before taking two cushions from a stack in the corner. She handed one to Vaughn. She placed the other in the center of the room and sat upon it, curling herself into a small, tight package.

Vaughn sat, cross-legged, self-conscious of his size and lack of grace in this tiny space.

When they were both settled on the floor, Tenzin Jinpa leaned forward. Holding Vaughn's gaze, she said, "When it comes to relationships, Buddhism is, at its core, about love. I have come to think of a relationship as a mirror. For many of us, we see not necessarily what *is*, but what we want to see. If we are wise, we learn to see people for whom they really are in that moment and love them anyway. We are all journeymen on the path, suffering alongside one another." She shifted her hips on her cushion and, now still, said, "But we are not always wise."

"No, we're not," Vaughn said.

Tenzin Jinpa smiled. "As a child, I wanted to see my father as a great man. Indeed, he was great in so many ways. He had what many might call vision. He dreamed of a great corporate empire and he pursued that vision with relentless focus and a healthy dose of paranoia."

"Creating Diamond Brands."

Tenzin Jinpa nodded. "First came Lily, named for my mother, whom my father worshipped."

"Worshipped is a strong word."

"Think of that mirror, Mr. Vaughn. My father wanted to see a beautiful, loving, selfless wife. Someone who would not only look good on his arm, but who would elevate him. For my mother was, in his view, at least, an extension of him."

Vaughn said, "That's a very narcissistic view of marriage."

She nodded. "Yes, it is. But that was how my father viewed Lily Diamond, my mother, until the day she died at the unfortunate age of thirty-seven."

"So young."

"It devastated my father. His view of my mother became even more elevated. She was the saint whom no other woman, no other person, could compare, either in selflessness or integrity."

"How old were you when she passed away?"

"Nine."

Which perhaps, Vaughn thought, explained the distant way in which she described her mother's death. He said, "It must have been awful for you."

"Then? Yes, of course. Now? Death is part of the cycle of life. We believe there is no death, really—only change."

"But at nine years old, to lose your mother—"

"My mother was not as my father would have the world believe her to be. I realize now that she was passive, weak-willed, and very sickly. For much of my youth, she was not around. Those preppy private schools to which you referred earlier? That was the only world I really knew growing up. My father was distant, my mother...challenged. Home was not a happy place."

The look on Tenzin Jinpa's face said despite Buddhism's teachings about relationships, this was not a topic she relished. And while her family dynamics echoed Allison's own family in many ways— if one replaced a distant father with an abusive one—this conversation was not moving him closer to understanding Diamond Brands and the issues in China.

Vaughn said, "How did this impact what happened overseas?"

"It didn't, at least not directly. But to understand Diamond Brands, and my father's reaction to what happened abroad, you must understand my parents."

Vaughn waited. He heard footsteps coming down stairs overhead, but if Tenzin Jinga heard them, too, she didn't react.

She said, "The company became, for my father, a symbol of his love for Lily. My father viewed himself as a strong Christian, an upstanding citizen. He gave money to charities, offered his employees generous vacation packages and maternity leaves. He became a champion of family and the American Dream."

"So to be associated with something as horrific as child slave labor would have been a personal affront."

"To him, and to my sainted mother." Tenzin Jinpa smiled. "So you see, he would have had nothing to do with polluting rivers or enslaving children. Unthinkable for a man like Ted Diamond."

"Yet it happened."

She nodded. "Yet, it happened."

"So your father would have had to either come to terms with what occurred, thus owning it, or he would have had to find a way to disassociate himself from the problems, thus denying his role? Maybe the spin-off was his way of doing that?"

"Perhaps."

"You don't sound convinced."

Tenzin Jinpa closed her eyes. She took a deep breath and said, "I converted to Buddhism at an older age. I wish I had found my calling sooner, but if I had, I may not have found the courage to pursue it."

Confused by the shift in topic, Vaughn said, "Because?"

"There is a Buddhist saying, Mr. Vaughn: 'Good to forgive, the best to forget.'"

Outside the door, a man was calling, "*Ani*? Are you okay?"

"In here, Chodak. You may enter."

The door opened and a young Asian man, also in robes, started to come inside. He bowed slightly when he saw Vaughn and began to back out of the room. Without making eye contact with either Tenzin Jinpa or Vaughn, he said softly, "Afternoon meditations will begin shortly, *Ani*."

"I'll be right there." Tenzin Jinpa looked at Vaughn. "Would you care to join us?"

Vaughn shook his head. "Thank you, but if I sit in this position any longer, you'll need a crane to lift me up."

The nun smiled. "Be well."

But Vaughn was still thinking about the quote. As they rose to leave the room, Vaughn said, "So your father spun off the family business in an effort to forget what happened?"

Tenzin Jinpa, the woman once known as Amelie Diamond, smiled ruefully. "I had not seen my father since the day I told him I was becoming a Buddhist. Neither forgiving nor forgetting was part of his character." She bowed. "Now good day, Mr. Vaughn. Continue to seek justice. It is a noble pursuit."

TWENTY-SIX

It was during the first weekend of what Eleanor had begun to view as her captivity that she found the first of the outbuildings in the woods. It was a sturdy affair, consisting of a concrete block foundation and heavy timber walls. Thick metal chains and a chunky metal padlock blocked entry, as did its positioning. Placed within a dense area of pines and deep into the woods, it wasn't visible from the road, the driveway or the house.

She'd gone for a walk in the woods, as much to clear her mind as to get away from Doris and those dogs. The shed intrigued her. Was it Doris's? It did seem to have her father's handiwork, and she wouldn't have put it past him to build it out here in order to store ammunition or valuables or even guns. But upon closer inspection, Eleanor realized the shed wasn't on Doris's property. A tree a hundred yards away had been tacked with a "Keep Out—No Hunting" sign and another marked the area as private property. Doris had no such signs. And taking the time to mark the perimeter of her property would take energy and effort, two things Doris seemed to lack.

Then whose shed was it?

Eleanor pulled at the lock. It wouldn't budge. The metal was rusting and the padlock showed signs of weather and age. The fact that it was still intact, though, said these woods were pretty deserted. Otherwise, kids would have broken in long ago and used the shed as a place to hang out, smoke pot or screw. Eleanor walked on.

Within another half mile, she came upon another building, a stone cottage of sorts situated in the midst of an overgrown clearing. Its rotting roof had fallen in and two of its eight windows were broken, with vines that wove their way around the exterior like a living shroud. Portions of the vegetation surrounding the building seemed denser and shorter than the others, and these shorter portions formed a swath that led from the cottage. She got down on hands and knees and felt underneath the weeds. *Bingo.* Blacktop. Cracked, faded and marred by plants growing up through the fissures, but blacktop nonetheless. There had been a road leading to this cottage. The road, though, looked like it headed farther into the woods. To where?

Eleanor pictured the area in her head. This must be the back side of Dunne Pond Resort. Growing up, it had been a place where wealthy Boston families summered. Now, it was abandoned.

The sun was sinking into the western horizon. The woods, so lush and full of peaceful promise in the summer months, felt cold and eerie. A harsh wind whipped through the trees, leaving Eleanor breathless. She pulled Doris's down parka tighter around her midsection, her mind swirling with possibilities.

She needed to get to her money and plan some type of escape. She couldn't hide at Doris's forever. But how? She had no doubt the authorities were looking for her, and after what she'd done, she had no doubt others were looking for her, too. Her sister was proof of that.

Eleanor scanned the clearing. It helped to know her surroundings. If things got bad, at least she'd have somewhere else to go. Somewhere away from Doris. Somewhere safe.

Allison had dropped Mia off at her car three hours ago, and now she found herself wandering aimlessly through her house. She'd changed into workout clothes and tried to go for a walk, but that didn't help. Instead of feeling calm or inspired, she felt more agitated. She wanted to do something, something that would put an end to the uncertainty about Scott and these photographs.

Upstairs, she placed a call to her sister's rehab center. She's doing the program, they told her. No, she couldn't talk to her, they told her. The woman on the other end of the line was sympathetic but reserved. She managed to give Allison almost nothing of substance.

Next, Allison called her sister Faye to check on Grace.

"She's doing great," Faye said. "Mom and Dad adore her."

Even Brutus was busy *not* needing her. The dog and his new best friend, Simon the cat, were curled around one another on her bed. When Allison slipped into her room to change into jeans and a sweater, Brutus opened one eye, thumped his tail stub on the comforter, and resumed his snoring.

"You're both worthless," Allison muttered. But she gave each of them a stroke before making her way to the office.

There, she called Jason while she flicked on her computer. Jason didn't answer. Disappointed, she left a voicemail and settled in to do some searching on the web.

A search on Eleanor turned up the same material she'd seen before: a Facebook page she couldn't access and dozens of race finishes. Eleanor's profile picture showed a grinning woman in her late thirties or early forties climbing the side of a cliff. Thin and muscular, Eleanor had the tan skin and bleached hair of a woman who spent a lot of time outdoors.

But there was a hardness in her eyes, even in her profile picture. She wore no helmet, and her bright blue eyes stared at the cameraperson with an almost startling intensity, as if she were daring them to say or do something.

Allison thought about Eleanor in the context of Scott's lovers. Unlike Leah, Eleanor didn't seem remotely academic. In fact, she seemed the antithesis of Leah's bookish, slightly arrogant persona. And where Julie was all soft curves and feminine smiles, Eleanor appeared sinewy and fit.

Allison changed her search terms and revisited Leah, Transitions, Doris Long, even Brad Halloway and his wife. She found nothing new...until she searched using terms related to Scott's murder. On a local news site, she saw the headline, "Three Arrested in Murder of Local Businessman."

The three kids suspected of killing Scott had been detained.

Allison stared at the photo. Three boys, all black, all between the ages of sixteen and nineteen. Two looked scared—terrified, really—and one had the deadened look of someone who hadn't cared in a long, long time. Such a tragedy, Allison thought, to have lost all hope and joy before your twenty-first birthday. Edith Myers had been right about one thing. What *were* we doing to our youth?

But then it struck her: these boys would go to jail, where they would be housed with hardened criminals. The likelihood of reformation was low. The likelihood of learning new antisocial behaviors, of becoming even more hardened to others' suffering, was high.

This is wrong, she thought.

Allison unlocked her filing cabinet and pulled out the file in which she kept the photographs and other information she'd accumulated on Scott's murder. From within, she pulled out the business card Detective Jim Berry had given her so many days before. She placed the file in her laptop bag and grabbed her phone and car keys and dialed Detective Berry's number on her way out the door.

TWENTY-SEVEN

Vaughn left the Buddhist Center feeling agitated. Why, he couldn't say. He only knew that something in Amelie's words set off a mental alarm. It wasn't so much what she'd said but how she'd said it. So distant, cool. As though Ted Diamond, his wife Lily and everything that had happened in her younger years belonged to someone else, and by becoming Tenzin Jinpa she had somehow escaped her past.

If only it were that easy.

Vaughn considered where to go next. His first thought was Mia, but then he remembered that she was no longer available to him and his sense of agitation deepened. He called Allison but his call went straight to voicemail. He decided to head to the boxing gym for a spell. Clear his mind, work up a sweat and think about what to do next. He started the BMW and was backing out of the spot when he thought of something else Amelie had said in reference to the problems in China: *Neither forgiving nor forgetting are part of his character.*

Could Scott have ticked him off? Had Scott been a part of the China fiasco? Unlikely—he wasn't even working there at the time. But perhaps they'd run into each other in the past. Vaughn realized he'd never asked Amelie if she knew Scott, or if it was possible her father had known the man. He started to call the center but remembered that Amelie—Tenzin Jinpa—was in afternoon meditation. Instead, he called Jamie. Angela answered right away.

"Have Jamie do me a favor," he said without preamble.

"What do you need, Vaughn?"

He asked her to ask Jamie to look for a connection between Scott

Fairweather and the Diamond family. "Anything," he said. "Business or personal."

Angela agreed. After a painful silence, she said, "Are you feeling better?"

"Just make sure Jamie knows it's important."

"Of course." Angela sounded wounded.

Vaughn didn't want to end the call that way. He said, "About this morning. The beer. I'd like to think I wouldn't have…well, thank you."

"You were hurting," Angela said. "Sometimes you have to accept your own weaknesses in order to move on."

"Yeah, well, I'm not so ready to move on."

After they hung up, Vaughn felt even worse than he had before. Like Ted Diamond, neither forgiving nor forgetting seemed to be in his wheelhouse. And apparently acceptance wasn't much of a strength, either.

Detective Berry agreed to meet Allison at the Starbucks on Sixteenth and Market in downtown Philadelphia. She spotted his red hair from outside the café. When she entered, he looked up from his high-top table in the corner. He didn't smile.

Allison took her time ordering a coffee. As she placed cream and sugar in her drink, she counted to ten and back again in an unsuccessful effort to quiet the dragonflies zooming around in her belly. She really didn't want to have this conversation, especially before talking to Jason, but he wasn't answering and she couldn't get the thought of those boys out of her mind.

Allison took a deep breath, grabbed a napkin, and did exactly what she told her clients to do in these situations: she projected the confidence she wished she felt instead of the nervousness she was actually feeling.

"Detective," she said, pointing to his tea. "I would have offered you something but I noticed you already had something to drink."

"Thanks for the thought." He glanced at his watch, making no attempt to hide his impatience. "You wanted to see me about the Fairweather murder? You said it was urgent, so here I am."

"Yes, you are. Thank you." Allison pulled the folder out of

briefcase. She had separated the nudes from the tamer photos and email and left them back in her car. There was no way she would pull them out here, and if he thought they were important, she preferred to give them to him in the privacy of her car.

She slid the folder to him across the table. He opened it, his eyes going from the semi-nude picture of Allison to the email and the envelope.

"I assume someone sent these to you?" He raised his eyebrows. "Blackmail?"

"That's just it, Detective. I don't think so. There have been no other attempts to contact me. I have several more, photos I didn't want to bring into Starbucks because of their X-rating. Plus, similar photos were sent to family members and a colleague."

"All of you?"

"Of me...and Scott."

Berry frowned. He picked up the email and re-read it, then stared at the photograph.

"You've handled all of these?"

Allison nodded. She looked away, toward the window, the faint hammering of a headache chipping away at her skull. "I didn't share these with you before because they seemed unrelated. But now that others have received them, too, and especially now that you've made arrests, I thought I should share." She frowned. "You can understand my reticence."

Berry sat back in his seat. He took off his reading glasses and, one end in the corner of his mouth, began to chew on the plastic. His silence was maddening. He was waiting for her to say more and she wasn't about to give him a thing.

Eventually, he said, "I could charge you with obstructing justice."

"For what, Detective? Nothing tied these photos to Scott's murder."

"Anything could be relevant. You're smart enough to know that." He put the glasses back on and again picked up the email. "And obviously you know that or you wouldn't be here today."

"It was the boys. They're just kids. I thought 'what if.'" Allison met his stare. "Truthfully, I can't see how these photos are connected. But I have come to learn that Scott had quite the active sex life and obviously someone," she pointed to the folder, "is not so happy about that. These pictures may point to a motive. Something other than drugs."

"So you think someone killed him out of jealousy?"

"I don't know what to think. The Scott I knew wouldn't do drugs. He was far too careful to do anything that could hurt him physically." She paused, thinking. "And then there's the fact of my name in his calendar. Why? I haven't seen Scott in years, since after that email was sent. Why would he want to see me?"

"Who took the photos, Ms. Campbell?"

Allison looked away. "I assume Scott did."

"Is it possible he was going to blackmail you? That the pictures, and the calendar entry, were part of a plan that, luckily for you, got interrupted by his murder?"

"But the pictures arrived after his death."

"And you've not received a single blackmail notice. Scott may have arranged the mailings before he was killed, but with him gone, there was no one to follow through with the plan."

"I guess it's possible. I've thought of that myself. But what about Eleanor Davies?"

"Eleanor?" Berry looked momentarily confused. "The girlfriend?"

Allison nodded. "She disappeared days after Scott's death. Why would she run?"

"Why do you say she ran, Ms. Campbell?"

"What would you call it, Detective? A woman stops showing up at work, leaves her home and cat behind?"

Berry resumed chewing on his reading glasses. He seemed to be deciding whether or not to tell her something. "How do you know all this?"

Allison tried to keep her face neutral. "I did some checking. I know some folks at Transitions. Brad Halloway for one. He told me the police know Eleanor is missing."

Detective Berry smiled. "If you talked to Halloway, then you also know Eleanor has a history with men. She's had more lovers than the Eagles have had losses. Scott was one of many. Why did she take off?" He shrugged. "Who the hell knows? Doesn't matter, though. We have our boys."

Alarmed, Allison said, "But what about her sister's murder?"

"In Florida?" Another shrug. "What about it? Rich single lady gets offed in her house. That's a problem for the Fernandina Beach police— not our jurisdiction. We looked into it but didn't see a connection."

"What if Ginny's murder had been a warning to Eleanor?"

Berry shook his head. "Allison, you have an active imagination, I'll give you that, but a detective you are not. There is no connection between the drug-related murder of Scott Fairweather and the break-in and murder of a rich white lady in Florida. She was a real estate agent. Imagine all the crazies she met on a regular basis."

Allison fought hard not to roll her eyes.

"With all due respect, Detective, between Ginny's murder and these photographs, don't you think there could be something else going on?"

"Shortest distance between point A and point B is a straight line. Kids with records, motive and opportunity. That equals a straight line in my book. The kids were selling and Scott was buying. The boys wanted the cash *and* the merchandise."

"Were there drugs in Scott's system?"

Berry wiped his mouth with a brown napkin and then tossed it on the table in front of him. "Look, you know I can't tell you that, but it doesn't really matter. He could have been buying them to sell them. And there's always a first time."

A jury may think it matters, Allison thought.

"What if someone paid them to kill Scott?"

"Who? These are street kids, not paid hit men." He shook his head. "Besides, if that had been the case, you can bet they would have squealed. They're a sorry lot. They would have done anything to shift the blame. Sorry, Allison. When things line up so neatly, we don't look to make complicated connections." He stood, handing Allison her folder. "Here you go."

"Don't you need these?"

"No. Unless you want to report them. Then I suggest you head to your local precinct."

"I don't want to report them."

"I figured as much." He gave her a jaded half smile. "If anything else comes up, don't sit on it this time."

Detective Berry opened the door for Allison. Outside, he stopped to button his overcoat, and she waited for him to finish before heading to her car.

"You know, Fairweather was a complicated man," he said while finishing the last of his buttons. "In any investigation, we look at not only the suspects, but the victim, too. Fairweather had created a lot of drama in his life. I would originally have said that he wasn't the man you used to know." Berry pointed at the folder. "But based on what you shared, I'm not so sure that's true."

"You really think those boys killed Scott?" Allison asked.

Berry took a pack of cigarettes from inside one of the pockets and tapped it against the palm of one hand to retrieve a cigarette. Frowning, he said, "I think Scott's life spiraled out of control. He made a series of bad choices that landed him in a heap of trouble. People don't really change as they get older. They just become more of whatever they were to begin with. Scott found out the hard way that bad choices meet with bad consequences."

Allison, thinking of her sister Amy, could understand his point of view. "That's a depressing perspective, Detective. I'd like to believe people can change."

Berry stuck the cigarette in his mouth and offered the pack to Allison. When she declined, he cupped the tip, lit it and drew a long breath. After blowing it out, he said, "In your line of work, I guess you need to believe in the ability to change. In mine," he shrugged, "we see the evidence every damn day. The shortest distance is a straight line. Simplicity. And the simplest answer is that people do what they've always done. A fact that helps us catch criminals again and again."

TWENTY-EIGHT

Mia hung up the phone. She knew he'd come through.

She put Buddy on a leash and ran out to the barn. The chickens were hungry and they let her know with their frantic squawking. She picked up Stevens, huddled in the corner, and stroked the chicken's head until she calmed down. Scalia, always a bully, strutted around the barn. As the only rooster, he was the loudest of all, and not for the first time, Mia considered getting rid of him. But she knew she couldn't. She'd never been good at ending relationships.

She wondered what Vaughn was doing now. A stab of loneliness and regret ran through her. She toyed with the idea of calling him. A call now would give him mixed messages, she reasoned. Better to let some time pass. As much as she loved him and missed him already, it had been the right choice for both of them. Of that, she was certain.

Mia scattered feed for the chickens, gave the nervous Stevens a last stroke, and loaded Buddy into the truck. She was meeting Svengetti at a bar not far from her house. She'd known he was in the area. She just didn't realize how close.

On her way, she received a call from Allison. Did she know where Jason was?

"He's not answering his mobile or his work numbers," Allison said. "I even stopped by his office, where he said he'd be, but no one was there. I'm worried."

And she sounded worried. "I talked to him this morning," Mia said. "He mentioned something about going for a bike ride or a hike after doing some paperwork at the office. He's probably out somewhere, letting off steam."

"Without telling me?" Allison asked.

"You've been pretty distracted."

"I have." Allison paused, and Mia heard traffic noises in the background. "If you talk to him again, let him know I'm looking for him?"

"I will," Mia said. "Allison?"

"Yes?"

"Have you given any more thought to what I said earlier? About giving the pictures to the police and walking away."

Allison sighed. "I tried. The police don't see a connection between the pictures and Scott's death."

"There you go—"

"But they're wrong."

It was Mia's turn to sigh. "And you wonder why Jason went for a hike without you?"

"Without *telling* me. There's a difference. Where are you, anyway?"

Mia debated telling her where she was headed but thought better of it. "Trying to get you information on Eleanor Davies," she said instead. "Like I promised."

"And how will you do that?"

"I have my sources."

"Svengetti?"

"That transparent?"

"He's sweet on you, Mia."

"*Please*," Mia said, but she felt a shiver of pleasure nonetheless. "Where will you be?"

"Here and there," Allison said cryptically. "I have a few things to check out."

"Nothing dangerous?" Mia asked, feeling her stomach tighten. After the events of last summer, Mia knew quite well that Allison's idea of dangerous and others' idea of dangerous were summer and winter.

Allison laughed. "Nothing dangerous."

"Famous last words."

*   *   *

Night was falling fast. Allison turned off Broad Street and onto Green Street, feeling conspicuous in her Volvo. This wasn't a great area of town, period. She shouldn't have come. But she needed to see the spot where Scott had been murdered.

On Green Street, Allison wedged the Volvo between an old Town Car and a newer Honda. She killed the engine. Based on what she'd read in the papers and what Edith had told her, this was the block. She climbed out of the car.

The night was still. Allison heard traffic noise, police sirens in the distance and the far-off beat of someone's jazz music, but here, along this block of Green, no one stirred. A row of connected homes lined each side of the street. On one side, the homes were largely intact. Rundown and dark inside, but intact. On the opposite side, across from where she'd parked, three-quarters of the homes were in utter disrepair. Roofing had collapsed, porches sagged, and stained glass windows were shattered reminders of what had once been. In the home on the corner, one of the few with an undamaged roof, a light shined from the basement. It flickered, went out and then came on again.

Squatters, Allison thought.

The wind picked up, scattering bits of litter across the sidewalk. A block and a half away, Allison could make out three silhouettes, all carrying lit cigarettes, coming down the street. In the pools of darkness between the street lights, she saw only the tiny red glow of the cigarettes bobbing in what looked like nothingness.

What *had* Scott been doing here? Allison wondered. Why the hell was he in this neighborhood on *that* day? She studied the houses on this side of the block. Although a few looked as though they might be occupied, there were no signs of life. Aside from the light in the basement of the abandoned house.

The bobbing cigarettes advanced. In the watery glow of the street light, Allison saw three young black boys, all dressed in baggy pants and hoodies. They barely glanced in her direction before they made a left at the crossroads and disappeared from sight.

Perhaps Berry was right. Perhaps Mia was right. Maybe Scott hadn't been reaching out to her for any reason other than blackmail. Or to rekindle an affair—an unwanted affair. Or for help. That was the bit she couldn't shake, that maybe Scott Fairweather had needed help.

Could she really have been that poor a judge of character? At one time, she'd thought she loved Scott. There had to have been some good in him.

Allison headed back toward her car. She was about to get in when movement caught her eye. A woman, teetering her way up the road, had come out from the abandoned house on the corner. She seemed to be headed this way.

Allison climbed in her car, waiting. The woman was alone. She wore spiky black boots, a skirt so short it could have been a bikini, and a sequined tank top. No coat. Long, unruly black hair framed an angular face hidden by shadows. As she neared, Allison saw multiple piercings in her ear, nose and lip.

Allison kept her hand on the ignition, her foot near the gas. She felt oddly calm. If the woman was packing, she was hiding the gun well. There was certainly no extra room in her clothing. When the woman approached, she leaned down so that her face was framed by the car window. She was older than Allison had first thought, maybe in her late twenties, but it was hard to tell. She had the far away, hollow look of someone who had been on the streets for too long. Sharp cheekbones, sunken eyes, and stained, rotting teeth indicated heroin or meth. The bruises on her pale arms screamed abuse.

The woman tried to smile, but the expression contorted into something painful and pathetic. She said something Allison couldn't hear. Allison cracked the window.

"What'd you need?" the woman asked.

"I just want to talk."

The woman grinned. "That's what they all say. Whatever your flavor, I can deliver—"

"Really, I just want to ask you a question." Keeping her eyes on the woman, Allison pulled a photo of Scott from inside her bag. "A man was killed here a few weeks ago. This man." Allison showed her Scott's picture. "Do you recognize him?"

The woman squinted at the photo, bending down to get a better view. "No, I'd remember him."

She looked certain, although Allison was unsure how much she could rely on her memory.

"Did you know about the murder on this block?"

The woman shifted from one foot to the other, either from cold or nervousness. She glanced again at the house and Allison figured there was a pimp in there, waiting for her to return with cash. She said, "Answer me and I'll give you twenty bucks."

A hungry nod. "Yeah, I remember. The cops were all over."

"Do you know who did it?"

"Gang kid."

"Did you recognize him? Is he one of the kids the cops arrested?"

The woman shrugged. The frightened look returned to her face. "Dunno."

Frustrated, Allison said, "Did you see anything? Anything at all?"

The woman shook her head slowly back and forth.

Allison pulled out a twenty and a ten. The woman's eyes widened. Allison glanced in the rearview mirror to make sure no one else was coming.

"Think hard for me. This is all I have, but you can have it if you help me."

"I didn't see it happen, but I hear things."

"What kind of things?"

"You can't tell nobody I told you. Understand?"

Allison nodded.

"Young guy did it. For money."

Not so different from what Berry said, Allison thought. Except that they pinned it on kids, not a kid. "Was he one of the young guys the cops arrested?"

The woman looked nervously back toward the house. A light had reappeared in the basement.

"Look," the woman said. "I didn't see it happen, but I hear things, like I said. Kid who did it got away. That's all I know."

"Was it part of a drug deal?"

"Don't think so."

"You don't know this kid's name?"

"Told you. No." She wrapped her arms tighter around her chest and rocked back and forth. Despite the cold, a line of sweat appeared above her lip. Goosebumps had sprouted along her arms. "That's all I know. Don't know his name, or why he done it."

"Did you tell any of this to the cops?"

Her snort said she never spoke to the police.

"But you're sure the kid wasn't one of the ones who was arrested?"

She nodded. Allison, still not sure whether to believe her, handed her the thirty dollars. The woman backed away from the car, lingering just out of reach. "Thanks."

"Do you need help?" Allison asked, thinking of Amy. "Do you want me to take you somewhere…somewhere safe?"

The woman smiled, a smile so sad and sweet that Allison felt tears well up in her eyes. "Ain't nowhere safe," she said. "But I 'preciate the offer."

Allison slipped her arms out of her coat and pulled it off. It was made of wool and cashmere, but built to withstand colder temperatures. She rolled down the window and held the coat out. "Take this. It's warm."

The woman stared at it, not comprehending. She held out her hands and tentatively touched the fabric. Allison saw track marks along her arms. She'd sell the coat to buy drugs, Allison knew, or her pimp would. But maybe, just maybe, she'd be warm for a night. Or the gesture would mean something to her some day in the future, when she could see her path more clearly.

"What will I tell…what am I gonna tell him?" the woman asked, sounding a decade younger than her late twenties. "How am I gonna explain a coat? Can't tell him I gave you information. He'd kill me."

"Tell him you negotiated well."

"He can see me from here. He'll know we didn't do nothin'."

"Then tell him I'm a missionary. A minister. Something like that."

The woman nodded. She slipped on the coat. It was several sizes too big, but she slid her hands gingerly down the length of the material.

Allison started the ignition. She pulled away from the curb and watched in her rearview mirror as the girl-woman fumbled her way back toward the house and whatever waited within.

TWENTY-NINE

Allison returned home to a dark house. Even Brutus took his time greeting her, coming down the steps with the startled, slightly dazed look of someone who'd been awakened from a deep sleep. The cat didn't bother with an appearance.

After giving Brutus a vigorous petting, Allison slid off her shoes and checked her phone. She had a text from Jason: "Heading back to my place. –J"

Odd, Allison thought. His normal routine was to stay here, or at least call. They never ended a day without an "I love you." It was only eight o'clock, so she tried to ring him. He didn't answer. She was about to put her shoes back on and head to his apartment when her phone beeped. Relived, she glanced down at the caller I.D. Only it wasn't Jason. It was Faye.

"Can you take the baby tonight?" Faye asked. "I'm sorry to call so late, but I forgot that Mom has an appointment first thing in the morning."

"Of course," she said to Faye, surprised but delighted, and more than a little apprehensive. "I can be there in an hour."

"Thank you," Faye said, sounding like a burden had been lifted. "You'll bring her back tomorrow?"

"Sure. What time?"

"Any time between twelve and three," Faye said. "Just in time for *Little House on the Prairie* reruns. We all watch those together."

*   *   *

Thomas Svengetti pushed away a half-eaten plate of Shepherd's Pie. "You want me to track down this Doris Long?" he asked. "Using federal tax records?"

Mia smiled at him from across the table. The spot he'd chosen for their rendezvous was a wood-paneled, noisy sports bar. But her veggie burger had been tasty and the beer in her hand, a local pale ale, went down easily. The company, she hated to admit, wasn't too bad, either.

"Can you do that?"

Svengetti nodded. "Sure, mostly public records anyway. But why do you need the information?"

"Favor to a friend."

Svengetti arched an eyebrow. "Why do I think you're up to something?"

"Me? What would give you that idea?"

Svengetti smiled, an expression Mia hadn't seen much on the man, and his vibrant blue eyes lit up. "You're a wily one, Mia Campbell." He ran a finger over a long scratch in the wooden table. He had strong hands, Mia noticed, and neatly trimmed fingernails. "You want to find this Doris Long? Why?"

Mia shook her head. "We want to find a woman named Eleanor Davies. She's forty-two and single, as far as I know anyway. Lives in Exton and worked at Transitions, Inc., a former brand of Diamond Brands, Inc. Disappeared from her home a few weeks ago."

"Foul play suspected?"

"Maybe," Mia said. "Her sister was murdered soon after Eleanor disappeared." Mia went on to explain Scott Fairweather's death and his relationship with Eleanor. "Something seems off."

"Heard about that. Man was killed in North Philly. Gang-related. They just arrested the perps." Svengetti raised his glass and frowned. "Sounds like a matter for the cops."

"I agree. Unfortunately, my friend does not."

"Why are you involved?"

"I'm not, really. This friend is worried. She thinks something happened to Eleanor. Or Eleanor knows something and ran."

Mia watched his face. While she wasn't lying, she wasn't being completely truthful, either. After everything that happened with the Benini and Edwards families almost a year ago, Mia trusted Svengetti. He was a smart man, and resourceful. But she also knew he was a maverick and he would do what he felt was right, not necessarily what someone else wanted him to do. She needed to play it cool.

"You're holding back on me, Mia," he said. "But I get the sense that you're not directly involved so I'll help you." He took a sip from his mug of beer, wiped his mouth with a white paper napkin, and leaned forward, eyes commanding. Mia found herself thinking he was a handsome man, in a Paul-Newman-in-his-later-years sort of way. "Don't go putting yourself in danger again."

Mia smiled. "This one isn't my fight, Thomas."

Svengetti stopped a waitress and asked her for a pen. She handed him one and he jotted the names down on another white napkin. "So you think that finding Doris Long may help you locate Eleanor."

"That's what my friend thinks."

Svengetti stared at her. "And your friend is Allison Campbell?"

"You're either smarter than you look or I'm an open book."

"You just seem to be *that* loyal."

"You say that like it's a bad thing."

Svengetti laughed. "Loyalty has its place, Mia. But it can also get you killed. Or worse."

Mia knew he was talking about his own life: his murdered wife, killed at the hands of the Russian mob, and others whom he'd seen gunned down or emotionally tortured over the years. She felt bad for bringing him into this.

"Thomas," she began.

But he waved away her concern. "I'm right where I want to be, Mia. So don't say another thing." He caught her eye, making the meaning of his words clear. "My hotel room is not far from here. If you want an answer right away, you're welcome to join me in the search. Otherwise, I can call you later."

Mia felt a warm flush creeping over her skin. "I think you'd better call later, Thomas."

He nodded, his expression unreadable. After a second he returned to his beer. "Doris Long," he said between sips. "Sounds like a good name for a serial killer. Or the murderer in a mystery novel."

*   *   *

Eleanor waited until Doris was asleep. With her ear to Doris's door, Eleanor fumbled along the counter where Doris kept her keys until she found what she was looking for: the tiny replica of a shotgun that held her car keys. An hour prior she had slipped each German Shepherd four Benadryl capsules wrapped in cheese and to her satisfaction both dogs were sleeping soundly on the floor by the couch. She'd slipped Doris a sleeping pill, too. Popped it into her evening beer. Just like giving steak to a lion.

As quietly as she could, Eleanor opened the front door and closed it softly behind her. It was a waning crescent moon, and without the moon's guiding light, it was nearly impossible to see. That was okay. Eleanor had made many nighttime treks across the western half of the United States and in parts of Europe and South America. She wasn't afraid of the dark, only the people who might be hiding out under the cover of night.

Eleanor slipped behind the wheel of Doris's Subaru and shut the door. She jammed the manual transmission into third gear and released the parking break, letting the car slide down the hilly driveway until she was far enough into the woods to turn on the ignition. The car bucked once, twice and then the engine caught. Eleanor waited until she was near the street and out of view of Doris's house before turning on the headlights. She'd walked this path so many times that she'd memorized the route and knew without looking every turn, every bump along the driveway. Still, she let out a breath when she reached the road and could finally see.

The headlights shined a swath of light onto the darkened road. Eleanor was careful to drive the speed limit. She couldn't afford an issue with the police or an accident with a deer or moose. Despite the cigarette-wet-dog smell of Doris's vehicle, it felt good to be back behind the wheel of a vehicle. It felt good to be driving. But if Doris awoke to find Eleanor and her car missing, Eleanor had no doubt she'd call the cops before she'd bother to read the note Eleanor had left for her. That's just how she was.

Eleanor had memorized the way to Route 1, her best bet for a twenty-four hour pharmacy or grocery store. Even along Route 1, though, it took her another thirty minutes to find a twenty-four hour drugstore. Before going inside the store, she took advantage of the cold and wrapped a wool scarf around her face, hiding her nose and mouth. To be extra careful, she looked away from the security camera as she entered. Just in case.

She found the disposable phones near the front, by the cameras. She chose one and paid in cash. Once in the car, she took a few minutes to set it up. With this, she could transfer money to her checking account and pay off Doris. The greedy bitch was getting antsy, and so was Eleanor. The money movement might set off some red flags, but by the time anyone caught on, she'd be long gone. The idea of spending Thanksgiving alone with Doris was depressing. Much better to be headed southwest, toward Mexico. She'd take the money, get a new car and cross the border. She could disappear in Mexico. Hell, with all her cash, she could disappear anywhere.

THIRTY

Allison awoke with the soft feel of little hands against her cheeks. She opened her eyes, momentarily startled, until she saw her niece staring at her. Grace smiled.

"Oh, good," the little girl said. "You're up."

"I'm up." Allison grinned. "Who wants pancakes?"

"Pancakes!" Grace giggled. Her long, dark hair was spread across Jason's pillow. Next to her, Brutus had wedged himself between the end of the mattress and the nightstand so that he was sharing Jason's pillow, too. The child didn't seem to mind. Only the cat wasn't in the family bed. He was sitting on Allison's dresser, by the window, looking disdainfully down at his new best friend Brutus as though Brutus's desire to be part of the melee was somehow an embarrassment.

"Nice to have you back in the fold," Allison said as she reached over to pet the dog. He snuggled closer to Grace and wagged his tail stump. Allison stuck her tongue out at Simon the cat and Grace giggled again.

"Can I watch television?" Grace whispered. "If I'm real quiet?"

"Tell you what," Allison said. "You can watch television even if you're real loud."

"Really?"

"Really!"

Allison tickled her niece, who laughed hysterically, which in turn made Brutus run in mad circles around the bed, barking.

"Look at him!" Grace screamed, laughing harder.

After a moment, Grace calmed down long enough to catch her breath. She looked up at Allison, still smiling. "You have a bad dog,

Aunt Allison," she said, hugging Brutus to her. The dog slurped at her face with his giant tongue. "But I sure like him."

"And he sure likes you," Allison said. Dog and child, she thought— all unbridled joy. As it should be.

Allison had been worried that Grace would be uncomfortable here. The house wasn't exactly kid-friendly. The closest Allison had to toys were a set of Russian nesting dolls she'd purchased during a trip to Eastern Europe a few years back. But one look at Brutus and Allison knew it was mutual love at first sight. Grace had been scared to sleep alone, so Allison had rented a kids movie On Demand and she, Grace and Brutus had cozied up in her bed. The child had fallen asleep twenty minutes into the show.

On impulse, Allison kissed Grace on the forehead. "I'm happy to have you here, Grace."

"I'm happy to be here, Aunt Allison."

Such grown-up words from such a little body, Allison thought. This child was so bright, so sweet. Clearly Amy had done something right. But she seemed much older than her years, what her mother would have called an old soul, probably a result of parenting her own mother. Grace needed playmates and school and the freedom to be mischievous now and again. Would she have that with Amy?

Allison pictured the prostitute she'd met the day before. Was that the life her sister was leading? Was Grace the child left behind while her sister partied? A vile thought.

"What's wrong, Aunt Allison?" Grace asked.

Allison sat up and swung Grace onto her lap. She tapped her nose gently with the tip of her finger. "Absolutely nothing." She kissed her again. "I love pancakes and I love having you here. And guess what? Brutus loves pancakes, too."

Grace laughed. "I bet Brutus likes everything."

"Brutus used to be homeless. Do you know what that means?"

Grace nodded. "It means he had no money and no house. That he had to live in a shelter."

"But that's all over now," Allison said. "Now he gets pancakes and syrup and a warm bed to sleep in."

"Those things are good, aren't they, Brutus?" Grace said. She patted his head, which was now lodged under her right arm. "Can we save some pancakes for Mommy?"

Oh, baby, Allison thought. She looked at her niece, hiding the ache with a smile. "We can freeze some. Would you like that?"

Grace nodded. "I miss her." A second later, she brightened. "Can I help you cook?"

"You betcha," Allison said. "Wouldn't have it any other way."

Allison kept Grace for as much of the day as she could. At First Impressions, she had back-to-back appointments, so Vaughn was called in as the makeshift babysitter, a job he took to with relish, if not skill.

"I stopped and bought crayons and coloring books," Allison said. "And here are the child scissors, in case she wants to make snowflakes or paper dolls." Allison looked at him sharply. "But don't give her adult scissors, even if she asks."

"Yes, Allison," Vaughn said with an emphatic roll of the eyes. "I do know the difference between a five-year-old and an adult."

"Then you know she should wash her hands before she has a snack." Allison pulled organic baby carrots and ranch dressing packages, along with raisins, hummus and pita chips, out of a Whole Foods bag. "Don't give her any of your Doritos. Even if she asks. Say something like—"

"Allison."

She looked up. "Yes?"

"Relax." Vaughn smiled. "Grace and I will be fine together. And if I need you," he pointed toward the client room, "I know just where to find you."

Allison frowned.

"I'm being a bit mental, aren't I?"

"You're just being a good aunt. But you can chill." Vaughn smiled at Grace. "We're going to color the walls with a black Sharpie, right after we run with grown-up scissors. Right, kid?"

Grace giggled. "I don't think so."

Vaughn grinned back.

"I don't think so, either. Not under the watchful eye of your Aunt Allison, anyway." He shooed Allison toward the client room and her waiting client. "Go. Make us some money. Right, Grace?"

Grace nodded solemnly. "That sounds like a good idea."

Five hours later, Grace was back with Allison's family and Allison was back at First Impressions. She'd sent Jason two texts with pictures of her niece and he hadn't responded to either. A call to his administrative assistant had been unproductive.

"He's acting odd," Allison said now. She was typing up client notes, but her mind was elsewhere.

"He's a busy guy, Allison." Vaughn said. "I'm sure you'll see him tonight."

Allison nodded, ignoring the ropes coiling in her gut. "I guess."

Vaughn plopped down on a seat in front of her desk. It was nearly seven, and they had just ushered out the last clients for the day: the ladies from Allison's recently divorced group. Allison took off her shoes, sexy red Manolos, and slouched back in her chair.

"I'm exhausted."

"Running Grace back and forth probably took its toll."

"Oh, it wasn't Grace. She and I had fun."

"Fun?" Vaughn asked, eyes narrowed. "Imagine that. How long will she be with your sister?"

Allison sighed. "That remains to be seen. Faye looked beat. And I think Amy will be out of rehab soon. Maybe by Thanksgiving." Allison pulled a hand through her hair. "I hate the idea of Grace going back to live with Amy."

"Maybe she and Amy can live with your folks."

Allison didn't think that was a long-term solution. "They barely have space for Grace. Plus, Amy and Faye would kill each other, and if history repeats itself, as it so often does, Amy will steal from them *and* take the child with her." Allison thought for a moment. "I wish there was some way to convince Amy to live with me for a while."

Vaughn looked at her, surprised. "You would do that?"

"You seem shocked."

Vaughn just stared at her, an infuriating half-smile on his face.

"Ugh," Allison said. "Not you, too." She stood and walked toward the window. Floodlights from the bank behind her small parking area cast shadows on the bushes and pavement in between. She thought of the street in North Philly, the street where Scott was murdered. She turned around. "Has Jamie had any success?"

"Yes...and no." Vaughn filled her in on Jamie's research: the Diamond family, the loss of the founder's wife, Lily Diamond, their daughter, Amelie, the child labor allegations and the spin-off of Transitions. "Amelie Diamond alluded to her father's vindictiveness. Apparently Ted Diamond saw himself as a sort of role model for other business leaders. He had two loves: his wife, Lily, and his company."

"Not his daughter?"

Vaughn mulled that over. "You're the one with the psych background, Allison, but if you want my two-bit analysis, Ted Diamond was a narcissist. The company and his wife made him look good. His daughter, not a pretty woman by most standards, would not have. And when she converted to Buddhism? The nail in the coffin, so to speak."

"That's a pretty harsh analysis."

Vaughn shrugged. "I told you I'm no expert."

Allison sat back down at her desk. "Well, you're probably not wrong." She fingered her day planner, thinking of her abnormal psychology book from graduate school and the DSM-IV description of Narcissistic Personality Disorder. She knew nothing about Ted Diamond, but she did know that many successful business people— many successful people, period—had narcissistic tendencies. And if that described Ted Diamond, what might he have done to get back at the folks, like reporters, who smeared his company and, in doing so, his wife?

Only Ted was dead. And it wasn't a reporter who had been murdered on the streets of Philadelphia.

"Jamie found no connection between Ted and Scott, outside of Scott's job at Transitions. The two had no former connection that he could tell."

"You read my mind."

Vaughn smiled. "It was the logical next question."

Allison considered that statement. *Logic*...she had failed to ask a logical question all along.

"Scott's calendar said he was meeting with me on Saturday night. There was no specific time, just my name scratched into the margin for the evening, around eight. That was also the night of Delvar's award ceremony. What if it wasn't me Scott wanted to talk with, but Delvar?"

"Why would Scott Fairweather want to talk with Delvar?"

"Clothing manufacturer...designer...maybe they're connected somehow."

Vaughn frowned. "I don't know, Allison. Feels like a stretch. Why not go to Delvar directly? Why go to the trouble of contacting you first?"

Allison considered that. "Delvar's celebration was the one place Scott could be guaranteed to get an audience with the reclusive designer. And he would have used me to make introductions."

Vaughn shook his head.

"Still not buying it. What would Scott want with Delvar?"

"Maybe he wanted him to design clothes for Transitions. If the company wasn't doing well, and Scott was getting heat, then having Delvar on board may have been a last-ditch effort to increase sales."

"Delvar designs edgy, sophisticated clothes for adults, not polo shirts for preppy teenagers."

"Then if not Delvar, who?"

"*You*. He knew you would be there, Allison."

"Scott could have easily found my home address. He could have found First Impressions—he was an ex-client. Why go to the trouble of crashing a private event just to get my attention?" Allison shook her head. The idea that it was Delvar's celebration that was key here struck her as right.

Vaughn tapped a pen against Allison's desk. "Could Delvar get the invitation list for the award ceremony?"

"Maybe," Allison said. "If he does, can Jamie cross-reference the list against important people in the clothing industry?"

"I don't see why not," Vaughn said. "Get it to me and I'll ask him."

Allison thanked him. "I'd like this to be behind us. I can't help wondering when another photo is going to show up. Part of me hates Scott for putting me in this position. Part of me wished he was around so I could ask why: why he took the pictures, why he shared them, why he was on that street in that section of town." She gripped the edge of her desk, fingers clutched against wood. "Makes me wonder whether I ever really knew him."

"The police believe they have their killers, Allison," Vaughn said. "This private investigation you're running, it's all about those photographs and your own morbid need to understand. You know that, right?"

"Actually, I'm not so sure the police do have their killers."

Vaughn cocked his head, waiting for more.

Allison had been reluctant to tell anyone about her conversation with the prostitute. She'd gone too far that time—she realized that. Vaughn would be right to be angry.

"I made another trip into Edith's neighborhood," she said. When he didn't look surprised, she described her encounter with the hooker from the abandoned house.

"You don't need me to tell you how stupid that was, do you?"

Allison shook her head.

He frowned. "She was sure? Just one kid?"

Allison nodded.

"Are you wondering what I'm wondering?" Vaughn asked.

"Whether a certain young man, a man with a temper issue, may know more than he's letting on?"

"Yep," Vaughn said. He glanced at his watch. "It's too late to head there now, but I think maybe another trip to see Edith and Duane Myers is in order. Agree?"

"Yes," Allison said. "Can you go tomorrow?"

Vaughn nodded.

"What are you going to do?"

"Tonight I'll check with Delvar to see if he can get that list. Tomorrow, I'm going to have another talk with Julie Fitzsimmons, Scott's colleague and another of his conquests."

"Why?"

"I have a few questions I need answered."

"And in the meantime? Dinner?"

Allison shook her head. "I'd love to, Vaughn, but I have something else I need to do."

He looked at her questioningly, no doubt wondering what predicament she was going to put herself into tonight.

"Nothing related to this," Allison said. "I need to see Jason. His sudden silence is scaring me. If he won't come to me, I'll go to him."

*   *   *

Jason's apartment was dark. Allison used her key to let herself in. Like the man himself, his apartment was simple: efficient and pleasing to the eye. Located on the first floor of an old estate house, it had wide-pine floors, ten-foot ceilings and glossy white trim. His space consisted of a living room/dining room, galley kitchen, bedroom and bath. The furniture was sparse but well-constructed, and competed for space with his sports equipment: two mountain bikes, a road bike, weights and an array of skis. A kid in a grown man's body, Allison thought. She smiled, getting ready to settle in to watch some television, but when her glance fell upon the dining table, that smile froze on her face.

A 9x13 white envelope. Someone had typed "Jason Campbell" on the front. Allison couldn't breathe. She knew what would be inside.

Slowly, deliberately, she removed a picture from the envelope.

It was the worst she'd seen so far, and not because of the explicitness of the picture—it depicted a fairly tame sexual embrace, more PG-13 than XXX—but because of the look of utter adoration on her face.

Allison was gazing at Scott with the expression of a woman in love.

Damn, Allison said to herself. Hot tears stung her eyes. She glanced down at her hand, at the finger that would soon display an engagement ring.

Oh, Jason, she thought. This should have been a happy time, but a photo like this would call everything into question for him. She'd told him about the sex shots, true. But in a man's view, wouldn't sex be one thing and love another? Clearly, Allison had once had deep feelings for Scott Fairweather. Even if she knew the picture was deceiving, that any feelings for Scott had been fleeting and rooted more in her grief over a failed marriage than respect for the man himself, to see something like this would be...devastating.

The unreturned calls, the unrequited texts. Jason was angry. He had a right to be.

And then it struck her. What if someone else had seen this picture, someone else who had a stake in this game? Leah Fairweather.

Was it possible that she'd killed her own husband—or had him killed—because of jealous rage? They'd explored the possibility before, but now, looking at this photograph and imagining her fiancé's ire, she could see how pictures of her husband's infidelities could push Leah over the edge.

Yes, Allison thought. The bereft widow might not be as grief-stricken as she seems.

But Allison knew she couldn't chase that tangent right now. She took off her shoes and settled into the small couch. She would wait here for Jason. All night, she thought, if that's what it took.

THIRTY-ONE

Only Jason didn't come home that night, nor did he go to Allison's house. At midnight, Allison wrote him a heartfelt email telling him where she was and what she was doing. His simple response was, "Go home, Allison. I just need some time."

Where was he spending that time? And what was he doing?

But she decided he deserved space *and* her trust, if that's what he needed, and she returned to her quiet house, thankful for Brutus and Simon the cat.

The next day, after three morning appointments that were difficult to get through because of a wandering mind and blanketing anxiety, Allison set off for the city and Julie Fitzsimmons. She'd called ahead, hoping that their sisterhood affiliation of Women Who'd Slept with Scott would buy her some time and some candor. She wasn't yet sure of the latter, but Julie agreed readily to the former. Only she was in the city for a conference and had to meet Allison downtown.

They met at the Corner Bakery on Seventeenth and JFK Boulevard. Julie smiled wanly as she took the seat across from Allison, a cup of steaming tea in her hand.

"This is about Scott, I assume?" Julie asked.

Allison nodded. "I appreciate your time."

Julie looked down at her hands as she flexed her fingers. "I can't stop thinking about him. Even though we were over before he died, he's always on my mind." She glanced up. "And I'm still receiving the photos. In fact, I got one yesterday."

Around the same time Jason would have received his, Allison thought. "Was there a note? Any written communication?"

Julie shook her head. "Just like before. The pictures delivered in a plain envelope. No letter, no handwriting." She sighed. "Eleanor. I still think it's Eleanor."

Allison wasn't so sure. "Has it occurred to you that whoever is sending the photos could have been involved in Scott's murder?"

Julie looked dumbstruck. She blinked once, twice. "Scott's murderers have been arrested. It was a bunch of kids. Why would they have these pictures? And if they somehow did, why send them to me?" She shook her head vehemently back and forth. "Plus, they're in jail, Allison. They were arrested earlier this week. How would they have sent me the last one?"

Allison agreed that the kids who were arrested would not have been involved with sending of the photographs. "But what if they didn't kill him?" Allison asked. "Or what if they were hired to kill him in order to make it look like a drug-related murder?"

Julie was quiet. "I hadn't thought of that." She chewed at one manicured nail, then stopped herself and placed her hand flat on the table. "But if it's not blackmail, why bother?"

"Maybe it's a warning."

"For what purpose?"

But Allison had no answer. She thought of the first package she'd received. The picture and the hole circled in red. "I guess that's what I'm trying to figure out."

Julie's eyes widened. "You've received them, too."

Slowly, Allison nodded. One more thing bonding them.

"It's awful, isn't it? Not knowing. Realizing that Scott betrayed your trust." She looked pointedly at Allison. "He did take them without your knowledge, right?"

"Oh, yeah. I had no idea."

"Me, either."

They sat for a few minutes, each lost in her own thoughts. It was nearing two in the afternoon and the local lunch crowd was trickling out. An older woman, her shorn hair covered with a pink headscarf, sat in the seat next to them. She pulled out a Stephen King novel and, book open in front of her, dug into a large blueberry muffin.

"I doubt you came here to talk about the photos," Julie said with a regretful sigh. "What else can I help you with, Allison?"

"Does the name Delvar ring a bell?"

"The designer?"

Allison nodded.

"Other than knowing who he is, no. Why, should it?"

"Do you know whether Scott knew Delvar?"

"Not that I know of," Julie said. "Although he may not have mentioned it if he did. When we were together, we didn't talk all that much." Her face reddened. "I just mean we didn't have a lot of time when we were together. Anyway, why do you ask?"

"Delvar was given an award and honorarium for a charity he's started. The award ceremony was the first Saturday in November. Do you know any reason why Scott may have wanted to attend that ceremony?"

Julie shook her head. "We weren't together then, though."

Allison considered the timeline. That would mean Scott had ended things with Julie shortly before he was killed. Had he also ended his affair with Eleanor?

"Julie, when Scott stopped seeing you, did he say why? I know it was because of Leah, his wife, but why now? What had changed to make him take that step?"

Julie turned her head in the direction of the older woman in the head scarf. Her pause was deliberate, and Allison sensed that she knew more than she was about to share. Finally, she said, "He didn't really say."

"He didn't say or you'd rather not tell me?"

Julie bit down on her thumbnail. "You have to swear not to tell anyone. Especially not anyone at Transitions."

"I promise."

"Someone caught us. We were...we were together in the copy room. I know it's cliché, but it was very early in the morning and no one was around. Scott thought it would be fun. The door was closed." Julie closed her eyes. "He slammed the door open and there we were. It wasn't pretty. After that, Scott was afraid for his job. His career was everything to him. Everything."

"He was afraid he'd be fired?"

Julie nodded.

"Yet you said he broke up with you at night. That was the morning."

"He came to my house later. We…we did it again. I thought maybe he had come to terms with being discovered. But after we slept together, he told me that was the last time. That he couldn't risk Leah finding out or losing his position at Transitions. He meant it. We were not together after that. In fact, he barely acknowledged me from that point on."

Scott's reaction to their discovery intrigued her. She recalled Mark Fairweather telling her that Scott had lost his position with Tenure Polk because of an in-house affair. Was this too close to history repeating itself, or was something else at play?

"Was Scott written up for what happened?" Allison asked.

"Not that I know of. I know I wasn't."

"And was Scott's position at Transitions secure?"

"As far as I know. He and I didn't really talk about work." Julie glanced at her watch. "I had better head back to the conference."

Allison nodded. She started to collect her coffee cup. "I appreciate your time, Julie."

"Sure, although I don't see how this helps you."

"It paints a picture of Scott. It's been a while since I've seen him. I'd forgotten…well, I figured he'd changed."

"I don't know about that," Julie said. She stood up, cup in hand. "Don't forget about Eleanor. Who still hasn't shown up, by the way."

"He was seeing her at the same time he was seeing you?"

Julie nodded. "I had no idea."

Which made Allison wonder: did Eleanor know about Julie?

"Who discovered you in that copy room, Julie?"

Julie's face contorted. "Brad Halloway, of all people. It was like being seen by my grandfather."

Brad? He hadn't mentioned it. But then, he wouldn't. "Has he treated you differently since then?"

Julie gave a sad smile. "It's like I don't exist. Before, he talked to me every day. Since that morning, not a word. I guess maybe that's bothered me, too. That Brad wouldn't give me the benefit of the doubt." Julie shrugged. "Like I told you before, it's hard to be the other woman.

The things you gain—companionship, passion—are an illusion in the end. The things you lose, well, at some point you realize that they're the things that matter."

Allison was merging on to the Blue Route when her cell phone rang. She hit the "accept call" button on her Bluetooth without looking to see who the caller was.

"Thomas is still trying to locate Eleanor's Doris Long," Mia said. "He said the name Doris Long brought up a gazillion hits. He's trying to triangulate based on age and her relationship with Eleanor's late father. But if the two never married and never owned property together, her location will be harder to pinpoint."

"Apparently this Doris Long is a huge gun enthusiast. Maybe that will help."

"Hmmm," Mia said. "Does she own a gun-related business? Something that would create a tax or registration trail?"

"I don't know. She participates in gun shows, for whatever that's worth."

"I'll let Thomas know."

Thomas. Allison didn't miss the use of Svengetti's first name. She was disappointed. She knew finding Doris wouldn't be easy. And even if they did locate the right Doris Long, there was no guarantee Doris would lead them to Eleanor. Or that Eleanor would be able to shed light on Scott's murder or the photographs. But it felt like the best hope they had, so Allison was determined to see it through to the end.

All of this had felt personal from the time she got that call at Delvar's award ceremony. But when Allison saw that photograph on Jason's table...well, that upped the ante. Now, there was really no going back.

"Thanks to you and Svengetti for the help," Allison said. "If he comes up with anything else, please let me know."

"He did find one other thing of interest, Allison. About your girl Eleanor."

Allison perked up. "What?"

"The woman has money."

After exiting the Blue Route, Allison made a right on Route 30 and headed east, toward her house. "She worked for a large company and was pretty far up the food chain. That could equate to large bonuses. And if she lived frugally—"

"Not that kind of well off, Allison. The kind of well off someone gets very suddenly. Thomas checked her bank records. Don't ask me how he got access. Frankly, I don't want to know. But what he found seemed compelling."

Allison waited for more. She turned into the Whole Foods parking lot and idled the engine, giving Mia her full attention. "Tell me," she said.

"She does not live frugally. The townhome? Paid cash. She's an adventure traveler, and she's been all over the world. Her last trip was to the Andes, where she did a two-week guided mountain trek."

"I saw some of that on social media."

"Know how much a two-week guided mountain trek to the Andes costs?"

"How much?"

"A lot," Mia said. "Which in and of itself is not news. But when you add in a new car, expensive housing, and a fat bank account, you begin to wonder." Mia paused. "Just in the last year, Eleanor made four deposits. One for $50,000 and another three for $25,000."

"Maybe she inherited the money."

"Not that Thomas could find. The money was transferred from a bank in the Bahamas."

While one hundred and twenty-five thousand dollars was not an earthshattering amount of money, the fact that it was deposited by an unknown source from an offshore bank *was* interesting. "Is there more?" Allison asked.

"Thomas found a brokerage account containing several hundred thousand in stocks and bonds. Plus, Eleanor owns property in California and Wyoming."

Allison mulled this over. "Maybe she's staying at one of those properties."

"He checked. Both are rented. Long-term arrangements, so it's unlikely she'd go there."

Allison considered the little she knew about Eleanor. "Does her job history match the money at all?"

"Svengetti is still looking at her background, but he doesn't think so."

"So what I'm hearing you tell me," Allison said, "is that Eleanor has unexplained wealth. Which could equate to unethical behavior."

Mia agreed. "At the very least, she has a sugar daddy or sugar momma out there somewhere, a benefactor who has been more than generous. Or—"

"Or she's being paid off."

"Either now, or for something in the past," Mia said. "Or she's embezzling money."

"Brad accused Scott of embezzling." Allison thought about Eleanor's job. Purchasing Director for Transitions. She'd have access to money, authority over its disbursement, and the connections needed to defraud her employer. "But with such large sums, I question that angle," Allison said, still thinking. "If you were embezzling, wouldn't you do it a little at a time?"

"But what if she had? What if the Bahamian accounts were where she kept the stolen assets?"

"And she transferred it to her U.S. accounts from time to time?"

"Exactly."

Allison put her head back on the leather seat rest. "If she has that kind of cash, she could be anywhere. Doris Long may be a dead end."

"I don't know about that," Mia said. "The money is still sitting there. Last night was the first time she'd attempted to transact in weeks."

The implications behind that statement hit Allison. "So wherever she is, she's planning to run again."

Mia said, "That very well may be her plan."

THIRTY-TWO

Back at the office, Allison was in for another surprise. Vaughn was back from his trip to Philadelphia to visit Edith Myers and her grandson. The Myers family had skipped town.

"We just talked to them recently."

"We did, but that doesn't change anything. They're gone." Vaughn had a mug-full of peanuts in his hand and was crunching them, one after the other. "No welcome mat, no cross on the door, no sign of anyone. I knocked on the front and back doors and waited. Nothing. I even hollered for Edith, which is why a neighbor came outside. A lady from two doors down."

Allison held a cup of hot coffee. She placed it on Vaughn's desk. "And what did she say?"

"Nothing kind." Vaughn popped a handful of peanuts in his mouth, chewed and swallowed. He glanced into the empty cup and frowned. "Always forget how much I love peanuts."

"The neighbor, Vaughn," Allison said.

"Yeah, the neighbor. Single woman by the name of Kaneesha. Despises Edith and is happy to talk about it. Called her a grouchy old woman—I'm rephrasing because there's a lady present. That would be you." He smiled. "Kaneesha may have used a few words that are sometimes selected to describe lady parts. Anyway, no love lost for Edith Myers."

"But did she know where Edith went?"

"She did not. Just said she hadn't seen either Edith or her grandson in days and wasn't that just great because now some junkie or pimp would move in and destroy that house, too."

Allison studied Vaughn. He had a cat-who-ate-the-canary look about him. "What else did you find out?"

"Kaneesha may have mentioned that Duane had been on the path to the straight-and-narrow, despite a childhood spent robbing, assaulting and participating in other unlawful activities. But she didn't believe he'd changed."

"Why was that?"

"She claims he assaulted her."

"He beat her up?"

"So she says."

"But she didn't report it?"

"Nah. Only thing she seemed to distrust more than Duane and his grandmother is the police. Said she 'handled him,' whatever that meant."

"So he's violent," Allison said. "We knew that, though. His temper, his behavior with his grandmother."

Vaughn grabbed his empty cup and stood. "Yes, but what we didn't know before was the steps Edith had taken to rehabilitate him. Ever heard of Wilderness Journeys?"

Allison shook her head.

"It's like Outward Bound, a leadership program for teens that focuses on survival skills and wilderness adventure. Only Wilderness Journeys takes some tough kids, kids other programs may not accept. Fire setters, rapists, the whole lot."

"How do they manage that?"

"Counselors include trained corrections officers, former cops and military personnel. Plus, they hire people skilled at adventure travel. Hikers, climbers, etc. Some volunteer, others are paid. It's a church-based charity that has some heavy-duty benefactors."

"Okay, you have my attention," Allison said. "Duane attended this program?"

"According to Kaneesha, he was there five years ago, when he was fourteen."

Allison narrowed her eyes. "And you think he may have had something to do with Scott's murder?"

"I think one of three things is going on. Edith and her grandson could be running scared because they pointed fingers at those boys. Gangs don't take kindly to narks, and the pair could be justified in running."

"Or?"

"Duane saw something he shouldn't have and ran."

"Or?"

"Duane killed Scott."

Allison sat down. She was weighing all of the information she'd learned from the prostitute against what she was hearing now. "Okay, even if this is true and it was Duane who pulled the trigger, not those boys, other than corroborating what the prostitute told me, it still doesn't explain some of the other discrepancies." Like who is sending the damn pictures?

"It does if someone paid Duane to murder Scott Fairweather."

"Someone who knew his background."

Vaughn smiled. "Someone who met him at Wilderness Journeys. Someone like Eleanor Davies."

"Eleanor?" Allison quickly added up the information she'd heard from Mia with this new bit of news. "You think Eleanor knows Duane?"

Vaughn nodded. "I had Jamie do some research. Duane's records are sealed, but going by the information Kaneesha gave me, it looks like the two were part of the so-called Southwest Adventure almost five years ago. Kaneesha said Duane was in the United States, and the other adventure that year took place in the Canadian Rockies.

"Eleanor helped design the program and procure resources. Jamie said that information was available online. She was also an 'adventure counselor' during the southwest trip. I am making connections here, but it sounds like she may have had the opportunity to get to know Duane pretty well. Small staff-to-kid ratio."

"Where was she living?"

"Not sure. The trip started in Wyoming and meandered south. Mostly Utah and Colorado."

Wyoming? "Eleanor owns a rental property in Wyoming." Allison filled Vaughn in on what Mia had shared, careful not to mention Thomas Svengetti. Her friend was not dumb, however.

"I guess Mia contacted Svengetti?" he asked.

Allison nodded. "He started with tax records and followed the trail. Eleanor is looking more and more interesting."

"Good work." Only Vaughn didn't *sound* like he thought it was good work. "We know a lot more than we did."

"What we *know* is that Eleanor has money and at one time worked for Wilderness Journeys. The rest is conjecture. But it all makes a certain sense. A woman who is willing to bend the rules for profit may be willing to proposition a boy who was once in her care."

"A woman who is willing to proposition a boy who was once in her care may be capable of murder." Vaughn frowned. "This is not someone you should be chasing on your own. Maybe it's time to involve the police."

"Tried that." Allison shared her conversation with Detective Berry. "I need something more concrete than conjecture and circumstantial evidence next time I talk to him. Plus, none of this is tied to Scott. We need to tie it to Scott."

"Infidelities."

Allison considered this. "I don't know. If Scott had debt issues, and we haven't found any real evidence that he did, how would blackmailing Scott over his affairs have resulted in over a hundred grand being placed in Eleanor's account?"

"Maybe that's why he was in debt. She was blackmailing him."

"I don't know." Allison picked up a pen and drew squiggly lines across a piece of yellow, lined paper. "Why kill the source of your income?"

"Maybe he was going to blow a whistle on something she did. That could be motive for murder," Vaughn said. "Or Leah Fairweather, in a fit of jealous rage, could have had him killed."

"But that doesn't work if the connection between Duane and Scott is Eleanor Davies."

"True."

Both were quiet for a moment. Allison was thinking through all they knew—about Scott, about his affairs, and about Eleanor Davies. A woman who would leave her cat behind.

Allison said, "Clearly Eleanor knows something. Whether she did it or not, she could be key. The money, the Wilderness Journey connection, her torrid affair with Scott. We need to find her."

Allison tossed the pen aside and stood. When she glanced down at

her doodles, she noticed she had unconsciously written the word
"whoring" on the page. It struck her that there were many ways to be a
whore. One could sell one's body for money, but one could also sell
one's soul. And there were lots of venues in which to sell a soul, not all
of them seedy.

"Can you ask Jamie for another favor?" Allison asked.

"Sure."

"Ask him to look again at the spin-off of Transitions from
Diamond Brands. Follow the money trail: who profited, who didn't."

"Are you thinking Eleanor may have been involved?"

"Worth a look."

Vaughn nodded. "Where are you headed next?"

"To prostitute myself."

When Vaughn looked at her funny, Allison smiled. "I'm heading
to see Scott's brother, Mark. He's a quid pro quo kind of guy."

On her way back into the city to visit Mark Fairweather's office, Allison
called her sister's rehab center. As with every other time she'd called, a
perky nurse told her no, she couldn't speak to Amy—protocol—and yes,
her sister was doing well. So well, in fact, that the center might agree
with Amy's request to an early discharge with follow-up appointments
and family counseling.

"Well, I'm her family," Allison had said.

"Yes, and we'll reach out when we have a discharge plan in place."

"What about her daughter, Grace?"

"She will be a critical part of the discharge plan."

"Shouldn't Amy have a few meetings with Grace beforehand to see
how she handles them? What if she regresses when she's with Grace?"

"Ms. Campbell?"

Allison forced herself to sound calmer. "Yes?"

"You can't be expected to be objective. This is your sister, your
niece." The nurse paused for effect. "Please leave this to the
professionals."

Allison hung up, dissatisfied and worried. The feelings didn't go
away when she pulled up to Mark Fairweather's office and parked in
the nearby garage. It was nearly seven-thirty, but a call to Mark's home

was answered by an annoyed wife who confirmed that Mark would be there until late tonight. So Allison expected to find Mark Fairweather. She didn't expect to find him at the office with Leah Fairweather.

Allison was buzzed into the office by the man himself. He smiled a snake's grin when he saw her, and opened the glass door to his office, which was nestled into the fifth floor of a building on Seventeenth and Market. There, Allison saw Leah Fairweather hunched in a chair, her face splotchy and tear-stained.

"Oh, I'm sorry," Allison said before Mark held up his hand.

"It's fine, Allison. Leah was just getting ready to go." He turned to his sister-in-law. "Weren't you, Leah?"

Leah stared at Mark for a pregnant minute before unfurling her long body. She was wearing brown dress pants and a beige linen button down shirt. Neither had been pressed and both needed it badly. Worse, her hair was unwashed and unkempt, and the shadows that had encircled her eyes the last time Allison saw her looked like rings of black crayon now. Despite her dislike for Scott's widow, Allison felt a frisson of sympathy course through her.

"I really don't want to interrupt," Allison said and backed out into the corridor.

This time it was Leah who stopped her. "We really are finished." Leah glanced back at Mark, her eyes hot pokers. "Clearly, I'm not going to get what I came for."

And what was that? Allison wondered.

Seconds later, Leah was gone and Allison was left alone with Mark.

"What do you have for me?" Vaughn asked Jamie. His brother was in his wheelchair by his desk, staring intently at one of the computer screens. Mrs. T was on tonight, although she seemed quieter than usual. Vaughn was used to coming home to the rich smells of Mrs. T's cooking and her broad smile. Instead, she'd nodded hello and retreated to a scentless kitchen.

NOT MUCH YET.

"Hey, what did you do to Mrs. T?"

NOTHING THAT I KNOW OF. SHE'S BEEN LIKE THAT SINCE

SHE ARRIVED.

"Did you ask her if everything was okay?"

COULDN'T. SHE WOULDN'T PAY ATTENTION TO THE DAMN SCREEN LONG ENOUGH FOR ME TO GET THE QUESTION OUT.

"No worries. I'll ask her," Vaughn said. "But first, how can I help?"

Jamie shook his head. YOU CAN'T. I'M ON THE SEC'S WEBSITE, GIVING MYSELF A CRASH COURSE IN SECURITIES FILINGS. LOTS OF INFORMATION ON THESE 8-Ks. JUST NEED TO KNOW WHERE TO LOOK.

"You're looking into Transitions and Diamond Brands?"

YES, AND SCOTT'S PREVIOUS EMPLOYERS. CURIOUS AS TO WHY HE LEFT THE LAST PLACE. Jamie removed his mouth from the controller and looked up at Vaughn. YOU KNOW I THINK THE WORLD OF ALLISON, he said, BUT SHE MAY BE OFF ON THIS ONE. I'VE READ THE NEWS REPORTS, I'VE LOOKED INTO SCOTT'S BACKGROUND. EVEN BY HER OWN ADMISSION, THE GUY WAS A SEX ADDICT. ADDICTIVE TENDENCIES CAN ENCOMPASS OTHER BEHAVIORS: DRUGS, MONEY, EVEN THRILLS.

"So you think the police got it right?"

I THINK THIS ONE MAY BE AS SIMPLE AS IT SEEMS.

"How do you explain Eleanor and Wilderness Journeys? Or the photographs?"

THE SIMPLE EXPLANATION IS THAT ELEANOR WAS CAUGHT UP IN WHATEVER SCOTT WAS. SHE'S WORRIED ABOUT SHARING HIS FATE, SO SHE RAN. AS FOR HER CONNECTION WITH DUANE? TENUOUS AND UNPROVEN. AND DUANE AND HIS GRANDMOTHER MAY HAVE LEFT FOR THE SAME REASON— FEAR. TURNING EVIDENCE ON GANG MEMBERS? BAD FOR LONGEVITY.

"How about Eleanor's sister? How do you explain her murder?"

THAT'S A LITTLE HARDER. THE BEST EXPLANATIONS IN MY MIND ARE THAT EITHER SOMEONE MISTOOK HER FOR ELEANOR OR THAT IT WAS A RANDOM KILLING, UNRELATED TO SCOTT'S DEATH.

"None of that explains the photographs."

MAYBE SCOTT SENT THEM BEFORE HIS DEATH. HE

INTENDED TO BLACKMAIL ALLISON AND THE OTHER WOMAN. THAT'S WHY HE WANTED TO TALK TO ALLISON. HE NEVER GOT THAT FAR, THOUGH. HE WAS KILLED BEFORE HE COULD. ELEANOR MAY HAVE EVEN BEEN PART OF THAT SCHEME.

"But the pictures were sent after he died."

SO MAYBE IT WAS ELEANOR. BEST GUESS? SCOTT WANTED TO MEET WITH ALLISON AS PART OF THE BLACKMAIL SCHEME—THAT'S WHY HER NAME WAS IN HIS APPOINTMENT BOOK. ELEANOR'S JUST COMPLETING WHAT HE COULDN'T FINISH.

Vaughn shook his head. "Only there haven't been any blackmail notes. No demands for money, no demands for anything."

MAYBE THEY HAVEN'T BEEN SENT YET.

Vaughn sat down on the loveseat by Jamie's bed. His brother made a certain sense. This could all be wrapped up pretty neatly without any grand scheme. But some things still didn't compute. The dots could be connected, but the figure they were outlining remained pretty distorted. Vaughn watched his brother flip through screen after screen on his computer monitors using the mouthpiece. It struck him that his brother could have done anything had life—no, had *he*—not dealt Jamie the blow of losing use of his body. Smart, handsome, personable, and trapped in a useless frame. But if Jamie didn't view his own life with such a pitiful lens, who was he to color it that way?

Yes, he had been the cause of Jamie's undoing. But maybe it was time to let go.

Guilt and shame had driven Vaughn to succeed where he may not have. But it had also driven him to, in his own way, hide from life. That was what Mia was trying to tell him, he understood that now. She believed he was as reclusive as she, and she didn't want to be his escape. She was letting go so that he could let go, too.

Vaughn rubbed his temples. Maybe Mia was right.

Jamie cleared his throat and Vaughn looked up.

THIS IS INTERESTING.

Vaughn stood to get a better look at the screen Jamie seemed to be focused on. All he saw were numbers and small text. Nothing jumped out at him.

THIS IS THE EARNINGS REPORT FILED BY TRANSITIONS.

Jamie glanced at him. THE COMPANY REPORTED MUCH HIGHER THAN EXPECTED LOSSES IN THE FIRST TWO QUARTERS, DESPITE A 22% JUMP IN REVENUE. ITS OPERATING MARGIN IS IN THE NEGATIVES.

"English."

THE COMPANY IS BLEEDING MONEY.

"Why?"

AT FIRST GLANCE, BECAUSE OF HEAVY INVESTMENTS IN U.S.-BASED SUPPLIERS. THIS MUST BE PART OF THEIR GREENER "MADE IN THE USA" CAMPAIGN. SCOTT'S BABY. Jamie looked troubled. ONLY SOME OF THESE NUMBERS DON'T MAKE SENSE.

He glanced at Vaughn in a way that Vaughn remembered from youth, a glance that said, I'm heading into The Zone; leave me alone.

"I'll leave you to your deciphering," Vaughn said. "While you read these reports, I'm gonna talk to Mrs. T and find out where our dinner is."

Vaughn found Mrs. T at the kitchen table, her nose buried in Elizabeth George's latest tome. She looked up.

"You startled me, Christopher," she said, giving him a half-smile. "That Barbara Havers, she does make some dumb decisions. I do like spending time with her, though." The older woman placed a worn marker in her book and closed the hardback. "What do you need?"

Vaughn sat down across from her. "What's wrong?"

"Why do you think something's wrong?" She tried to look affronted by his question but couldn't quite pull it off.

"Because you're sitting in the kitchen reading a book, for one. Usually you'd be in there," he motioned toward Jamie's room, "reading to him. Secondly, I don't smell anything. When was the last time I came home and you didn't have some delightful concoction cooking away on the stove or in the oven?" He mock-peered into her face. "So tell me what's wrong."

Mrs. T sat back, looking worried. Her hair was done in neat plaits that were wrapped in a bun on her head. She was a large woman, but today she wore a soft orange dress that complemented the ebony tones in her dark skin. Despite that, she looked tired to Vaughn. Tired and sad.

"Milton is sick," she said. "Cancer."

Vaughn let the words sink in. "Karen." He had never used her first name, but it seemed right in this context. He held out his hand and she placed hers in it. It felt small and soft and frail. "I'm sorry."

She shook her head slowly back and forth. "What needs done, needs done, you know that as well as I. I am giving myself exactly one day to get used to this news and then I will make sure he and I find the good in this God-awful situation. This is only a call to arms."

"I know you'll fight."

Mrs. T stood. She placed her book neatly on the corner of the table and walked toward the cabinet that held the pots. "In the meantime, don't you tell that boy what's going on. He doesn't need to be burdened with this at a time when he's so happy."

Happy? Vaughn looked at the nurse questioningly.

"Angela and Jamie are an item," Mrs. T said. This time her smile was heartfelt. "Your brother's in love." She bent to pull a cast iron frying pan from the cupboard. "And if you could stop worrying that Angela is going to break that boy's heart, maybe you could feel happy for him yourself."

Vaughn just stared at her, too startled to speak. How did she know?

"Because he told me," she said, reading his expression. "Don't look so surprised, Christopher. Jamie and I talk."

"Then you should tell him about your husband."

"In time," she said, now at the refrigerator. She pulled out eggs and cheese. "Once I can tell him without crying, I will. For now, let him be lost in whatever nonsense he's researching." She turned abruptly, her face on the verge of collapse. "And I will make you an omelet, Christopher. Not because you need it—I think I see a little fat around your middle—but because I need to *do* something."

"Well, don't let me stop you."

Mrs. T laughed. "You always did support charity work."

THIRTY-THREE

Mark's office was a stark contrast from her own. Utilitarian, dirty and crowded were words Allison would have used to describe it, and that would be generous. He had a small reception area, a conference room that doubled as a law library and his own cramped office. The place smelled of Italian hoagie and stale cigarette smoke. The hoagie smell came from the crumpled wax paper in the trashcan, presumably Mark's dinner remnants, and the cigarette smell emanated from the man before her.

Mark folded himself into a chair in the meeting room. "Sit. Talk. Unburden yourself."

"I won't take up much of your time. I'm still trying to understand what happened to Scott and—"

"Sounds like you never got over my brother."

"To the contrary," Allison said. "I hadn't thought of him in years. Until...until Leah called me, after he was killed."

Mark waved his hand dismissively. "Leah. He should never have married her. Scott should never have married anyone. He wasn't meant for that life."

"Because of his philandering ways?"

"Because he couldn't keep his dick in his pants, to put it simply," Mark smiled. "My brother had a thing for women. I'm afraid being his wife wasn't easy."

"Is that why she was here?"

Mark's facial expression hardened. "What do you want, Allison?"

Allison studied the man before her. It was hard to believe he was Scott's brother. Where Scott had been all hard angles and muscle,

Mark was soft and squishy. He may have been attractive once, but his jowly face, red nose and beady eyes gave him the look of a longtime alcoholic.

"The police have arrested three boys for your brother's murder."

Mark nodded. "And?"

"Do you believe they did it?"

"Why wouldn't I?"

"You told me before he wasn't into drugs."

"I also told you he was probably in the wrong place at the wrong time. I still believe that."

Allison cocked her head. "What would Scott have been doing on that block on that morning?"

Mark sat back, stretched his arms over his head. "How the hell would I know? A hooker? Lost? But clearly he was. And it got him killed."

Allison wasn't buying it. "Scott's latest fling, a woman named Eleanor Davies, is missing. Did you know her, Mark?"

"Did I know her? No. Did I know of her? Yes. My brother was rather fond of Eleanor, at least in the carnal sense. She had, shall we say, few boundaries."

"He told you that?"

"Scott told me a lot of things."

"Is it possible that Eleanor had your brother murdered, Mark?"

Mark laughed, a hearty, mean laugh. "Are you joking? Why would his girlfriend want him dead?"

"I don't know." And that was the sad truth of it, Allison realized. She didn't know. She had just come here hoping something would connect for her, that her intuition would begin sending off alarms. Her mobile buzzed, indicating a text, but Allison ignored it. "Maybe he'd recently ended the relationship and she hadn't accepted that well."

"So she killed him for revenge?" Mark scowled. "I don't think so." Mark leaned in and, from across the desk, Allison could smell onions on his breath. "Why are you really here, Allison?"

"I just told you why I'm really here. Lingering questions. That's all."

"You can't let go."

"Of Scott? I let go long ago. Of a need for the truth?" Allison looked away. Her mind wandered to Jason, to her sister's daughter, to a cat left out in the cold. "No, I suppose I can't."

"Then I am going to tell you something very important. Scott was a no-good bastard. He didn't care about his family, including me, and he especially didn't give a rat's ass about his wife. The only thing he cared about, really cared about, was his job. Things were slipping, he was getting heat, and he made stupid decisions based on that. He succumbed to the pressure."

The disgusted look on Mark's face told Allison exactly what he thought of people who succumbed to the pressure.

"For what? That's what I can't wrap my arms around." And why the photos, Allison thought, why send them now? But she couldn't share that. Not with Mark, of all people.

"He was human."

"The job—was it too much for him? You were the matchmaker for the position. Did you have doubts?"

Mark sat back. "I'm the older brother. Do you know what it's like to see a younger sibling make bad choices again and again and be helpless at stopping them?"

Indeed, Allison did, but that was something else she wouldn't say.

"That's how it was with Scott. He had such talent: good looks, charisma, brains. But he always did something to screw it up."

Something in the way Mark spoke caused Allison to wonder whether his brother's shortcomings were less a reason for concern than a source of self-worth. As long as his brother made bad choices, Mark could be the better person and have something to lord over him.

"So yeah, I had doubts," Mark said. "Scott had screwed up at his last job. He had a series of extramarital affairs that could have ended poorly. And my ass was on the line with this job, too. I'm the one who convinced Brad Halloway to hire him in the first place."

"You and Brad are friendly?" Somehow Allison couldn't see it.

That stopped Mark. "You know him?"

"Yes. He helped me with some charity work years ago."

Mark looked at her over steepled fingers.

"Really. Wouldn't have guessed that." He shrugged. "Doesn't matter. The bottom line is my brother was a fuck-up, plain and simple. And now he's dead. There's a moral there, but I'm still trying to figure out what that moral is."

Mark's desk phone rang. "Excuse me," he said and answered it. "Sure, come up," he said into the receiver. To Allison, he said, "My son."

Allison rose, happy for the exit strategy. "I appreciate your time."

"I didn't tell you anything new."

"It all helps." And it did. Allison felt like maybe buried in this discussion was a nugget or two that might offer some insight. "If you hear from Eleanor, please give her my number." Allison passed her card. "I have her cat."

Mark smiled.

"Perfect. You have her p—"

"No," Allison didn't let him finish. "Don't do that. None of this is a joke, Mark. None of it."

Mark looked offended. Before he could fire back, the glass door opened and Mark's son, Shawn, walked in. His jeans were covered in bright splotches of paint, and a forest green hoody was ripped at the cuffs. He carried a large leather art portfolio in one hand and a camera bag across his shoulder. He stopped short when he saw Allison.

"Didn't know you had company, *Dad.*"

"She's leaving."

Allison nodded to the younger Fairweather. "That, I am."

Allison headed toward the door, aware of two sets of eyes on her back. She wasn't sure which of the Fairweather men made her more uncomfortable, Mark or Shawn. Happy she didn't have to choose, she walked back into the night.

The text was from Mia. *Call me immediately.* Allison did but got no answer. In frustration, she checked her email. Nothing from Mia, but Delvar had sent her a note. In it, he'd attached the guest list for the award celebration. Hope you find what you need, he'd written. Let's lunch soon. The attachment was hard to read on her phone, so Allison saved it for later. She got back on the road, dreading a trip to a Jason-less house. Feeling sorry for herself, she put on some Jack Johnson and let herself feel mellow. She needed to think. She needed a plan.

About twenty minutes into the drive, her phone rang. Mia.

Mia said, "Thomas found two addresses. Both properties belong to Doris Ann Long, originally of Connecticut. Your tip about her interest in guns was the answer. She'd created an LLC a few years ago, probably to shield herself from liability. Shrewd woman. Really hasn't used the company since. She has no losses or income."

"Two addresses?"

"One's in Connecticut—maybe her childhood home?—and the other is in Maine. Rural Maine. I just texted you the addresses. The Maine location may be hard to find. A quick Google Maps search showed that it's somewhere inland, off the mid-coast."

"Was Svengetti able to tell where Doris currently lives?"

"He thinks it's the Maine address. The other is listed as a rental property, although she hasn't claimed any rental income in some time. I bring it up because it's possible Eleanor is staying there."

Allison considered her options. She had a fairly open day tomorrow, and Jason wouldn't be home anyway. But if Eleanor was there, that could spell danger. After the last encounter with danger, she was in no mood for more violence.

"Can you watch Brutus and Simon the cat?"

"Promise me you're not going alone."

"I'll take Vaughn, if he can go."

"Then yes, I'll watch the animals." Mia hesitated, and Allison picked up on the undercurrent of maternal concern. She was grateful, but she'd been down this path before and trusted herself to do it again. "You promised," Mia said eventually, "that this would be the last avenue. There is no guarantee that Eleanor will be with Doris Long. If Eleanor is a dead end, no pun intended, you stop."

Allison was slow to respond. She *had* promised, though, and she would keep her word. And Mia was right: there were no guarantees. But she had a hunch, and she was also learning to trust her hunches. "You're right," she said. "If I don't have any luck with Eleanor, I will put this whole issue to bed. Pinky swear."

Vaughn wasn't available.

"Sorry, Allison," he said, sounding genuinely upset. "Duty calls. I told Mrs. T to go home early, she has some family stuff going on, and now it's Jamie and me for the night."

"That's okay," Allison said. She'd just fed Brutus and Simon and left detailed instructions for Mia on the kitchen island. Her bag was packed, and she was ready to go. "What does tomorrow look like?"

"Just wait a minute, okay?"

While she held, Allison watched Brutus and Simon. Brutus was licking the cat's face, one eye on her, one on the cat's leftover food. Her heart swelled with affection for that dog. He'd been in her life for less than two years, but when she considered how terrified she had been of dogs, of anyone or anything that needed her so totally, she realized she owed him a debt of gratitude. "A whole box of treats when I get back," she told him. "And a new toy."

She could have sworn Brutus smiled.

"I'm back," Vaughn said. "I was hoping Angela could come tonight but she's away. Chicago. She'll be here in the morning, though. We could leave then."

Allison wanted to get an early start. If she left now, she could at least see if the Connecticut house was a non-starter, as Mia seemed to suspect.

"How about this," she said. "I'll head to the Connecticut house tonight. If it's not occupied, there's no sense in wasting time. Then you can meet me in Maine. Also, I'm going to forward you the list of attendees at Delvar's award ceremony. Can you ask Jamie to cross-reference it against Scott's co-workers at Transitions?"

"Sure." Vaughn hesitated. "Wait for me before you go into either house. If the Connecticut house is promising, wait for me there. Please don't go in alone."

Allison was hopeful, but her instincts said the Connecticut house wouldn't be promising. "I will," she said. "I reserved two rooms at a little hotel in Maine, about five miles from Doris's residence. I'll email you the details. If you don't hear from me otherwise, meet me there tomorrow afternoon."

"Okay," Vaughn said. He didn't sound sure, but Allison wasn't going to give him time to change his mind. She hung up with a "thank you" and reached for her coat. Brutus glared at her balefully. "You know I'm leaving, huh boy?"

Brutus put his head between his paws, holding her gaze. Simon was now asleep beside him.

The last thing Allison did before leaving was to call Jason. He didn't answer, and she hadn't expected him to. "I love you," she said. And then, at a loss for words, "That's all I called to say."

THIRTY-FOUR

It was after midnight when Allison arrived in New Haven. She made due with a Motel 6 off the highway and climbed into her queen-size bed. Her body ached. It struck her that in her desire to get on the road, she'd failed to bring her Fairweather file with her. No matter. If she met Eleanor, she could articulate her questions without the information she'd gathered. It was all in her head.

She lay down, thinking of what she'd ask and how she would approach the other woman. Allison should be a pro at this. Instead, she felt anxious and jittery, ready for it to be over.

Silently, she cursed whoever had been sending those photographs, especially the one sent to Jason. He was hurt, she knew that, and it tore at her soul.

Maybe he's better off if I just walk away, Allison thought.

She realized that the mere concept of life without Jason was maddening. She wanted more. And she would wait until he was ready and could trust her again. It was her turn to be patient. If he opted out, it would be devastating. But how could she blame him?

Outside, a steady drizzle tapped the window. Between the rain, her nerves and the traffic sounds emanating from along Route I-95, Allison couldn't sleep.

She considered her conversation with Mark Fairweather. Something about him and his son, Shawn, struck her as particularly odd, but she couldn't say exactly what. It was as though some element of that meeting had clung to the edges of her psyche like toilet paper on a shoe. She couldn't quite see it, nor could she shake it.

It was hours before her eyes got heavy enough to close. Just as she was drifting off to sleep, she heard her phone. The insistent *buzz, buzz* became interwoven with her dreams, and instead of answering the call, she saw a colorful parade of images in her mind's eye: Jason, Mia and baby Grace, all staring at her, accusing her, against the backdrop of a vast construction scene. None of it made sense, and Allison's final thought before the bliss of unconsciousness took over was that she'd better wake up. Someone was in trouble.

Vaughn was ready to go by seven the next morning. He'd packed clothes for every contingency: a winter coat (wasn't Maine cold? He'd never been there), hiking boots, and even a coat for Allison, in case she'd run out of her house before thinking through what she'd really need. His boss was level-headed and calm under pressure, but she also became almost a savant when chasing a trail, all focus and limited common sense. It was his job to make sure the details were secured.

Vaughn checked in on Jamie. He was in bed, sound asleep. Vaughn knew his brother had been up late, researching Transitions and Scott Fairweather and tracking down the names on that list Allison had received from Delvar. He'd been unusually quiet, and Vaughn had no idea of what Jamie had found, if anything. His brother was as dogged about following a trail as Allison was. And Jamie was usually reluctant to speak until he'd pieced together what he thought was a rational picture.

So they would wait until Jamie was ready.

At 7:30, Vaughn started to get restless. Angela was supposed to have flown in from Chicago last night. She should be here by now.

He forced himself to make some toast and sit down for breakfast. She'd be here. And until then, Allison would be fine.

Allison was up by eight. After a brief and unsatisfying shower—lukewarm water and weak pressure—she dressed quickly in jeans and a black wool turtleneck sweater. It was still drizzling out, and the sky looked overcast and angry. It would be an unpleasant drive, especially if the rain turned to snow or sleet as she headed north.

She quickly packed her bag. She was pulling a few bills out of her wallet to leave for the cleaning staff when she remembered her phone. A few seconds of wishful thinking—maybe it had been Vaughn with news from Jamie—were quashed when she glanced at the caller ID. A number she didn't recognize.

The caller left a message, one she listened to with a heavy heart.

Amy had signed herself out of treatment AMA. Against medical advice.

The administrator who called said they had also contacted Faye because they believed Amy's first stop would be to get her daughter. Allison called the center back. They were recommending Grace stay with relatives until child protective services could be called in. They had concerns about her safety given Amy's erratic behavior and lifestyle choices.

A call to Faye went unanswered.

Allison sat down on the bed. This was bad news, for her sister and her niece. For all of them. Could things get any worse?

Retract that, Allison thought hastily. Experience had told her that things could always get worse.

By eight-fifteen Vaughn was worried. He called Angela's phone again and got no answer. Jamie was still asleep, but he couldn't be left alone. If something happened, Vaughn would never forgive himself. He toyed with calling Mrs. T but opted not to. She needed time with her husband right now. Angela would come through. He had to have faith. In the meantime, Allison was a smart woman. She would be fine.

Allison stared at the building before her. It was a three-story house on the outskirts of New Haven, in a neighborhood that had once been solidly middle class but was now what some might call ghetto. It was clear no one was living here on any legitimate, permanent basis. The front door was shuttered closed and a condemnation notice had been posted on it next to a "No Trespassing" sign. The windows in the front, too, were boarded up. A broad front porch was covered in leaves and litter. The small yard in front of the house was overgrown with thistle and Johnson grass. Allison thought about going door-to-door, but a glance around changed her mind. Most of the houses were in similar states of disrepair.

Allison climbed out of the Volvo and locked the doors. A peek through the boards hammered to one of the front windows revealed an empty living room. Hardwood floors had been swept bare. Such a shame, she thought. High ceilings, nice floors, old trim. This could have been a beautiful residence. Instead...decay.

Allison made her way to the side of the house to get a better look inside. Every room told the same story. Nice house with good bones, abandoned. She didn't see any signs of squatters, either. Disappointed, she finally admitted defeat. She'd move on to Maine.

THIRTY-FIVE

Allison had stopped at a rest area somewhere along I-495 in Massachusetts when Vaughn called to say that Angela was delayed due to a cancelled flight. He'd meet her at the hotel sometime this evening. He had information to share, but it would have to wait until he could lay it all out for her.

"I can't wait," Allison had said. "Fill me in."

But Vaughn wouldn't budge. "I have something to check out first. I'll know more when I see you."

"Call me later."

"Only if you wait for me to get there."

In the end, Allison promised not to go to Doris Long's house alone.

But she *didn't* promise not to scope out the area.

Angela finally arrived, breathless and full of apologies, at eleven that morning. Vaughn had thanked her, but he didn't wait around to chit chat. He'd needed to get on the road.

Now, staring at the complex in front of him made him contemplate his brother's sanity. The address for Mills Manufacturers took Vaughn to a lot in a small industrial park outside of Camden, New Jersey. The park itself was a sprawling commercial wasteland not far from the Schuylkill River. At the mouth of the park, two factories sat side-by-side, separated by a small field of high, brown weeds and litter. The first factory was surrounded by a u-shaped parking lot, half full with cars. Plumes of steam streamed from two smokestacks. The other factory appeared abandoned. High walls of barbed-wire fencing protected three white buildings with red roofs. Most of the windows in the facing building were broken. Despite the barbed wire, graffiti tattooed the paint. A tilted sign had been boarded over so that the company name was no longer visible. Vaughn drove on.

Deeper in the industrial park, he passed several additional small factories. Like the first, these seemed to be operating. He kept going until he found the address he was looking for, set back at the end of a dead-end road. Mills Manufacturer shared a field with another abandoned factory. This one, identified only as Brown & Co Metals, was encased by two layers of barbed wire fencing, which extended beyond the monstrous, ivy-covered walls of the outbuildings.

Unlike Brown & Co, Mills Manufacturing's single building was pristine and occupied. A parking lot in front of the building contained a dozen cars.

He was here at Jamie's behest. Jamie had given him strict instructions: don't give your name and park where your license plate is obscured. He hadn't explained what he wanted Vaughn to look for, though. He'd just asked him to pay close attention to the building and its surroundings, and to see what the company was producing. He said he'd fill him in on everything he found once he had information on the manufacturer. Vaughn felt anxious to get moving north, but Jamie had been insistent.

After parking in a corner of the lot next door, Vaughn walked over to Mills Manufacturing. A metal gate at the entry blocked his admittance, and he couldn't see an intercom or any way of communicating with the folks inside. He finally spotted a small camera hiding in the eaves of the building, on the other side of the gate.

"Hey!" he shouted, hoping to get someone's attention. He had a story prepared—he was a reporter doing an article on abandoned factories and wanted to ask about the property next door—but that would only work if someone let him the hell in.

After a few minutes of shouting, the front doors opened and a beefy man with a crew cut came to the gate. He wore maintenance khakis and carried a walkie talkie. "Yeah?" he grumbled.

Vaughn explained his reason for being there, adding a little flair to make his cover story sound believable. "So I was hoping to get some information on Brown & Co, maybe from someone who was here when the factory closed."

The guy shook his head. "Sorry, none of us has been around here that long."

"New business?" When the man nodded, Vaughn glanced around the factory grounds, pretending to notice this building for the first time. "Taking advantage of cheap rent?" he asked with a nod toward the abandoned factory next door.

"I dunno," the guy said. "Just the maintenance crew."

"Hard work," Vaughn said. "My dad was maintenance back when Exelon was Philadelphia Electric. Backbreaking." He made a grimace that he hoped came off as sincere. The only work his dad had done was lifting the belt to swing it toward Vaughn's behind.

With a grunt, the guy said, "Yeah, not appreciated, either."

"What do you guys make? Car parts?"

"We'll make textiles, once we're up and running. Right now, we're primarily a machine shop."

Vaughn nodded, not wanting to push it and cursing his brother for not telling him specifically what he was looking for. "How long you been here?"

"The machine shop has been around for a few years."

"And you're expanding for the textile business?"

The guy's eyes narrowed. "This part of your article?"

"Nah, just curious."

The guy shrugged. With a backwards glance at the front of the building, he said, "Supposed to be up and running soon. Got no idea when it'll happen, though. Until then, as long as they keep paying me, I show up." He touched his walkie talkie, which sat silent on his hip. "That it?"

Vaughn nodded. "Appreciate your time."

The guy stayed put, waiting to make sure Vaughn headed back in the direction of his vehicle. Vaughn walked without looking back, but once he got to the field that adjoined the two factories, he checked to make sure the maintenance man had gone inside and then he followed the abandoned building's perimeter around back to get a glimpse of the rest of Mills Manufacturing. He saw nothing out of the ordinary. The factory, which extended far back into the field beyond, looked in good repair, and the property seemed secure.

Maybe Jamie's losing it, Vaughn thought.

Halfway through the industrial park, Vaughn dialed Jamie's number. He reached Angela. "Put me on speaker," he said. "I called to give Jamie an update on Mills Manufacturing."

Allison arrived in Camden, Maine, a little after three in the afternoon. She stopped for a basket of fish and chips and a beer, hoping the combination would calm the snakes twisting in her gut. It only made her bloated. With only an hour of daylight left, Allison headed toward Dunne Pond. The sky remained clear, although the rain she'd encountered in Connecticut and Massachusetts threatened. Soon it would be cold and stormy. For now, it was just cold.

A few miles from the Dunne Pond Road, Allison located the small motel where she'd booked two rooms. It was called The Beach Hut. Well, they got it half right, Allison thought. A little far from the beach, but definitely a hut. She checked in and paid cash for her room and Vaughn's. The innkeeper, a guy in his early twenties with more pimples than facial hair, tried insisting on a credit card for incidentals but a one-hundred dollar bill seemed to quell his need to follow the rules.

Allison made her way to a cramped room with dated furnishings. Immediately to the left of the door was a bathroom. Beyond that was a full-size bed, dresser, chair and an old-school television. Flowered wallpaper did little to cheer worn wooden furniture and a matted beige carpet. A ceiling fan swirled overhead. The room smelled of disinfectant and mildew, but despite that, and despite the room's careworn appearance, Allison was happy to have a home base. She washed her face, brushed her teeth and popped two Excedrin to ward off the tension in her temples. Then she was off.

Dunne Pond Road was a meandering country lane that headed west, toward central Maine. Moose crossing signs were the only traffic warnings, and the forest, consisting mainly of coniferous trees, large boulders and whatever weeds sprouted up through rich peat, infringed on the asphalt so that Allison felt she was the only driver making her way through a fairy tunnel. Several miles along Dunne Pond Road, Allison passed a peeling sign advertising "Dunne Pond Resort, a

Summer Community." The sign, like the guard house at the mouth of the resort, had seen better days.

Allison saw no indication of a house or the driveway that might lead to Doris's place. She made a right into the old resort entrance and turned around. The sun was dipping below the western horizon and the thought of being alone in an abandoned resort gave Allison the chills. She headed southeast on Dunne Pond Road, scanning the left side for an entrance to a dirt road. Doris's drive didn't even exist on Google Maps. She finally spotted the entrance on the fifth pass. It was almost exactly across from a small, crooked sign for the old resort.

Allison kept driving, making a mental note about the location of that sign.

In the winter, Doris's driveway could be impassable without four wheel drive. On a day like today, it should be fine, although, Allison realized, there would be no way to drive down that driveway without giving herself away. It was better either to hike in or to wait for Vaughn, as she'd promised.

Despite her desire to talk with Scott's former lover, and ignoring a growing sense of urgency, Allison kept going, back toward the motel.

Night was pressing in. And Allison, having kept her promise, expected Vaughn to keep his. She'd call him once she was in the room so that he could explain his mysterious references.

She glanced at the car's clock. Only five-thirty-seven, but it felt like ten. No stopping for a real dinner tonight, she decided. The call to Vaughn and then bed. She wanted to be ready to come back here early tomorrow, before Doris Long—or Eleanor—had a chance to leave.

THIRTY-SIX

The sun had set fully by the time Allison arrived back at The Beach Hut. She'd stopped at a nearby gas station to purchase a bottle of iced tea and a Snickers bar. Armed with her well-balanced dinner, she locked the door of her room and settled in at her laptop. First order of business was a call to Jason. She knew he wouldn't answer, but she wanted him to know she was thinking of him. To her surprise, he picked up.

"Where are you?" he asked.

She hesitated. "In Maine."

"Scott." His voice was flat. Not accusatory, but...flat.

"I'm not here for Scott, Jason. I want the photos to stop. I want my life back." She paused, hoping he'd respond. When he didn't, she said, "Besides, I'm convinced three boys will go to jail for something they didn't do. That doesn't seem right, not if I can help it."

Allison waited through the silence. She could tell he wasn't happy, but at least he had answered the phone.

"Always saving the world," he said. With a sigh, he continued. "We need to talk."

Her heart skipped a few beats. "Do you want to call off the engagement, Jason?"

"Allison, why would you even ask that?"

Caught off guard by his tone, Allison realized she was holding the phone in a death grip. "Because you haven't spoken to me in three days. Because of the photograph. Because I'm always off trying to save the world, to use your words."

"Yeah, well...I'm sorry, Al. I needed space and time to think. It wasn't easy seeing that picture. I had some soul-searching to do. But I believe you when you said you have no feelings for him."

Allison said, "I love you."

Jason made a sound, something between a snort and a laugh. "That's it? 'I love you'? Well, I must love you, too, Al. Otherwise, I would have found some nice, normal woman who prefers yoga and needlepoint to saving the world, one crime at a time."

Allison smiled. "You'd be bored."

"I don't know," he said. "Boredom sounds pretty damn good right now."

Two attempts at reaching Vaughn ended in voicemail. She left a message for him to call immediately and booted up her laptop. First order of business was the email Delvar had sent her. A quick scan of the two-hundred-plus names rang no bells. She stared at that list, realizing that she was missing from the list, as was Delvar's mother, Vaughn and Jason. If they were missing, maybe others were, too.

She called Delvar and explained her concern.

"Just the board and their guests," he said. "And Mama. Everyone else was a paid invitee."

"The board of Designs for the Future?"

"Allison, sweetheart, what other board would I be on?"

Allison laughed. "Can you send me those names, too?"

"Sure."

Staring at her laptop screen, Allison asked, "Does the name Scott Fairweather ring a bell, Delvar?"

"No, never heard of him." He paused. "What are you up to, Allison? Why do you want these lists all of a sudden?"

"Would you believe me if I said I'm just curious?"

"No."

Allison's phone buzzed. Vaughn.

"Well, hopefully I explain everything eventually. For now, though, I have to go."

Allison hung up with Delvar and answered Vaughn's call. "About time."

"Yeah, well, my GPS seemed to think going through Manhattan

was the most efficient way to get there. I couldn't talk when you called. Too busy honking, like everyone else in this city."

Allison smiled. "Everything okay with Jamie? Angela finally show up?"

"She did. She looked exhausted, but she was thrilled to see Jamie." He hesitated. Before she could respond, he continued. "But that's not what we need to talk about. First thing: Jamie cross-referenced Delvar's list against everyone at Transitions and he came up with a blank. Society types, local academics, a bunch of philanthropists, some fashion folks from New York—no one of consequence—but no hits. In other news, though, things seem a little weird."

Allison settled against the bed.

"Tell me."

"I can't explain it as well as Jamie—he's the one who pieced it together—but hear me out. Remember the spin-off of Transitions from Diamond Brands?"

"Of course."

"Transitions had a lot of cash poured into that spin-off in order to make it successful and to reinvent the brand."

"Right, the LEED-certified buildings, the local contracts, the socially conscious agenda."

"Exactly. Let's start with the contracts. Jamie thinks they're bullshit."

"They're not making product in the U.S.?"

"The contracts they have entered into in the United States, the ones that are allowing them to say their products are made in the USA, don't seem legitimate."

Allison pulled her legs up under her on the bed.

"Wow, that's a damning allegation. How does Jamie know that?"

"Now you know why I didn't want to talk about this as I was driving through Brooklyn. It's complex. I stopped by one of the manufacturers that Transitions has contracted to make clothes here in the United States. Despite more than a year of hefty payments from Transitions, they're still not operating."

"The business is a front?"

"I don't know about that, but something is odd. It's an existing factory, so on the outside it looks legit, but when I stopped by, there was nothing really happening. That was Jamie's hunch from looking at the securities filings and researching the companies Transitions had entered into contracts with—that nothing is happening. At least not yet."

Allison thought about that.

"Who signs those contracts?" she asked.

"The head of purchasing."

"Eleanor." Allison's mind churned. "But to get away with it for so long—"

"There would have to be others involved. Exactly." Vaughn paused. "There's more, Allison. As you requested, Jamie looked at the spin-off itself: who was affected, who got fired, etc."

"And?"

"And Amelie Diamond was right. Her father neither forgave nor forgot."

"Those involved were let go?"

"To the contrary. None of them was fired. Ted Diamond made a big show about standing behind his people. At least to the public."

Allison was getting frustrated.

"Then how were they penalized, Vaughn?"

"I'm getting to that. From what Jamie could tell by the two companies' securities filings, one person was demoted but remained at Diamond. Craig Cummings. He has since left. Two others, the CFO and the COO, were spun-off with the company."

"So they kept their jobs?"

"Yes. But—"

"They took a salary cut?"

"Not exactly. Again, Jamie spent a lot of time sifting through securities filings. You would be amazed at the information available online, if investors are patient and savvy enough to look. What Jamie found is a trail of renegotiated agreements. Certain agreements with company officers have to be filed with the SEC. For the COO and the CFO, much more lucrative arrangements were cancelled and replaced with much less valuable terms."

Allison thought about that. She had some experience with executive contracts just based on her work with officers and directors from various companies. "In essence, Ted Diamond let them keep their jobs, but in return, they had to agree to new terms. Essentially, pay cuts."

"Not pay cuts, exactly. Their salaries didn't move much. But had they retired from Diamond Brands or been let go due to a change in control of the company, they would have been very rich. Now, under Transitions? Not so much."

"They were punished."

"Yes," Vaughn said quietly. "Looks that way."

"Reason for revenge?" Allison asked.

"Maybe."

She stood, pacing the length of the small motel room.

"But neither Scott nor Eleanor worked for Diamond."

"True, and that's where this becomes a little of a so-what proposition. What Jamie found is interesting, but nothing ties it to Scott."

"Other than Eleanor."

"Yes," Vaughn said. "Other than Eleanor."

"Who wasn't even part of Diamond Brands?"

"Right."

"So what does Jamie think?"

"He thinks something smells when it comes to Transitions. The company is losing money, and he believes many of the U.S. contracts it's entered into are bogus."

"Someone is committing fraud."

"And based on her history and the unexplained money in her bank account, that someone would seem to be Eleanor."

Allison climbed off the bed and walked to the window. She looked out over the motel parking area. The lot was poorly lit and, other than Allison's car and two others, empty. The encroaching forest coupled with the darkness lent to a feeling of isolation. Allison closed the drapes, giving in to a sudden chill that tingled its way down her spine.

"What if there is a conspiracy going on, Vaughn?" He started to say something and she said, "Hear me out. What if the men who were demoted to Transitions—because that's what it sounds like, a demotion—are colluding to defraud the company? What if Scott found out about it and was blackmailing them? It would have been in their best interest to make sure he couldn't tell."

"So they set him up? Made it look like he was living dangerously and took a hit."

"Right."

"But what about Eleanor?"

Allison sat back down, pulling her computer back on her lap. "My first thought is that she's in on the blackmail scheme, too, which is why she's on the run. But her connection to Duane doesn't support that."

"A coincidence?"

"Could be, yes, but do you really think there are any coincidences here?"

"So you think she set Scott up?"

"What if she and Scott had cooked up the scheme? She got greedy and wanted it all? She could have had him killed and run, taking the money with her."

Vaughn made a "hmmm" sound. "How do you explain Eleanor's dead sister?"

"The Philly police think it's unrelated."

"No coincidences, remember, Allison? You said it yourself."

"I did." Allison moved the computer mouse to get her screen running again. "And then there's the matter of the photographs. How do they fit in?" Allison yawned, exhaustion taking over. "Hopefully Eleanor will have some answers."

"If she's there."

"If she's there." Allison thought of something Vaughn said earlier. "The men who were transferred from Diamond Brands to Transitions, who were they?"

Vaughn became suddenly very quiet. "You won't like this. The Chief Operating Officer was a man named Brian—Bic—Friedman."

That name sounded familiar. "I met him. He was with Brad...oh, no..."

"And Brad Halloway was the CFO."

Allison closed her eyes. Of course he was. That was his current role at Transitions. "Then we have our story wrong," she said. "There's no way Brad would be involved in something like this. He's one of the most honor-bound men I know."

"As was Diamond."

"What are you getting at?"

"What if Halloway and Friedman truly believed they had done nothing wrong? Spent years helping to grow Diamond? The shit goes down overseas and suddenly their golden geese are cooked and their golden eggs are made of concrete. For a man like Halloway, a man who feels justice should always prevail, bringing down Transitions could feel like the right thing to do. He could convince himself he's acting for good."

"I don't know." I don't want to even contemplate that, is what I mean, Allison thought. For a period, Brad had been like a father to her. The thought that he could be behind corporate fraud...unthinkable. Allison recalled her last visit at the Halloway home. His wife's worsening condition, Brad's unrelenting cough.

"He's sick," Allison said, knowing in that instant it was true. "Brad's sick and he's worried about making sure Antonia can be cared for after his death."

"Perhaps. But how does running the company into the ground assure that his ill wife will be taken care of?"

"The change in control agreements. They're only triggered if there is a change in control of the company. Maybe he's trying to force a buy-out. The company does poorly, and someone comes and takes over. Happens all the time."

"But his agreement isn't that lucrative." Vaughn was quiet for a moment. "But there may be another piece to this. A piece I had dismissed until now."

Allison, a feeling of dread creeping up her spine, said, "What's that?"

"The third guy, Cummings. His new career? He left and started a venture capitalist firm."

Allison processed this new bit of information. "He comes in and buys the company. Suddenly things go rosy and everyone shares in the fruits. Brad and Bic get their severance and maybe even a behind-the-scenes cut in the new ownership structure."

"And they have the last say over Diamond."

"Scott learns all of this and he and Eleanor blackmail the company."

"She gets greedy and has Scott killed," Vaughn says.

Allison still wasn't so sure about that last part, but she didn't argue. "I bet if Jamie looks at that company Transitions hired to be the U.S. clothing supplier, buried below somewhere he'll find another shady connection. This time to Cummings."

"Mills Manufacturing. I'll have him look."

"This is starting to add up, Vaughn. We'll talk to Eleanor tomorrow, but even if she's not there...I think we're on to something."

Allison remembered her promise to Mia—that she would stop after Eleanor Davies. But that was before now, before this new information. If Eleanor wasn't there, she would turn all of this over to Berry. The detective might dismiss it, but she would have done her job.

She just wished she understood the photos. If their hypothesis was right, who was sending the pictures? And why? Was Scott reaching out beyond the grave, another element of his blackmail scheme gone awry? Had her name been in his calendar so that he could hit her up for money, only he was murdered before he had a chance to talk with her? If that was the case, maybe Eleanor had sent the photos, and she sent them anyway. But then why no demand for money? The information Jamie had found was critical, but things still didn't quite come together.

"Where are you now?" Allison asked.

"Stopped to get gas and coffee. I'm somewhere in New Hampshire, near Portsmouth."

"So you won't be here for a few more hours?"

"I guess," Vaughn said, sounding tired.

"You're checked in and paid for. I'm going to hit the sack." She gave him her room number. "Let's plan to get up early—say six?—and head over to Doris's place."

"Six? Fine, fine," Vaughn said jokingly. "I thought my first trip to Maine would be a vacation. Guess I was wrong."

"Yeah, things don't turn out as we think they should, do they?" Allison asked, thinking of Brad Halloway. "Keeps things interesting, I guess."

"That's one way to look at it."

"Be careful, Vaughn," Allison said before they hung up. "And thank you."

Vaughn laughed. "End of year is fast approaching. I see a bonus in my future. And all I want to do after this is get that Sexy Senior group started. Never thought I'd be so happy to work with Midge Majors." His voice became serious. "You be careful, too, Allison. And wait for me. I'll see you in the a.m."

THIRTY-SEVEN

Allison was ready to shut down her laptop and head to bed when a new email arrived from Delvar. It contained the list of the board members for Designs for the Future along with any of their guests that attended the ceremony. Allison scrolled through the names on the list. The board members were all familiar. As a board member to the fledgling group, Allison had met each of them at least once. But she hadn't met the guests. One person caught her eye.

Betty Diamond, guest of Beth Duvall.

A quick internet search explained the connection. Betty Diamond was Ted's elderly mother. Beth Duvall was his new wife. Beth Duvall *Diamond*.

She went by her maiden name professionally, so Allison never made the connection.

Allison's entire body went rigid. Suddenly things made more sense. She thought of Scott at Thirtieth Street Station: the way he'd tried to get her attention. Her trip to New York had been planned and very public. She always took the train, and he'd known that. But based on the photo of Allison and Scott at the station, someone had been watching him. He may have been afraid to go to her home or office, preferring the anonymity of a public place.

He'd also known about her connection to Delvar. Designs for the Future had been in the paper. Connecting Allison and Duvall to the charity wouldn't have been hard. He could find them all at the celebration. That was what the appointment book was about.

Scott wasn't trying to blackmail anyone. He'd been using Allison to get to Beth Duvall. Diamond Brands—specifically, the Diamond family—still owned a good portion of Transitions. Scott knew he was in danger. He was trying to tell Beth Duvall what was going on.

He wasn't a crook; he was trying to be a hero.

But what about the pictures? Whoever took that photo in Thirtieth Street Station knew about her history with Scott. Leah? Eleanor? If I'm right about Scott's motives, Allison thought, was Eleanor his partner in the quest for justice or was she in on the scheme? Or had she learned of the scheme and decided to profit from it through blackmail on her own?

Eleanor's history said she was an opportunist, and her role at Transitions said she had access and opportunity. Plus, there was the money trail and her connection to Duane Myers. If Duane pulled that trigger, not the boys who were arrested, it would have been because Eleanor paid him to do it. If Scott was threatening to blow the whistle, Eleanor may have had reason to kill him.

But then who killed Eleanor's sister? And why?

Ginny's death left Allison with the unsettling thought that there was a second murderer out there.

Allison shut down the computer and turned off the lights. After making sure the door was closed and the window secured, she climbed into bed. Sleep didn't come easily, the iced tea and knot in her stomach saw to that, but when it did come, it hit her hard.

Vaughn arrived at ten minutes to midnight. The clerk at the front desk, a thin, anemic-looking woman with ghostly-pale skin and knotted knuckles, handed him a key, an actual key.

"Room nineteen," she said with a raspy voice. She avoided eye contact, preferring instead to keep her eyes glued to the television. She was watching one of those home shows where people have to choose between three properties. Vaughn didn't wait to see which French apartment they picked. He was too tired to do anything but head to his room.

There, he stripped out of his jeans and long-sleeved t-shirt and put on sweats. He had a bad feeling, one he hadn't been able to shake since getting off the phone with Allison. He told himself it was left over from fighting traffic in unknown territory. He knew better. And this place out in the middle of nowhere didn't help.

Vaughn was a city boy. Too much fresh air made him antsy.

He set his alarm for five-thirty. One night in the woods would be enough. He was already ready to go home.

Allison awoke at three-fifty with a burning need to pee. It took her a hazy moment to realize where she was. She rolled out of bed and fumbled her way to the bathroom. Finished, she was washing her hands when something stopped her.

A man's refection in the mirror.

Allison blinked, her vision constricting. Her breath caught in her chest. Had she imagined it? She was suddenly afraid to move. No, someone was in the motel room. She started to turn on the light but stopped herself. Whoever it was might not realize she knew he was there. Surprise was her only weapon. *Think.* Silently, she reached for a can of hairspray. Weak, but it was all she had. She tucked it behind her and walked out of the bathroom, toward the door. She might be able to escape before he could reach her.

She had her hand on the knob when she felt an arm around her neck. She tried to turn, hitting her attacker in the ribs with her elbow, but his grip was too strong. He reached down and pulled the hairspray from her grasp before she could use it. She struggled, but it was no use.

She was trapped.

THIRTY-EIGHT

Eleanor set her alarm for four a.m. Today was the day, one way or another. The money would clear. Doris was primed. She had dollar signs in her eyes, so she was only too happy to cash those checks and be rid of Eleanor. And Eleanor would be off, ready to cross the border and start a new life.

She was tired, angry and nervous, but she welcomed the adrenaline pumping through her system. Adrenaline would get her where she needed to go. But for now, she needed a release. She'd go for a run.

In the dark, she slipped off her pajamas and put on a sports bra and her insulated running tights. She ruffled through her bags until she found her Under Armour top, a gray hoodie and insulated socks. Then she slid a headlamp over her forehead. Lastly, she secured a GPS watch onto her wrist, tied her running shoes and put on Doris's parka.

With a glance at Doris's door, still closed, she headed out. She didn't feel remotely guilty for drugging Doris and the dogs last night. Even if she wasn't trying to sneak around, the drugs meant Doris went to bed earlier. That meant no stupid television shows, and Eleanor could get to sleep.

On the landing, the cold air hit her like a shotgun blast. Eleanor pulled gloves from her pockets and pulled them on as she jogged toward the back of the property. She turned the headlamp on and, with the help of the strong beam from the lamp, headed toward the trail.

She was three feet from the forest entrance when she noticed the car parked on the dirt road that led to Doris's house. It was around the bend, not visible from the house. But from this angle, she saw the glint of silvery paint through the trees.

Momentarily panicked, she started to run, unsure where she was headed.

Something hit her in the back. She stumbled, then fell to the ground.

"How many times have I told you? You can't run from your mistakes, Eleanor."

The voice stopped her cold. Before she could react, she felt a sharp blow to the head. Then nothing.

Allison struggled all the way to the car. She couldn't speak—a hand gripped her mouth—and she couldn't see because whoever her attacker was kept her facing forward, away from him. She tried to kick at walls as she was forced through the motel, but with each attempt, her assailant increased the vise on her arms.

Vaughn. She knew he was here. She just wished she had some way to scream.

She tried biting the hand over her mouth but her assailant was clamping down on her mouth so hard she could barely breathe.

Outside, the air was frigid. Her attacker pulled her toward a waiting vehicle, a plain black Chevrolet Malibu.

It was there that he let go, jamming a gun between her ribs. The metal was hard, adding injury to the cold wind that pummeled her half-naked body. She turned to face her attacker, ire in her eyes.

Mark Fairweather.

Of course. The matchmaker. Allison spit on the ground, ridding herself of his taste. "You bastard. You betrayed your own brother."

"Get in the car."

"No."

He jammed the gun harder. "Now."

Allison thought about running, but she was barefoot. If she stumbled, he would shoot her. She considered screaming, but a glance at the sleepy motel told her no one would come to her rescue. Unless Vaughn could hear her. By then, she could be dead.

The look in Mark's eyes said he wasn't screwing around.

"That's a girl," he muttered as she climbed into the front. He kept the gun aimed at her through the windshield as he made his way around. "Nothing will happen if you cooperate. Now, hold out your hands."

Allison did so and Mark placed a pair of metal handcuffs securely on her wrists. "When we get there, I'll take them off." He looked at her almost apologetically. "You are a hard-headed bitch."

"Don't call me a bitch."

Mark's eyebrows arched up. "All this, and that's what offends you?"

"What offends me is that you betrayed your brother. You got him that job at Transitions. Tell me, Mark, did you know from the start that Brad and Bic were scheming to get back at Diamond, or did that come later?" Allison shook her head. "And Eleanor, were you banging her all along?"

Mark smiled. "Sorry, you got it wrong." He started the car. "Eleanor and I were never together."

"Then where are we going?"

He glared at Allison, but instead of responding, he steered the car out toward the road. Allison fought a rising sense of panic. "Stop," she said. "If you go back, I'll give you the evidence I've collected."

"Evidence of what?"

"Evidence that you, Brad Halloway and Bic Friedman have been conspiring to defraud Transitions' shareholders, including the Diamond family."

Mark's jaw clenched. He slammed on the gas, causing the car's tires to squeal as he raced from the parking lot. "You have no evidence, Allison, because it's not true."

"Securities filings are public. All it takes is someone smart enough to connect some dots, and a picture emerges. One of greed, retribution and carelessness. Because telling Scott was careless."

"No one told Scott anything."

"Then he figured it out. And when Eleanor couldn't convince him to blackmail you, she had him killed." Allison waited for the surprise she knew would cross his features. "I know about Duane Myers. I know Eleanor paid him to kill Scott. I know that you're after her."

Mark looked at Allison with an odd mix of frustration and pity. "You've dug yourself quite a hole. My brother was crazy about you. Did you know that?" He shook his head. He reached out one hand and stroked Allison's cheek. She pulled away. His face reddened and for a second Allison thought he would slap her, but he lowered his hand.

"No more talking, or I put something in your mouth, too."

"I—"

"Uh-uh. No more." He turned on the radio. The only thing he could find was a gospel music station. He drove along to *Amazing Grace*, one hand clamped to the wheel, the other holding the gun. "Just be a good girl and stay quiet. I'd like to say we can make a deal on this one, but I'm afraid the time for that is over."

Vaughn had been sleeping restlessly, but the squeal of tires on gravel jolted him awake. He sat up, startled, and fumbled for his glasses. He looked outside. Both his car and Allison's were still in the lot. Probably kids, he thought. Still. He traded sweats for jeans, brushed his teeth and packed his bag. The clock by his bed read 4:08. Too early to wake Allison.

He looked out the window again. Why were kids driving around so early?

It was dark, and by the weak light of the parking lot spotlights, he could only make out a few cars. The motel office lights were on, though. Maybe there'd be coffee.

He opened his door and stumbled into the hallway before remembering that he had to go outside to get to the office. He'd forgotten his coat. He headed back in, and that's when he noticed it: a small can of hairspray on the ground, by Allison's room.

Vaughn pounded on the door. "Allison, are you okay?"

No answer.

He knocked again, then tried the doorknob. Locked.

Adrenaline coursing through him, he sprinted down the hall and outside. He slammed the door to the office open so that it ricocheted against the back wall. The lights were on, but no one sat behind the small counter. A sign next to a pile of Maine brochures indicated that those arriving late should ring the bell. Vaughn rang the bell, and then he shouted, "Hey! Wake up! I need some help out here."

A few seconds later, the skinny woman from earlier came out

from behind a partition. "No need to yell," she scolded. She squinted at Vaughn. "What?"

"Room twelve. I need to get in."

"You, too?"

"What do you mean, 'you, too'? Who else was here?"

"The woman's husband. About two hours ago." She frowned. "I don't know what's going on here, but I'm not getting into the middle of some love triangle—"

"Let me into the room."

"I'm sorry, but I can't."

Vaughn took a threatening step in her direction. "Someone's life is in danger because you are an idiot. That man was not her husband. Let me in the damn room."

Looking frightened and confused, she took a second to make up her mind. Finally, she reached beneath the counter and grabbed a set of keys. "I'll take you," she said.

They found the room just as he was afraid they would—empty. Allison's bag was still on the dresser; even her shoes were there. What he did not see were her phone or her laptop.

"Describe the man who came by."

Like a hand-shy dog, the woman edged away from Vaughn. She said, "Medium height, forties, a little paunchy." She shrugged. "Nothing special."

Vaughn fought a losing battle to keep his temper in check. "Why the hell would you give him a key?"

"He said she was expecting him, but he didn't want to wake her. He knew the make of her car. I just thought—"

The flush in her face and her downcast eyes gave her away. Whatever she thought, it had been helped along by cash.

"Damn, damn, damn," Vaughn said. He glanced around, trying to figure out what to do next. The description of the guy didn't sound familiar. Someone Allison knew? Someone who'd followed her up here? Whom had she been talking to lately? He realized he didn't know. It could be any one of a dozen people.

He'd start with Eleanor. And on the way over, he'd call the police.

THIRTY-NINE

The dogs really were worthless. Eleanor thought maybe they'd at least bark, but the interior of Doris's cabin was as quiet and serene as a Christmas card photo, while out here Eleanor sat against the side of Bic's car with her head cradled in her hands. She regretted drugging them. Her face hurt, her skull hurt and, perhaps most of all, her ego hurt. She had been so close...so damn close to escaping with both her money and her life. How the hell had Bic and Brad found her here?

How, indeed?

She didn't have to wait long for the answer to that question. Within minutes, a second car pulled into the driveway. A plain Chevy that screamed rental car, the vehicle swerved around the man standing in front of Eleanor with his gun poised, and parked next to Doris's Subaru. Eleanor recognized the driver as Mark Fairweather. She recognized the blond beside him, too, as the image consultant Scott had slept with, Allison Campbell. Scott had been obsessed with her, convinced she was the way out of his mess.

Instead, she was their undoing. And now, Eleanor was pretty certain this woman had led the others to her.

Eleanor waited until Mark got out of the car. He came and stood in front of her, aiming a gun at her head.

"I should just finish this now," he said.

"Mark," Brad said in a warning tone. "Not yet."

Mark looked back at Brad, then Bic. There was tension between them, tension she'd tried hard to use to her advantage over the past eighteen months. She'd been successful, making them doubt their plan, making them doubt each other. Although that friction had backfired. Their jumpiness made them trigger happy. First Scott, then, as a warning to her, Ginny.

Maybe she could use that friction now.

"That's right, Mark," she said. "Listen to your puppet master. Wasn't this whole thing your idea? Yet somehow you seem to be the one always taking orders."

"Shut up," Bic said. "Or I'll let him pull that trigger." Bic nodded toward the car. "You have the other one?"

With a wary glance in Brad's direction, Mark nodded. "I followed her from Pennsylvania, after she left my office. She's alone."

"Did you touch her?" Brad asked.

"No." Mark pulled open the door to the sedan and helped the woman out of the car. She was cuffed. "She's fine."

"For God's sake, she's wearing pajamas," Brad said. He coughed and it took a minute for him to regain his breath. "You are truly an asshole."

Eleanor looked at Brad sharply, a smirk on her face. "Kettle, black," she said.

But Brad didn't respond. Ever since this started, she'd been *persona non grata* to him. Someone to use and discard, only he would never see it that way.

Bic said, "Give her a coat."

"She's barefoot."

"Really, Brad? Does it matter? We're going to kill her."

Brad looked from Bic to Allison and back again. Even with limited light thrown by the flashlights, Eleanor could make out Brad's expression: sorrow.

"It matters to me," he said. Brad looked at the Campbell woman. "I'm sorry you're mixed up in this. Sometimes, you have more ability than sense, my dear. You have always been like that."

Allison said simply, "Why, Brad?"

"Because life is not fair."

"That's an excuse, Brad, and you know it," Allison said. "I would have expected so much more of you." She paused. "I always had such respect for you. And now...?"

But Brad had turned away. "Get those handcuffs off her," Brad said to Mark. "And get her clothed." He looked at Eleanor, acknowledging her for the first time. "If you would be so kind, Eleanor. Your coat and your shoes, please."

"No way."

"Oh, Eleanor." Brad motioned to Bic, who raised his gun higher. "I have no time for your nonsense. Take off your shoes and coat."

"I don't want her shoes or coat," Allison said. But even as Allison was saying it, Mark was on top of Eleanor, pulling off her parka.

"Fine. Here."

She shoved Mark away and took off the coat. She tossed Allison her sneakers, too. She was thankful for the Thorlos padded socks. She'd be warm for a while, at least.

The other woman rubbed at her wrists. Only at Brad's insistence did Allison put on the shoes and coat. She looked ridiculous, standing there in her cotton flannel pajamas with Doris's coat and Eleanor's oversized running shoes.

"What now?" Eleanor said. "You want the money back? I can give you that."

Brad shook his head slowly, back and forth. "Both of you, come."

"Where are you taking us?" Allison asked.

"The woods, my dear. I'm afraid we're heading into the woods."

Vaughn drove ninety down Dunne Pond Road. It was still dark, and the road was completely unlit. He knew Doris Long's house was somewhere along the long stretch of country road, but he couldn't make out a damn thing. On the third pass, he slowed down and looked for light, movement, anything that might indicate people.

He saw nothing.

At the mouth of some kind of old resort, he turned around to try again. Doris's house was here. Somewhere.

Allison was terrified, but she refused to let her terror show. She followed Brad and the others toward the darkened tree line, about a hundred yards away. Mark had a gun to her back; Bic had a gun aimed at Eleanor.

She was cold. The wind swept through the small clearing. Her pajama bottoms did little to warm her legs, and her head and hands remained uncovered. She knew that was the least of her worries. Nevertheless, that, and guilt for wearing the other woman's ill-fitting clothes, still occupied her mind. It's the little things, Allison thought. In the end, it's always the little things.

Her mind was catapulting in a thousand directions, trying to get a handle on what was happening and why. Her hunch that Brad and Bic were working to defraud the company seemed right. She hadn't expected to see Mark, but now that she thought back, it made sense. He'd been the one to get his brother the job. And if this scheme had been his idea, he would have wanted someone he could control. Scott would have been controllable because of his vices and his status as the younger brother. Scott had been a perfect choice.

Until he wasn't.

"Move," Mark hissed. He shoved the gun into her back. Brad reached out and smacked him in the head.

"Stop. I warned you, Mark." To Allison, he apologized. "Antonia would never forgive me if she knew."

"You don't need to do this, Brad. Please. Think."

"I'm afraid I really have no choice."

He looked suddenly old, much older than his sixty-some years. "Cancer?" Allison asked, not unkindly.

"AIDS."

Allison glanced at him sharply.

"But there are so many treatments, Brad."

"Not once it's advanced to this degree." He smiled a dying man's smile. "I told you, life is not always fair. It's not easy being married to an invalid, no matter how deeply you love her. One time I strayed. One time too many. Unforgivable."

"And Antonia?" Even in the midst of this crisis, Allison found she cared.

"Negative for HIV. But then, she would be."

His scorn for Eleanor, even Julie, made more sense.

"Brad, it doesn't have to end this way. You do have a choice."

"I'm afraid it does. There's just too much at stake."

"Whoever let Mark into my motel knows I'm here. There's a trail.

First Ginny, now us. You won't be worth anything to Antonia in prison."

Brad turned suddenly to Mark. "Is this true about the motel?"

"I had to get to her somehow. Don't worry. They think I'm her husband. No one will make a connection."

Still, Brad seemed unsettled. Allison was thinking of a way to take advantage of the situation when from somewhere in the darkness, two shots rang out.

"What in the hell?" Brad shouted.

"I'll tell you what will be in hell!" A woman's voice screamed. "Your sorry asses!"

Another shot blasted from somewhere near the house. Allison stared in the direction of the sound. She saw light emanating from the small cabin. A woman was standing in the driveway with a rifle pointed in the air.

The woman lowered the rifle and aimed it in Bic's direction.

"What the hell do you think you're all doing on my property?" She screamed. "Three seconds to answer."

No one moved. She shot Bic, hitting him in the leg. He screamed.

"Answer me!"

Eleanor took off, into the woods. As the irate woman aimed the gun toward Mark and Allison, Mark dropped for cover. With only a fleeting glance in the shooter's direction, Allison fled. She headed for the woods, following Eleanor's lead. She could see the metallic stripes on Eleanor's sweatshirt.

Allison ran hard, harder than her lungs could handle, trying not to trip over the rocks and branches that littered the forest floor, and cursed every gym class she had skipped as a kid.

She heard running and heavy breathing behind her. It was Mark, who had scrambled up to chase her.

"Stop!" he yelled.

But Allison kept going. She knew from self-defense classes that when you're in the sights of a gunman, you should weave back and forth. Make him work for it. Allison did that—or tried to. She used the trees as shields, running from one to the next.

It was getting harder to keep up with Eleanor, though. "Please wait," she yelled at one point. She was almost as terrified of getting lost in the woods and dying of exposure as she was of being shot. Eleanor glanced back but kept going.

Mark was gaining on her. He fired. The sound rang out, hurting Allison's ears and making her stumble. She righted herself, using a tree as a crutch, and kept going. Tears stung her eyes. Her breathing was ragged and burned.

She thought of Jason and asked silently for his forgiveness.

She thought of her niece, who she would never get to know.

She thought of Vaughn. *Vaughn.* Mark wouldn't have known about him because he arrived so late. Would Vaughn follow her here? Would he put two and two together?

That was her hope. She kept running, propelled by the knowledge—the faith, really—that her friend was nearby.

FORTY

Vaughn heard gunshots through his open car windows, but he still couldn't find the damn turn-off. It was just too dark. He had a sense of where the road should be, though. Using the sounds of the shots as guides, he parked and started hiking along the road. Eventually, he saw a gap where the trees didn't quite meet. He bent down and touched dirt. *Bingo.* He sprinted back toward his car.

Where were the police? They'd sounded unconvinced but had agreed to send a car. Hopefully they'd arrive soon. Vaughn would call again, once he saw what was going on. If they had Allison...he didn't even want to consider that possibility. The thought of explaining all this to Jason left him cold.

He pulled the BMW onto the dirt road, following it as fast as his chassis would let him. If these situations continue, he thought, I'm getting myself a more rugged vehicle.

And a damn gun.

Allison's lungs were searing. Mark was still behind her. He fired off another shot, then another. She stumbled, almost fell. He was gaining on her. She dug deep, willing herself forward.

"Damn," she heard Mark hiss. She closed her eyes when she heard the click of the trigger. Then nothing.

He was out of bullets. Allison swung behind a tree, resting her back against the rough surface of the trunk to catch her breath. Her eyes, now fully adjusted to the darkness, could make him out, down below on a small ridge. He was bent over double, staring at the gun he'd flung to the ground. Giving a silent prayer of thanks, Allison took off again, heading in the direction Eleanor had gone.

She didn't get far. About fifty yards away, she found Eleanor kneeling on the ground, her hand covering her upper left thigh. As Allison approached, Eleanor said, "He got me."

Allison looked behind her, debating. Finally, she squatted beside Eleanor. The woman was shivering, and while Allison couldn't see the extent of the damage, she saw enough blood to know it was serious.

Rustling from below caught her attention. "He's coming," Allison said.

"Don't leave me."

Allison stood. She should leave her, just like Eleanor had gone ahead without her. But she couldn't. If she was going to die tonight, Allison didn't want her last act to be one of cowardice. With a resigned huff, she put her arms around the Eleanor and helped her up. "We need to wrap that leg," she whispered. "But not here."

"I know a place," Eleanor said. "Go that way."

Eleanor pointed off to the left and Allison followed her direction. Eleanor was leaning on her, which made going tougher, but the woman was still strong. Allison soldiered on.

A few hundred feet later, Eleanor whispered, "Over the ridge. There's a shack. Beyond that, there's an abandoned cottage. Go there."

But Allison couldn't make out anything other than more trees. The sun was rising over the horizon, but in this pocket of the woods, it was still dark.

Although, she reminded herself, as the hunted, not the hunter, darkness was an advantage.

Together, they crossed the ridge. As Eleanor had promised, they came upon a small shed and, beyond that, a dilapidated cottage. Evoking memories of another time, another murder, Allison headed reluctantly toward the cottage. What choice did they have? At least there they could hide.

The scene was pure chaos. Two men down, one woman shot. Vaughn rushed to the woman first. She was older, out of shape, and had the dull look of someone who spent way too many hours watching television, but she was alive. A gunshot wound to the shoulder had rendered her helpless. Vaughn grabbed her rifle and jogged toward the other two forms. One he recognized as Brad Halloway. The other, a dark-haired man in his thirties, was a mystery. Bic Friedman, maybe. Didn't matter now. He was dead.

Brad was alive, but with the wound in his stomach, maybe not for long.

Vaughn ran into the house and called 9-1-1 from the house phone. Maybe now the cops would show. He should help Doris and Brad, but he had other things to attend to first, like finding Allison.

Allison helped Eleanor to the back of the cottage. With all the might she could muster, she pushed open the rear door and dragged Eleanor into what had once been the kitchen. Allison got three feet inside and stopped. She heard rustling.

"Raccoons," Eleanor whispered. "Look in the pocket of my parka."

Allison felt around and found a head lamp. She put it on, directing the light into the room's interior. Two beady eyes stared back at her from underneath an old table. More rustling, and it was gone.

After gunmen, raccoons were nothing.

"Here." Allison pulled over an old chair and eased Eleanor down on it. "I think we lost Mark. For now. Let's look at your leg."

A cursory examination showed a small wound and a lot of blood. Allison was no doctor, but she could tell Eleanor was close to shock from cold and blood loss. She peeled off the parka and wrapped it around Eleanor. She had nothing to staunch the bleeding, though, unless she wanted to risk hypothermia herself.

"Stay here," she whispered. "I'll be right back."

Eleanor put her head back against the wall and shut her eyes. She nodded.

Allison skirted her way around the spot where the raccoon had been and walked gingerly through the rest of the downstairs. Like the kitchen, the house was semi-furnished and full of clutter. Allison went from room to room as quickly as she dared.

In the bedroom, she found what she was looking for: rags, in the form of old sheets. She grabbed them and went back to Eleanor, who was alive but weakened.

Allison used a ragged piece of wood from the old cabinetry to make a tear in the sheet. She ripped a piece off lengthwise and tied a tourniquet, or as close as she could get to a tourniquet, above the wound in Eleanor's leg.

"Thanks," Eleanor said.

Allison didn't respond. All she could think about was Jason. If she made it out of here alive, and that was still a big *if*, she had some soul-searching to do. This whole mess was her doing. If she hadn't had the affair, she wouldn't be here now. It was possible she'd never see Jason again.

"I loved him, you know," Eleanor said. Her voice was so low that Allison had to strain to hear her. "Before he left me, that is. He wasn't like other men."

Allison latched on to the second part of her statement. "Is that why you had him killed? Because he left you?"

Eleanor's heavy eyes widened. "You think I had Scott killed?"

"Yes, you. You knew Duane from Wilderness Journey—" But even as the words were out of her mouth, she knew she was wrong. Yes, Eleanor knew Duane, but now that she'd met Eleanor, Allison realized she was hardly the type to befriend a kid, needy or not. But Brad was. And who had been involved with more philanthropic activities than Brad and Antonia? Wilderness Journey was just the type of nonprofit Brad would support. Hadn't Brad taken Delvar under his wing? Perhaps he'd tried with Duane as well, personally or financially. And if Duane hadn't come around after Brad's ministrations...well, in Brad's view, maybe getting him to commit something like murder was justified. A lost cause.

Like Allison.

How easy it would have been to get Scott into the city. How easy to set him up and have him killed?

Eleanor nodded. "Brad," she said. "All of them, including Mark. Scott had become a liability."

"Because he was threatening to blow the whistle."

"Scott had put bits and pieces together." Eleanor grimaced through some unseen tremor of pain. "He had enough information to have an idea what was going on. Nothing concrete. He called the SEC, but they didn't listen. He couldn't offer them anything but theories."

"So he asked you about it. You'd been in on it all along."

Eleanor nodded. "After the smear campaign Mark and the others put Scott through, no one would believe him. He needed evidence."

"And you told him the truth."

"I saw opportunity. Mark hadn't been fair."

Allison suddenly understood. "This was all Mark's idea?"

"Mark's a cunning bastard. Brad was looking for legal advice after the news about China came to light. Brad says he knew nothing about the pollution or the labor law violations, and on that point, I believe him. Brad had been blamed. He was angry, hurt, and, most of all, worried."

"About Antonia. Because of the AIDS diagnosis."

Eleanor nodded. "I'd known Brad from Wilderness Journeys. I'd had some...relationship issues...with a rich donor. It was a fun fling. The program got money, I got a new house. A win, win from my point of view."

Eleanor spoke glibly, as though she were discussing a delayed flight.

"The man's wife didn't see it that way," Allison said. She'd been leaning against the far wall so that she could see out the back window, but now she moved closer to the back door, senses alert.

"No, she didn't. I'd raised a lot of money and positive attention for Wilderness Journeys, so Brad took care of things. I did well in the arrangement. In exchange for my silence."

"Ultimately branding you as a harlot and a criminal in Brad's eyes."

Eleanor nodded. She closed her eyes again, this time for longer. Allison knelt down, risking light from the headlamp to look at Eleanor's leg. It was still bleeding, although not nearly as badly.

"When they needed a purchasing agent who would look the other way, he thought of me." She shrugged. "In exchange for quarterly payments, I didn't bat an eye when Brad signed purchase orders with companies that existed only on the fringes of the imagination."

"But you got greedy."

Eleanor's eyes opened. Allison saw the first flash of real emotion. "I got wise. Between Friedman, Mark, Brad and Cummings, they were going to make a killing. Their plan was so deviously simple: reduce the value of the company, sell it to Cummings' venture firm, recoup on the backside. My tiny slice didn't seem fair."

"But Scott found out, and he wouldn't play along."

"Surprising everyone," Eleanor whispered. "Even himself." She closed her eyes again. "He'd been pushed too far."

Eleanor stopped talking. Allison watched as the sun peeked over the eastern horizon, illuminating Eleanor's complexion, which had gone from white to gray. Allison was starting to believe Mark Fairweather wasn't waiting in the trees for them to emerge. She was starting to believe they would make it.

She bent to check on Eleanor. Her breathing was labored and slow. She needed medical attention.

Allison looked around. There was no way to carry her in this condition. She'd have to hike out to the road alone. She looked around for a weapon, eventually spying a sledgehammer in the corner. The handle was broken. Allison stepped on it, completing the break, and took the jagged piece with her. It was something.

She covered Eleanor with the sheet, tucking it carefully around her. She felt nothing but pity. To look at the life only through the lens of self and to have such a limited view of love...sad.

Allison walked outside. She felt tired and cold, but also happy to have some closure.

Not everything was settled, but she knew how to handle that, too.

About a quarter of a mile down the road that paralleled Dunne Pond, Allison heard a car. Pulse racing again, she backed into the tree line, blending into the woods, her stick at the ready. But it was Vaughn.

She wasn't surprised.

FORTY-ONE

Thanksgiving was a bittersweet celebration.

Mia had gone all out: turkey and all the trimmings, dessert, a fire in the large fireplace and enough fine wine to please a Frenchman. Nevertheless, the atmosphere was charged with tension.

Vaughn seemed alternately happy and sullen, staring at Mia with an almost spiteful gaze. Jamie was clearly concerned about his brother. With Angela beside him, there was something different about Vaughn's twin, something Allison couldn't quite pinpoint. And Allison's parents had refused to leave their house, so Allison would be heading there afterwards. They had agreed to let her bring Grace, though, and now Grace and Mia's dog Buddy were playing fetch in the yard under the watchful eye of Jason.

Allison was washing dishes and Mia was drying in the tiny kitchen overlooking the yard. Both women gazed out at Jason and Grace.

"He's good with her," Mia said.

"He wants children badly."

Mia knelt to put a pie pan in a lower cabinet. "And you?"

"I do, too," Allison said. "I think."

Mia didn't say anything. She straightened, grabbed a plate and continued drying. "And I hear you're engaged."

Allison smiled. "We were waiting to make an announcement. Jason told you?"

Mia nodded.

"There are no secrets around here." She looked at Mia with

affection, relieved the cat was out of the bag. "Do you approve?"

A smile blossomed slowly across Mia's face. "I couldn't be happier."

They worked in silence for a few minutes until Allison said, "So I guess you and Vaughn are talking again?"

"Depends on the day." Mia sighed. "Lots of change for him. Me, Jamie. You."

"Me?"

"Don't underestimate the affect your marriage will have on Vaughn." Mia added quickly, "Don't look so shocked, Allison. I'm not saying he has feelings for you, but you're family to him. Vaughn comes across as tough, but you and I both know he's a marshmallow underneath. Whenever there's a change as immense as this, there's bound to be anxiety." She put the dish away and wiped her hands on her apron. "So be patient with him."

Allison smiled. "Of course." How could she be anything else? He was her brother, closer to her than her own flesh and blood.

The door to the kitchen banged open and Jason flew inside. His face was red from the cold. He had a giggling Grace under one arm and his cell phone in the other. He held the phone out to Allison.

"Faye. She tried your phone but couldn't reach you."

"Thanks." Allison kissed him, then Grace, before accepting the phone. "Hi," she said.

"What time are you coming back?" Faye asked.

Party pooper, Allison thought. "What time do you want us?"

"Grace goes to bed at seven-thirty."

"It's Thanksgiving, Faye. How about if I get there by nine?"

"She needs a routine."

"Fine." Allison didn't bother arguing. She'd learned long ago that arguing with Faye didn't get her anywhere. She would arrive when she arrived and Faye would have to deal with it.

She hung up, determined not to let Faye's dourness affect the few remaining hours. "Who wants to feed the chickens?" she asked with a glance in Mia's direction. Mia nodded her consent.

"Me!" Grace screamed.

And out they went.

*   *   *

The next day brought a grouchy sky and wintery cold. Allison drove north thinking of Antonia, Brad's wife. Brad was now in critical condition at Einstein and Antonia was alone with her nurse. All Brad's efforts to protect Antonia and, in the end, she'd be left with a caretaker and the knowledge that her husband was a murderer.

With a strong sense of resolve, Allison turned into Lofty Acres. She knew the Fairweather house by now. Leah had promised to be home. Her car was in the driveway—she had kept that promise.

"Come in," Leah called in response to Allison's knock.

Inside, Allison found Scott's daughter asleep in a portable crib and her mother on the couch. Leah was holding a stack of large envelopes. "Sit," she said to Allison.

Allison chose the seat across from Leah, where she could see her face and Scott's daughter. The baby was beautiful, all pink cheeks and mewing snores.

"You can stop sending the photos now," Allison said without taking her eyes off the baby. "It's over."

"It will never really be over."

"I think that's in your hands." She looked at Leah, needing to know. Needing closure. "It was because of Mark, wasn't it? He threatened Scott, said he would tell you about Scott's affairs if Scott exposed their scheme to defraud Transitions and its shareholders. Before that, you had no idea Scott was still cheating."

"I thought it ended with you." Leah shifted in her seat, angling her body away from her child. "I should have known." She shrugged. "Maybe I did know, deep down."

"Scott confessed. He even gave you the pictures. His way of making restitution." When Leah nodded, Allison said, "What a horrible burden to place on you."

Leah's face was a blank canvas, devoid of emotion. "Mark helped Scott with the photography. It was their sick little hobby." She stared at Allison. "You were the first."

The idea, as repulsive as it was, came as no surprise. It was why Mark had recognized her at Scott's funeral.

Someday she would get over the feelings of shame and betrayal.

Someday.

"Was Shawn involved?"

Leah shrugged. "Probably."

That was Allison's hunch, too. Thinking back to that fateful trip to Mark's office in the city, she realized she'd honed in on the camera bag around Shawn's shoulder. What a sick family. What a sick way to live.

Allison said, "The important thing is that Scott had vowed to change. He came clean, he broke off his affairs. He tried to right the wrongs. All of them."

"It was too late."

"That was a huge step for him, Leah. You have to hold on to that. I think he loved you." Allison glanced at the baby. "And his daughter. As best he could."

Leah didn't say anything else. She stood up and handed Allison the envelopes. "That's all I have. I'm certain Mark has more, but the bastard wouldn't turn them over."

Allison reflected back to Leah's meeting with Mark in the city. *Monster*. It had been about the pictures for her all along. Leah wanted closure, too.

Allison said, "Mark will be in prison for a very long time."

"We both know that may not matter."

True. Allison would have to take her chances. It had been Leah after all, not Mark, who was delivering the pictures, so perhaps that chapter really was over. Leah had wanted Scott's mistresses to feel her pain and her shame. She wanted to hurt others like she'd been hurt.

Allison stood. "Thank you," she said. "For these."

But Leah had already tuned her out.

Back at home, Allison was welcomed by Brutus and Simon the cat. Eleanor would recover, but she'd have to fight Allison to the death for Simon—and she couldn't very well do that from prison. Simon was Allison's now. Actually, Allison thought, with a glance at the pair of greeters, he was Brutus's.

Brutus barked. Simon meowed.

"Food. Yes, I know...you two only use me for my thumbs." She scooped food for each of them before taking off her coat. Dinner with

Jason tonight, just the two of them. He was still sensitive about the pictures, and still smarting over her close call in Maine. But when she'd returned, he too had welcomed her. And she thought she saw something like grudging admiration in his eyes. So dinner tonight would be special, their first real night alone in days.

What to make?

Allison was about to head upstairs to change when she heard the doorbell ring. Pleasantly surprised to see Faye and Grace on her front step, she ushered them in. Grace ran toward the kitchen with Brutus at her heels, but Faye stood in the entryway looking pensive. It was then that Allison noticed the luggage on the porch. There were two large black bags and a pillowcase stuffed with what looked like dolls and toy animals.

"Amy came by again last night," Faye said. "She was high. It's too disruptive for Mom and Dad." Faye glanced toward the kitchen. "We can't do this anymore."

"You want me to take Grace?"

"Until Amy can." Faye's gaze challenged her. "Can you do that?"

"Of course I can. I would love to have Grace."

Allison walked outside to retrieve the bags, thinking. After Faye's lectures, this came as a shock. She looked over at Grace, now on the hallway floor with Brutus, her coat still on. The move made sense, especially given the battles with Amy that were sure to come. Yes, she would take her. Of course she would. But once this little girl came into Allison's home, Allison knew she wasn't going to let go without a fight.

Allison lined Grace's belongings up along the foyer wall and asked, "Is this all she has?"

Faye nodded. "Most of it is stuff I bought." She called to Grace. "You're going to stay with Aunt Allison for a while."

Grace's eyes lit up. "With Brutus, too?"

"Yes, with the dog," Faye said. Her eyes welled with tears. Allison realized how hard this was for sister. It probably felt like giving up, and Faye was not one to give up.

Allison put her arm around Faye. Her sister stiffened and pulled back. "I'd better go," she said. "I have a nurse staying with mom, but her shift ends soon."

Allison watched her leave. As she stood in the doorway, looking out into the street, she felt warm, tiny fingers latch on to her own.

"It's hard to say goodbye," Grace said. "Mommy always says that."

Allison took a deep breath. She knelt down and took Grace in her arms. "How about helping me make dinner? Your Uncle Jason is joining us."

"Pancakes?" Grace asked, excited. "With sprinkles this time? Sprinkles make everything better."

Allison smiled. "Pancakes sound perfect. I think your Uncle Jason could use some sprinkles, too."

Photo by Ian Pickarski

WENDY TYSON

Wendy Tyson's background in law and psychology has provided inspiration for her mysteries and thrillers. Originally from the Philadelphia area, Wendy has returned to her roots and lives there again with her husband, three kids and two muses, dogs Molly and Driggs. Wendy's short fiction has appeared in literary journals, including *KARAMU, Eclipse, A Literary Journal* and *Concho River Review*.

In Case You Missed the 1st Book in the Series

KILLER IMAGE

Wendy Tyson

An Allison Campbell Mystery (#1)

As Philadelphia's premier image consultant, Allison Campbell helps others reinvent themselves, but her most successful transformation was her own after a scandal nearly ruined her. Now she moves in a world of powerful executives, wealthy, eccentric ex-wives and twisted ethics.

When Allison's latest Main Line client, the fifteen-year-old Goth daughter of a White House hopeful, is accused of the ritualistic murder of a local divorce attorney, Allison fights to prove her client's innocence when no one else will. But unraveling the truth brings specters from her own past. And in a place where image is everything, the ability to distinguish what's real from the facade may be the only thing that keeps Allison alive.

Available at booksellers nationwide and online

Visit www.henerypress.com for details

In Case You Missed the 2nd Book in the Series

DEADLY ASSETS

Wendy Tyson

An Allison Campbell Mystery (#2)

An eccentric Italian heiress from the Finger Lakes. An eighteen-year-old pop star from Scranton, Pennsylvania. Allison Campbell's latest clients seem worlds apart in every respect, except one: Both women disappear on the same day. And Allison's colleague Vaughn is the last to have seen each.

Allison's search for a connection uncovers an intricate web of family secrets, corporate transgressions and an age-old rivalry that crosses continents. The closer Allison gets to the truth, the deadlier her quest becomes. All paths lead back to a sinister Finger Lakes estate and the suicide of a woman thirty years earlier. Allison soon realizes the lives of her clients and the safety of those closest to her aren't the only things at stake.

Available at booksellers nationwide and online

Visit www.henerypress.com for details

Henery Press Mystery Books

And finally, before you go…
Here are a few other mysteries
you might enjoy:

CIRCLE OF INFLUENCE
Annette Dashofy

A Zoe Chambers Mystery (#1)

Zoe Chambers, paramedic and deputy coroner in rural
Pennsylvania's tight-knit Vance Township, has been privy to a
number of local secrets over the years, some of them her own. But
secrets become explosive when a dead body is found in the
Township Board President's abandoned car.

As a January blizzard rages, Zoe and Police Chief Pete Adams
launch a desperate search for the killer, even if it means uncovering
secrets that could not only destroy Zoe and Pete, but also those
closest to them.

Available at booksellers nationwide and online

Visit www.henerypress.com for details

WHEN LIES CRUMBLE
Alan Cupp

A Carter Mays Mystery (#1)

Chicago PI Carter Mays is thrust into a house of lies when local rich girl Cindy Bedford hires him. Turns out her fiancé failed to show up on their wedding day, the same day millions of dollars are stolen from her father's company. While Carter takes the case, Cindy's father tries to find him his own way. With nasty secrets, hidden finances, and a trail of revenge, it's soon apparent no one is who they say they are.

Carter searches for the truth, but the situation grows more volatile as panic collides with vulnerability. Broken relationships and blurred loyalties turn deadly, fueled by past offenses and present vendettas in a quest to reveal the truth behind the lies before no one, including Carter, gets out alive.

Available at booksellers nationwide and online

Visit www.henerypress.com for details

DEATH BY BLUE WATER

Kait Carson

A Hayden Kent Mystery (#1)

Paralegal Hayden Kent knows first-hand that life in the Florida Keys can change from perfect to perilous in a heartbeat. When she discovers a man's body at 120' beneath the sea, she thinks she is witness to a tragic accident. She becomes the prime suspect when the victim is revealed to be the brother of the man who recently jilted her, and she has no alibi. A migraine stole Hayden's memory of the night of the death.

As the evidence mounts, she joins forces with an Officer Janice Kirby. Together the two women follow the clues that uncover criminal activities at the highest levels and put Hayden's life in jeopardy while she fights to stay free.

Available at booksellers nationwide and online

Visit www.henerypress.com for details

FATAL BRUSHSTROKE

Sybil Johnson

An Aurora Anderson Mystery (#1)

A dead body in her garden and a homicide detective on her doorstep...

Computer programmer and tole-painting enthusiast Aurora (Rory) Anderson doesn't envision finding either when she steps outside to investigate the frenzied yipping coming from her own back yard. After all, she lives in Vista Beach, a quiet California beach community where violent crime is rare and murder even rarer.

Suspicion falls on Rory when the body buried in her flowerbed turns out to be someone she knows—her tole-painting teacher, Hester Bouquet. Just two weeks before, Rory attended one of Hester's weekend seminars, an unpleasant experience she vowed never to repeat. As evidence piles up against Rory, she embarks on a quest to identify the killer and clear her name. Can Rory unearth the truth before she encounters her own brush with death?

Available at booksellers nationwide and online

Visit www.henerypress.com for details

SHADOW OF DOUBT

Nancy Cole Silverman

A Carol Childs Mystery (#1)

When a top Hollywood Agent is found poisoned in the bathtub of her home suspicion quickly turns to one of her two nieces. But Carol Childs, a reporter for a local talk radio station doesn't believe it. The suspect is her neighbor and friend, and also her primary source for insider industry news. When a media frenzy pits one niece against the other—and the body count starts to rise—Carol knows she must save her friend from being tried in courts of public opinion.

But even the most seasoned reporter can be surprised, and when a Hollywood psychic shows up in Carol's studio one night and warns her there will be more deaths, things take an unexpected turn. Suddenly nobody is above suspicion. Carol must challenge both her friendship and the facts, and the only thing she knows for certain is the killer is still out there and the closer she gets to the truth, the more danger she's in.

Available at booksellers nationwide and online

Visit www.henerypress.com for details

THE RED QUEEN'S RUN

Bourne Morris

A Meredith Solaris Mystery (#1)

A famous journalism dean is found dead at the bottom of a stairwell. Accident or murder? The police suspect members of the faculty who had engaged in fierce quarrels with the dean— distinguished scholars who were known to attack the dean like brutal schoolyard bullies. When Meredith "Red" Solaris is appointed interim dean, the faculty suspects are furious.

Will the beautiful red-haired professor be next? The case detective tries to protect her as he heads the investigation, but incoming threats lead him to believe Red's the next target for death.

Available at booksellers nationwide and online

Visit www.henerypress.com for details

Made in the USA
Middletown, DE
11 April 2015